Initiation

A Novel

By

Phil M. Williams

Initiation
By Phil M. Williams
Copyright © 2016 Phil M. Williams

Printed in the United States of America
Second Printing, 2018

Phil W Books
www.PhilWBooks.com

ISBN: 978-1-943894-14-7

Cover design and interior formatting by Tugboat Design

Contents

A Note from Phil

Dear Reader,

If you're interested in receiving my novel *Against the Grain* for free, and/or reading my other titles for free or discounted, go to the following link: http://www.PhilWBooks.com. You're probably thinking, *What's the catch?* There is no catch.

Sincerely,
Phil M. Williams

– 1 –

The New Kid

Carter heaved a cardboard box from the back of the truck. His name was scrawled in black magic marker across the box. He walked down the metal plank to the sidewalk. Tiny treeless postage stamp lawns and faded vinyl siding shriveled in the heat. Most of the townhouses had bay windows and one-car garages. The end units could fit two, but most kept their cars outside.

He was average height, athletic, and chiseled. The brim of his dirty white baseball cap was pulled low. He waited on the lawn, the veins in his arms bursting out of his skin. He watched two scraggly-haired movers position an armoire through the front door frame of his new home. A couple, mid-forties, big smiles, marched on the sidewalk toward him. The woman carried a covered dish. A teen boy scurried behind.

"Hello … I'm Jill Wheeler," the woman said, her right hand outstretched, her left still cradling the dish.

Jill Wheeler had the look of the prototypical mom. She was pretty enough, but not so pretty that she'd become the lewd fantasy of every neighborhood boy. She had an oval-shaped face, small blue eyes, and brown hair down to her shoulders.

Carter smiled and repositioned the box so that it sat between his left arm and hip. "I'm Carter," he said, shaking her hand.

Jill stepped aside and motioned to the man and the teen behind her. "This is my husband, David, and our son, Ben."

David Wheeler was thin and small, with dark, deep-set eyes. His chestnut hairline was receding, and his glistening forehead dominated his face. He wore round wire-frame glasses.

Mr. Wheeler grinned and stepped forward. "It's very nice to meet you, Carter." They shook hands. "We live just seven houses down that way." He pointed down the street. "We wanted to welcome your family to the neighborhood. We've been living here for eight years now. I think we've been here longer than anyone. People are so transient around here. We've become kind of like the unofficial welcome wagon."

"I doubt he cares," Ben said.

Ben was small and thin like his dad, with the same dark, deep-set eyes. His nose was too large for his face, and his teeth were too large for his mouth. He had more overbite than he could hide.

Mr. Wheeler smiled at his son. "You're probably right." He looked at Carter. "Ben's the voice of reason. He's probably about your age—sixteen, just got his driver's license and, well, I'm sure you can imagine that Mrs. Wheeler and I are still getting used to the idea of our son behind the wheel of a car."

"Dad," Ben said, frowning.

"I'm sixteen too. It's nice to meet you," Carter said to Ben.

"Isn't that wonderful," Mrs. Wheeler said to her son. "You have someone your age just a few houses down. I'm sure you guys can hang out and do whatever it is you guys do."

"Mom," Ben said, shaking his head.

"That sounds great, Mrs. Wheeler," Carter said. "I don't know anybody around here."

"I'll be busy getting ready for football season," Ben said, "and once the season starts, you have no time, especially on varsity."

"Our Ben here is quite the little quarterback," Mrs. Wheeler said.

Ben exhaled. "It's *corner*back. I play defensive back, not *quarter*back."

Mrs. Wheeler laughed. "Shows how much I know about football."

"What the hell you doin'?" a booming voice said from the front door.

The Wheelers turned wide-eyed toward the sound. Carter stared into the sky, as if he were looking for answers written in the clouds. The hard-set jaw and scowl on the beefy bald man loosened at the sight of company. He smiled, showing a large gap in his upper teeth as he jogged down the front steps.

"How are you folks doin'?" he asked.

Mrs. Wheeler repeated the introductions.

"I'm First Sergeant Jim Arnold," he said, "and I assume you met Carter."

First Sergeant Jim Arnold was a mountain of a man, built like a linebacker. His skin was pale, his nose wide, and his ears stuck out from his domed head.

Mr. Wheeler smiled and snapped a salute.

The First Sergeant narrowed his eyes. "What branch did you serve in, sir?"

Mr. Wheeler's smile flattened. "Oh, I didn't. I was just kidding. I'm a computer programmer."

The First Sergeant nodded, and crossed his bulging arms, his eyes still narrowed.

"This is for your family," Mrs. Wheeler said, handing the casserole to the big bald man. "I know how hard it is to cook when your stuff's still in boxes."

"Thank you, ma'am," he said, taking the dish. "Come on in and meet my wife and daughter. You'll have to excuse the mess of course."

The adults disappeared into the house. Carter set the cardboard box down in the grass. Ben looked around as if he was expecting someone.

"So," Carter began, "how good is the football team?"

Ben smirked. "Virginia triple A state champs last year."

Carter shrugged. "Is it a big school?"

"Triple A has the biggest schools in the state. We have like three thousand students."

Carter nodded. "How many kids are on the football team?"

"Freshman, J.V., or varsity?"

"All of 'em."

"The freshman team usually has fifty, J.V. forty, and varsity … maybe as many as a hundred this year. Everyone wants to get another ring."

Carter smiled. "It'll be a hundred and one then."

Ben cracked his knuckles. "What position do you play?"

"Running back and free safety, plus special—"

"You can't play both ways here. You have to pick one position to go out for."

"Doesn't the coach decide?"

Ben shook his head. "If you're one of the good players, but if you're brand new, they won't care. You'll just pick a position group to go to. The head coach probably won't even know your name for at least a year."

Carter nodded. "I think he'll know my name a whole lot quicker than that."

Ben frowned. "I wouldn't be so sure. You've got two seniors ahead of you at free safety. Noah Lambert was all-district at safety last year. Running back is even worse."

"I'm not worried."

"You should be. Where'd you play last year?"

"Panama."

"Wow, Florida. There's some pretty big football down there."

Carter shook his head. "No, Panama, like in Central America. My dad was stationed down there. He just retired."

Ben laughed. "They have football there? I can't imagine it's anything like here. I hope you're ready for a rude awakening. We only have a month until camp."

Carter grinned. "I think that Noah kid is in for a rude awakening. It's gonna suck sitting on the bench his senior year."

Ben smirked. "You must either be good or delusional. Did anybody ever tell you that you're cocky?"

"If you don't believe in yourself, who the hell will?"

Ben turned toward the ring of a bell. A red-headed teen girl pedaled her banana seat bike on the sidewalk toward them. She smiled and pressed the bell again on her curvy handlebars. She wore paisley printed shorts to mid-thigh, a gray T-shirt, and enormous specs with dark frames. She slammed on her brakes and skidded, stopping just shy of the boys.

"What's up, douchebag?" she said, still smiling.

Her face was soft, her skin bright white. The sun seemed to radiate from her. Under her specs, her eyes were big and blue, surrounded by long lashes. Carter stared, his mouth partly open.

Ben smiled, trying to keep his teeth in check. "Hey, Sarah, are we still on for tonight?"

"Is your mom cooking?" she asked.

"Who else would?"

"As long as you're okay with the knowledge that our friendship is purely based on your mother's culinary talents."

"Whatever."

She grinned at Carter. "Who's this hiding under that hat?" She grabbed his cap from his head, revealing blue eyes, a long thin nose, and a strong chin. She placed the dirty cap on her head and pulled the brim low, mimicking Carter.

He smiled at the thief. "I'm Carter—"

"He just moved here," Ben said. "He thinks he's gonna take Noah Lambert's starting position."

"I hope he does," Sarah said, handing back his cap. "Noah's a total asshole."

Carter curved the brim and pulled his hat low over his eyes.

"Since when do you care about football?" Ben asked.

"I don't." She turned to Carter. "I'm Sarah, *by the way*. I live on Crestleigh two streets back that way." She pointed with a dimpled smile.

"That's an interesting bike," Carter said.

5

She pushed her bike toward him. "Take it for a spin."

Carter hopped on the bike and blasted into the street.

"That didn't go the way I thought it would," Sarah said to Ben.

Carter drove in tight figures of eight with a plastered smile. The handlebar's pink streamers flew in the wind.

"You look so gay," Ben called out.

Sarah laughed in hysterics.

Carter popped a wheelie, driving the banana-seat bike on one wheel. He flipped the front wheel three hundred and sixty degrees before landing back on the asphalt. He hopped the curb and stopped next to Sarah.

He dismounted. "That was fun."

"You're ridiculous," she said with a grin. Sarah turned to Ben. "You should invite Carter tonight."

Ben bit the inside of his cheek. "It's probably too late. My mom bought food for one extra person, not two."

Sarah cocked her head and frowned. "You and I both know—"

"It's cool," Carter said. "I have a lot of unpacking to do anyway. Maybe next time."

"We should get going," Ben said to Sarah.

"Why?" Sarah said.

"Carter probably needs to get back to work. Don't you?" Ben eyed Carter.

"Yeah, I do," Carter replied.

"I guess we'll see you later then," Ben said.

"I'm gonna get my weights unpacked tonight. Do you wanna come over and lift tomorrow afternoon?"

"I normally lift at school. One of the coaches opens the weight room every day, except Sunday."

"I was gonna run in the late morning. There's a steep hill I saw in that neighborhood with the big houses. It'd be good for hill sprints. Not much traffic either."

"I don't know. We had speed training yesterday."

Sarah narrowed her eyes at Ben.

He sighed. "I guess I could do that. What time?"

* * *

The hill was at least a hundred meters long, and steep enough that most cyclists would dismount at the bottom. The asphalt sidewalk was swollen with the summer heat. Carter bent over and touched his toes.

"The jog over here had to be a mile. Aren't you warmed up yet?" Ben asked.

"Almost done," Carter said. "Gotta take care of your body if you want it to take care of you."

Ben exhaled. "That doesn't make any sense. Your body and you are the same thing."

Carter smiled and put one knee in the grass, pushing his pelvis forward. "I strained my hip flexor last year, and it was a pain in the ass. Not doing that again. Flexibility's important."

Ben shrugged.

Carter stood and shook his legs, one after the other. They looked up at the wide asphalt path rising up to the crest of the hill. An occasional luxury car passed by on the adjacent road.

"I'm gonna do ten sprints to the top of the hill," Carter said, his eyes trained on the slope. "The recovery period is the walk back down. The intensity level should be ninety to a hundred percent. I'll probably start at ninety percent for the first few until I'm really loose."

"I don't see the point of going all the way to the top. When do you ever run that far in a football game? That's why we run forty-yard dashes, not hundred-yard dashes."

"Then you can stop halfway."

Ben rolled his eyes. "Who says go?"

"I'll go on you. When you move, I'll move."

Ben and Carter stood side by side at the bottom of the hill with one foot forward and one back, their knees bent. Ben pushed off and sprinted ahead. Carter exploded, his legs pumping up the hill as if he'd been shot from a cannon. He raced past Ben. Carter slowed and stopped past the crest of the hill. He put his hands on top of his head as he walked back down. His gray T-shirt stuck to his skin. Sweat accumulated in dark rings under his arms.

At the bottom of the hill Ben said, "I thought you weren't going full speed on the first one."

"I wasn't."

Carter hung his shirt on a nearby tree. He was tanned from the Panamanian sun. His torso was sinewy, with athletic shoulders and a thin waist. He looked like he was carved from granite. Ben tossed his shirt in the grass. His skin was white, except for the farmer's tan on his arms and neck. He was lean, with narrow shoulders and thin arms.

"You all right?" Carter asked.

Ben's eyes were red, his face flushed. "I'm good. I'm just sore from the speed training with the team."

Carter continued to motor up the hill like it was a flat surface. Ben stopped midway. After eight sprints, Carter was dripping with sweat from head to toe. His brown hair looked black and slick. Ben's face, no longer flushed, had turned pale green.

"I'm gonna sit the last two out," Ben said.

A topless Jeep honked.

"Faggots!" a gang of teen boys jeered, middle fingers extended, as they past.

Ben grabbed his shirt from the grass and put it on.

"Do you know those kids?" Carter asked.

Ben nodded with a frown. "I should've kept my shirt on. It does look gay … us running together without shirts."

"It's a hundred degrees. My shirt just turns into a wet rag. Besides, who gives a shit what those kids think?"

"Everybody."

Carter looked at Ben with a smirk.

8

"Seriously," Ben said.

"I don't."

"You will. That's Zach Goodman's Jeep. He's the only kid we have that plays both ways. He's a lineman, six-foot-five, probably two-seventy-five or so—solid muscle. He's a lock for a D-1 scholarship. He'll probably play in the pros like his dad."

"Big deal."

Ben frowned. "Luke Brewer was in the passenger seat. He's our quarterback. He's really good too, but not as big a prospect as Zach. All the girls are in love with him. They both live in this neighborhood. Zach's dad lets him have parties at his house. They have a pool and a movie theatre. Lots of girls go."

"Have you ever been?"

"They don't let the J.V. in. This year I'll go."

"What about the kid in back?"

"That was Noah Lambert. Remember the kid *you're* gonna have to beat out?"

Carter grinned. "Noah who?"

Ben shook his head. "He actually lives in our neighborhood, but he mostly hangs out over here."

Carter looked beyond the hill to the neighborhood, noticing as if for the first time the McMansions, the swimming pools, and the checkerboard lawns. "You can't blame him for that."

Carter and Ben jogged back toward their neighborhood with their shirts on.

"Did you wanna stop at 7-Eleven, get something to drink?" Ben asked, his breathing elevated.

"If you want to," Carter replied.

They entered the convenience store, the air conditioning freezing in contrast to the sweltering heat. Ben made a beeline for the refrigerator. He opened the glass door and removed a bottle of orange Gatorade.

"Did you want one?" Ben asked Carter.

"I didn't bring any money."

Ben grabbed another one. "I got you."

Outside Ben and Carter guzzled the orange electrolytes.

"Thanks," Carter said raising the plastic bottle.

"I have to admit, you are pretty fast."

"Thanks."

"It would be cool if we could both start this year." Ben took a swig of Gatorade.

"It'll happen." Carter half-smiled and took a drink.

Ben exhaled. "I hope so."

– 2 –

Three's a Crowd

Carter opened the refrigerator and grabbed a gallon of milk. He filled his glass and his bowl of cereal. He sat on a stool at the counter bar in the open-plan kitchen. From the next room he could see a rerun of *Magnum P.I.* playing on the thirty-six-inch television. He heard light steps from the adjoining stairway. He saw thin legs, short shorts, and a tank top with exposed bra straps. The girl carried a duffel bag.

"Where are you going dressed like that?" he asked.

"None of your business," Alyssa replied.

Alyssa Arnold was short and thin, bumps developing on her chest. Her body reflected her twelve years of age. Her face was cute, from her button nose to her round blue eyes. Her hair was dyed blonde, the ends heated into curls. Her smile was loaded with metal.

"Dad's right downstairs," he said.

She put a hand on her hip, the other clutching her bag. "So."

"If he sees you wearing that—"

"I got a change of clothes." She held up the duffel bag.

"Don't say I didn't warn you."

"What do you care?" She slammed the front door behind her.

Carter finished his cereal, drank the sugary milk from his bowl, and washed it in the sink. The front door opened. His mother appeared, loaded down with shopping bags from clothing outlets. Her thin arms were taut from the weight.

"Hey, Mom," he said.

"Hey, sweetheart," she said as she breezed into the kitchen.

Grace Arnold was proud of the fact that she'd stayed thin into her late thirties. Her dark hair was shoulder length, parted on the side, no bangs. Her face was caked in high-end makeup, her small blue eyes enhanced by the optical illusion of the eyeliner. She wore designer jeans that were more high school than mom. Her low-cut T-shirt exposed her protruding collarbone and skin that had seen one too many tanning bed sessions.

She kissed Carter on the cheek with tacky lipstick.

Carter discreetly wiped his cheek on the shoulder of his shirt.

"What are you doing, standing here all by yourself?" she asked, her head cocked.

"I just finished eating. I was gonna go over to Ben's in a few minutes."

She was quiet for a moment, listening. "What's your dad been doing?"

He frowned. "When I went running this morning, he was on the computer. When I was lifting this afternoon, he was on the computer. Wanna guess where he is now?"

His mother exhaled and pursed her lips. She stomped downstairs to the basement.

Carter heard sharp voices.

"Is this what you're planning to do with your life?" she said.

"I'll do whatever the hell I want. I'm retired," his dad said.

"We can't live on your retirement. Especially not around here."

"You'd better get a job then."

"I thought D.C. was full of defense contractor jobs?"

"You need to get off my *fuckin'* back."

"I knew this was going to happen. It would all fall on me. I can't count on you for anything."

Carter heard the squeak of the computer chair, and the slamming of something against the wall.

"What did I just say?" his dad said.

Carter gripped the handrail at the top of the basement steps, his knuckles white. He took one step down.

"If you ever fuckin' talk to me like that again," his dad said.

Carter released the handrail, turned around, and marched out the front door. He stood on the stoop, humid air settling on his skin. The sun was setting, the sky a searing orange. He took several deep breaths. There was a faint crash from the basement. Carter jumped from the stoop and dashed down the sidewalk. He stopped at the end unit townhouse, just seven lots down from his own. The front door was on the side of the house a floor up. He took the steps two at a time to the landing and rang the doorbell.

The door swung open. The spicy, sweet smell of cooking oregano, basil, and tomato wafted outside. "Carter, honey, how are you?" Mrs. Wheeler asked.

"I'm good," he said, looking away.

"Come in, come in. Ben's in his room." She stepped aside and motioned with her hand.

Carter stepped inside. A black cat with white paws rubbed in and around his legs in a figure of eight. He bent down and petted her head.

"Would you like to stay for dinner? We're having spaghetti and meatballs."

He stood up. "It smells really good."

She smiled. "It's settled then. I'll add a chair to the table."

"Thank you, Mrs. Wheeler."

"Tell Ben it'll be ready in twenty minutes."

With each step up the stairs, the scratching of records and the pumping of bass grew a little louder. Carter knocked. Ice Cube rapped about goin' toe to toe with the police. He knocked harder.

"Come in," Ben said over the bass.

Carter opened the door and stepped into the room, closing the door behind him. A single bed sat along the right hand wall with a disheveled Washington Redskins comforter. The walls were covered with football heroes and bikini models. A desk with a computer sat in one corner, while a Kenwood stereo with stacks of CDs and tapes stood in the other. Across from the bed there was a forty-eight-inch television and a black leather chair. Ben sat holding a game controller, scoring touchdowns with tiny pixelated football players. He wore a North Potomac Marauders Football T-shirt with the sleeves cut off. His arms were veiny.

Ben glanced at Carter and lifted his chin, then went back to his game. Carter turned the music down, wheeled over the chair from the desk, and sat down next to Ben.

"You don't like N.W.A.?" Ben asked, his eyes glued to the screen.

"N.W.A.?"

"Niggaz Wit Attitudes. That shit gets me pumped."

Carter smirked. "Are white people allowed to say that?"

"It's not the N-word. It's niggazzzz, with a Z."

"Seems like the same thing to me."

"Damn, Panama must really be behind the times."

"Would you say it to one of the black kids on the team?"

"Well, no. But if I did, it'd be cool."

Carter nodded.

Ben glanced at Carter's loose khaki Bermuda shorts and his black "Cerveza Panama" T-shirt.

"What do you listen to? Panama salsa or some shit?" He looked back at his game and called another play.

Carter shrugged. "Your mom said dinner's gonna be ready in twenty minutes."

"You're not staying, are you?"

"Your mom invited me."

Ben paused the game and tossed the controller to the floor. He turned to Carter with a scowl. "Sarah's coming over. I can't have you cock-blocking."

Carter smiled, shaking his head. "Have you told her how you feel?"

"I'm working up to it."

"She thinks you guys are friends."

"If she didn't like me, she wouldn't be hanging around all the time."

"Maybe."

"Seriously, man, I'm sorry, but you need to go. She gets all weird when you're around. It's like you're this novelty, being the new kid and all."

"All right." Carter stood up.

The door burst open. "What up, *bitchez*," Sarah said with a grin. She wore short blue athletic shorts and a white T-shirt.

Ben turned toward the door. "You could knock," he said.

"Afraid I might catch you jerking off?"

Ben blushed. "Funny."

"Hey, Sarah," Carter said with a smile.

Sarah smirked, pushing her red hair off her glasses. "Hey, Carter." She looked at Carter, then to Ben, back to Carter, and then back to Ben. "You two don't have something going on, do you? If you want to come out to me, I'll be cool with it." She glanced at the stereo. "Now Dr. Dre on the other hand, he might have an issue with it."

Carter laughed.

Ben shook his head. "That's enough with the gay, Sarah. It's really not funny anymore."

"Carter's laughing," she said.

Ben narrowed his eyes at Carter.

"I was just leaving," Carter said.

He started toward the open bedroom door. Sarah stood with her arms spread apart, blocking his exit. She had a crooked smile, her dimples on display.

"Not without the magic word," she said.

"Abracadabra?" Carter asked.

"No."

"Please?"

"No."

He looked at the ceiling, then back to her. "Sarah's the coolest girl in all of Virginia, and I wish I was as cool as her."

She blushed and put her hand over her chest. "What a good guesser you are. I thought you'd be stuck in here forever … with your *lover*." She smiled wide.

Ben scowled.

"So where are you going?" she asked.

Carter shrugged.

"What kind of an answer is that?"

He shrugged again. She punched him in the arm.

"You hit like a girl," Carter said with a grin.

"Didn't want to hurt you. If I did, your mom would be upset. She'd call my mom. My mom would get mad at me and tell me how I'm not supposed to use my superpowers. Then I'd have to explain that I was just trying to toughen you up for football, that it was for your own good. Then the government would find out about my powers and I'd be on the run for the rest of my life, living in the shadows, fighting for justice. It would've been a big mess."

Carter laughed. "Clearly … I'll see you guys later."

"No seriously, where are you going?" She pressed out her lower lip.

"I have work to do at home."

"Oh bullshit. Mrs. Wheeler made you a place for dinner. She already thinks you're staying. It would be super rude to leave now." She looked at Ben. "Don't you think Carter should stay?"

Ben shrugged.

"Not you too." She frowned.

"He can do whatever he wants," Ben said.

"At least stay for dinner. Then you can go do whatever boring shit you have to do. *Pleeeeeeze*."

Carter shook his head. "Okay."

Ben exhaled and returned to his game.

Sarah and Carter strolled to the computer chair and stood next to Ben.

"You can sit," Carter said. "I'll sit on the floor."

"Nope!" She put her hand on his chest and pushed him into the chair. "We can sit together."

"Wait."

Sarah sat down on his lap, her curves in all the right places. Carter felt the blood rush to his groin. He wasn't sure where to put his hands. She felt warm on his lap. Ben gaped at them, his eyes narrowed, his face beet red.

Sarah looked at Ben. "What's wrong?"

"Nothing," he said, turning back to his game.

"Since when did you start cutting off your sleeves?" Sarah asked.

Ben ignored her.

"Sun's out, guns out." She giggled. "You look all veiny. Were you pumping up for me?"

Ben's face went red again. He smacked the controller buttons unnecessarily hard.

Carter couldn't contain his erection. He needed a graceful exit.

"Can I turn you?" Carter asked, hoping to get her groin off of his. "You're kinda hurting me."

She blushed and stood up. "Oh sorry. It's just my fat ass. I'm going to go help Mrs. Wheeler set the table. I'll leave you two lovebirds."

And with that she was gone.

Ben threw his controller, bouncing it off of his Nintendo. He eyed Carter, his jaw set tight. "Nice job, asshole."

− 3 −

Two-a-Days

Carter sat on the wooden bench in front of his locker. He was bent at the waist, tying his cleats. A thick haze of body odor hung in the air. It was quiet except for the rustling sound of pads being shoved into pants and girdles, the plastic parts of shoulder pads smacking together, and the click-clack of cleats across the tile floor. He tied a double knot and sat up straight. Ben sat next to him, rigid, his face pale, his cleats tapping the tile.

"Are you all right?" Carter asked Ben.

Ben was dazed.

"Are you all right?" Carter asked again, louder this time.

"Huh?" Ben said.

"You look a little pale."

Ben's eyes blinked into focus. He shook his head and grabbed a handful of his white jersey. "This jersey's bullshit."

"What's wrong? It doesn't fit right?"

Ben exhaled. "You don't know, do you?"

Carter shrugged. "Know what?"

"Your jersey color."

"What about it?" Carter looked down at his white number 20 jersey.

"Look around," Ben said. "You'll figure it out."

Carter glanced around the locker room. Zach, Noah, and Luke

stood in the center talking, paying no attention to the traffic jam they were creating. Zach and Noah wore black, Luke wore red. The biggest, most athletic kids wore black jerseys. Others, slightly smaller, wore gold. Everyone else wore white.

"They already decided?" Carter asked.

Ben glowered. "They act like everyone has a chance. Coach Pitts said last year that I had a good chance to start if I worked hard. It's bullshit."

"It's not a big deal. It's only the first day of full pads. They haven't seen anything yet."

Ben shook his head. "You're delusional. This isn't Panama. Those black jerseys rarely change hands. We never lose, so the coaches never have a reason give anyone else a shot. Once kids get that black jersey, they never give it up. Occasionally a gold jersey moves up to black, but never us."

"Us?" Carter raised his eyebrows.

"We're the scout team. So get ready to get your ass handed to you every day for the rest of the season. Don't worry though. On Friday nights, we'll get a good view from the sideline."

"You're looking at this all wrong."

"How so?"

"We're gonna have an opportunity every day to make the first string look bad." Carter stood up and slammed his locker shut. "Eventually they'll have to move us up."

Luke Brewer strutted past, his helmet in hand.

"Hey, Luke, what's up," Ben said, smiling.

Luke scowled in response. He was tall, tan, and chiseled. He had a square jaw and a symmetrical face.

"What about the red jersey?" Carter asked.

"That's for kids you can't hit, like the quarterback, or Dwayne over there." Ben motioned to a tall, muscular dark-skinned kid checking himself out in the mirror on the inside of his locker. "He was second team all-state last year, but he's got shoulder problems."

"So?"

"So he's really good, and the coaches don't want him getting hurt in practice."

Carter grabbed his helmet from the bench. "I'll see you out there."

Ben glanced up at the analog clock on the wall. "We still have twenty minutes."

"I need to warm up and stretch. Flexibility's important, remember?"

"Whatever." Ben stood up and slammed his locker shut.

Carter was shouldered from behind as Zach and Noah walked past.

"Hey, Zach, Noah," Ben said. "You guys look like you're ready to hit someone."

Zach looked Ben up and down as if he were calculating his value. "You look like you're about to shit a brick."

Ben looked down.

Zach had long, white, beefy limbs and a blond crew cut. His face was full, his blue eyes small and deep set.

"If you're scared, say you're scared," Noah said.

Noah was short and stocky: the physique of a bodybuilder. His face was young and bright, more boy-next-door than meathead.

Carter glared at them.

"What the fuck you lookin' at?" Zach said.

Carter stood silent, his eyes locked on Zach. His knuckles were white where he clutched his helmet. Zach and Noah laughed and left the locker room. Ben's eyes hadn't left the ground. Carter turned to him, smacking him on his shoulder pads.

"Hey, forget it." Carter smiled. "First day of hitting, let's have some fun."

Carter jogged from the locker room to the practice field. The morning sun burned bright. He passed racially segregated groups of his teammates walking.

"What you runnin' fo?" a gigantic dark-skinned kid said, his gut hanging over his belt. "Ain't no coaches 'round to impress." *Mike Townsend* was scrawled across a piece of athletic tape stuck to his helmet. The three hundred-pounder had a plump face and eyes that were mere slits.

Carter continued jogging. He stood on one foot at the edge of the practice field holding onto a chain-link fence. He pulled his leg back, his heel touching his butt. A group of black kids sauntered by, joking.

Mike Townsend said, "Coach Ware's so black that if he had a red light, he'd be a motherfuckin' pager." The kids laughed.

"I got one," Dwayne said with a grin. "Coach Ware's so black that the oil light turns on when he gets out the car." They laughed with bright white smiles.

"No, no, no," Mike said. "Coach Ware's so black when he goes outside the street lights be comin' on." Laughter erupted.

Dwayne shook his head with a smile and said, "Coach Ware's so black Oprah Winfrey says, *damn* you're purple." Raucous laughter ensued.

Dwayne eyed Carter.

"Hey, white boy," Dwayne said. Carter looked over. "That Jane Fonda shit ain't gonna help you today."

Carter nodded, still stretching.

A whistle blew. A handful of coaches marched onto the practice field. The players sprinted to arrange themselves neatly along the white lines. Carter stood in the back, white jerseys all around him. They spelled Marauders with jumping jacks and performed various stretches to a ten count. Head Coach Cowan and the offensive coordinator Coach Ware paced between the lines, inspecting players for defects.

"It's awfully quiet today, huh, Coach?" Cowan said.

Coach Cowan was broad, above average height, with a salt and pepper mustache.

Coach Ware smiled. "I heard a lot a trash-talkin' these past three days. Ain't nobody got nothin' to say now, huh?"

"Today we separate the men from the boys."

The players weren't exaggerating, Coach Ware's skin was as dark as his shades. He was tall and muscular, his hair cut tight to his head.

Coach Ware erupted, stopping the stretch. "Townsend got two buckles undone. That's twenty pushups for everyone. Count 'em out!"

The team groaned and assumed the pushup position.

After stretch, the lines converged and they did fifteen yards of high knees, butt kicks, shuffles, bounding, and backpedals. Halfway through, Coach Ware flipped out.

"I'm tired of watchin' this lack of effort! Do it over," he said. "We'll stay here all day if we have to."

After three tries, Coach Ware finally seemed satisfied with the team's effort. Coach Cowan blew his whistle.

"Eye openers, everyone to the bags," Coach Cowan said.

Six soft rectangular bags, each the size of a man, were laid on the ground about three yards apart. The team huddled in front of Coach Cowan.

"Now listen up, because I'm only gonna explain this once." Coach Cowan looked around at his players, his Bike shorts tight to mid-thigh. "Runners make a line behind the bags, and defenders make a line here." He pointed in front of him. "It's simple, runners will pick a hole and defenders will fill it. This is one hundred percent live, full contact. Let's see good hard tackles with your heads up. We'll do this drill first thing every morning through camp. We call it eye openers because, well." The coach smiled and looked around. "'Cause it's gonna wake you up."

Lines were formed on both sides of the bags. Three identical drills were set up ten yards apart to accommodate the mass of players.

"Let's go. Even those lines up," Coach Ware said.

Runner after runner picked a hole and sprinted through, their shoulders lowered. Defenders crashed through, meeting them in between the bags. Some were stopped cold to the sounds of ohhhs, ahhhs, and damns. Others were planted by the runner, run over like roadkill.

Some players, Ben included, jockeyed for a "favorable" position in line. They counted their position, then the corresponding position in the opposite line to find their opponent. If they'd drawn a particularly intimidating opponent, they switched places in line. The brave or foolhardy would always end up with the toughest adversaries. Carter was destined to face all two hundred and seventy-five pounds of Zach Goodman. He made no attempt to switch places.

Carter stood facing Zach across the bags. He watched Zach's waist as he moved. Carter mirrored him, waiting to see which hole he'd choose. Zach dipped his shoulder and rumbled into the third hole like a battering ram. As soon as Carter saw the dip of his shoulder, he burst into the hole to meet him. At the last moment, Carter lowered himself and crashed into Zach's kneecaps, upending him.

Coach Cowan blew his whistle. "Individuals," he said.

The players sprinted to different corners of the field to their position groups. Carter and Ben ran to the bottom corner. Coach Pitts stood holding a football. Two squares were marked out with cones to form areas about fifteen yards across. Coach Pitts had dark skin, balding short black curls, and a weightlifters physique.

The defensive backs stood in front of their coach.

"What are y'all waitin' for?" Coach Pitts said with a toothpick in the corner of his mouth.

"What are we doin'?" Noah asked.

Coach Pitts smirked. "What do we always do? The course, of course."

The players backpedaled along the square denoted by the cones, jogged across and came back down.

"Turn and run to the left," Coach Pitts said. "Let's go, Ben. That turn's gotta be lower and faster."

A short, thin black kid backpedaled, turned his hips, and in the blink of an eye sprinted to the end of the square before easing up and coming back the other way.

"It's Devin, right?" Coach Pitts asked, looking at the athletic tape on his helmet.

Devin nodded, his facemask bouncing up and down.

"That's perfect. You'll never get beat deep with a turn and run like that."

They backpedaled, planted, sprinted forward, and backpedaled again.

"Y'all should be tired right now," Coach Pitts said as the kids labored. "Especially if you've been sittin' on your ass all summer." Coach Pitts watched Noah slog through the drill, his hips stiff and his body upright. "Lower, Noah. That's way too high."

Carter backpedaled, his arms swinging comfortably, his body low and loose. He planted and sprinted forward. "That's nice, Two-Zero," Coach said to Carter.

Coach Pitts blew the whistle and started to jog toward the opposite end of the field. "Let's go, one-on-ones with the receivers," he said. The defensive backs followed.

Luke and the backup quarterback stood together on the goal line in the middle of the field with Coach Ware. Wide receivers and defensive backs lined up near each sideline. One defender from each line jogged onto the field to cover the receiver. Carter was behind Ben in line. He counted the queue, hoping to draw Dwayne.

Carter tapped Ben on the shoulder. "You wanna switch?"

Ben looked at the line of wide receivers, counting. "Hell yeah." They switched places in line. "He's fast, and he'll catch anything up high."

Carter nodded. "No problem, it'll be a lot of exposed ribs."

Ben frowned. "You can't hit him, remember?"

Carter smiled.

Coach Pitts marched over. "For you corners, I want you practicing your press man technique. Safeties, seven yards off in a backpedal technique."

Carter jogged into position, stopping seven yards from Dwayne. The all-state receiver stood, one foot forward, one back. Carter focused on Dwayne's belt buckle.

Luke said, "Set, go."

Dwayne exploded forward and cut inside. Carter turned and sprinted downfield, mirroring him. After three hard steps inside, Dwayne planted and reversed course, headed outside to the corner. Carter flipped his head and hips, turning one hundred and eighty degrees, losing sight of Dwayne for a split second, but ending up glued to the wide receiver. Dwayne tilted his head up, looking for the spiral hanging in the air. Carter looked up. The ball was high and deep, out of Carter's reach. Dwayne leaped into the air. His basketball hops, long arms, and six-foot-two frame put him over ten feet off the ground. His long fingers cast a net that cradled the football. Carter leaped as gravity tugged on the receiver. He shoved his right arm between Dwayne's arms, wrenching the football from his grasp. Their bodies tangled and they fell to the turf. The ball fell next to them—incomplete.

Coach Pitts clapped his hands. "There you go, Two-Zero."

Coach Ware stood with his arms crossed, staring under dark shades.

Dwayne hopped to his feet, pushing his hands out in front of him, signaling like a referee. "That was pass interference."

"Looked clean to me," Coach Pitts said.

"He was all over me," Dwayne replied.

Carter jogged toward the end of the defensive back line. Ben came out to take his place.

"Hey, you," Coach Ware called out.

Carter turned around.

"Yeah you, number twenty. Get your ass back in there. Go again."

Ben returned to the line.

Carter lined up on another receiver, this one slower and shorter. He ran three steps and cut inside on a slant pattern. As the ball touched the receiver's hands, Carter drilled his facemask into the kid's sternum. The ball jarred from his grasp—incomplete.

"Go again," Coach Ware said.

Coach Pitts covered his grin with his fist.

Carter stepped in front of an out route—interception. He drilled another receiver on a hook route. He knocked down a deep pass on a go route. Carter put his hands on his knees, catching his breath.

"Again," Coach Ware said. "I know you ain't tired yet."

Another receiver, another incompletion. Carter wheezed for air, his legs weak. He was back to the top of the order: Dwayne.

"Ready to get burnt?" Dwayne said.

The receiver sprinted forward five yards and stopped on a dime. Carter stuck his cleat in the turf and blasted forward with malicious intent. Luke started to throw, but the ball stuck to his hand.

Shit.

Dwayne sprinted downfield on the hitch and go. Carter turned and chased, two yards behind. Dwayne put his hands up, the ball falling from the sky. Carter leaped forward and wrenched the receiver's right hand down just as the ball touched his hands. The superstar receiver simply caught the football left-handed—touchdown.

Dwayne smiled wide. He held the football in one hand like a loaf of bread. "What's that smell? Is that you, white boy? You smell like some burnt toast."

Coach Ware blew his whistle. "Team scrimmage. Down at the far end zone, comin' out. Don't be last."

Carter and the rest of his teammates jogged toward the opposite end of the field where lineman, linebackers, and running backs waited. Devin Starks, the small but lightning quick cornerback with a white twenty-one jersey, jogged next to him.

"I heard you just transferred here?" Devin asked.

Carter spoke between heavy breaths. "Panama ... dad's in the army ... you?"

Devin grinned. He had a gap between his upper teeth. "Germany. Army brat too. You did pretty good in one-on-ones."

"Thanks."

"I had a feeling they were gonna do a double move on that last one."

Carter shook his head. "I shoulda known."

They stopped on the sideline with the rest of the white jerseys.

He held out his hand. "I'm Devin."

"Carter." They shook hands.

Devin motioned with a nod toward the first team that was walking through plays. "What do you think of the safeties in front of you?"

Carter shrugged. "I'll be starting week one."

Devin laughed. "I don't doubt it."

"What about you?" Carter asked. "What do you think of the corners?"

"I'm faster than anyone here."

"I believe that."

Coach Cowan blew his whistle. "First O on the ball goin' out. Give me a scout D."

Coach Pitts jogged over to the sideline.

"Devin and Ben, you're in at the corners. You, number twenty." He pointed at Carter. "You're in at free safety."

Coach Pitts signaled in the play. Carter relayed the play in the huddle.

Luke placed his hands under the center, looking left and right. On "go," the center jammed the football into his hands. He pivoted and tossed the ball to the running back behind him. Kevin Lewis motored for the sideline, his thick legs pumping, the ball secure in his outside arm. Devin and Carter converged with a crack, stopping the stocky back for no gain. Kevin popped up without a word. Coach Ware stalked to the scene of the crime. He grabbed a slender wide receiver by the facemask.

"Who are you supposed to block?" Coach Ware said.

The receiver pointed to Devin, his head stuck in the coach's grips.

"And who made the tackle?"

The kid pointed to Devin.

Coach Ware shook the kid's helmet with his head still in it. "Then block the goddamn corner!"

The next play, Dwayne was blanketed by Devin on a post route. Luke forced the ball. Devin tipped it to Carter for an interception.

Coach Cowan took off his hat and shook his head at his quarterback. "Why'd you throw that? Kevin was wide open on the arrow."

"It was a mismatch," Luke said, referring to the height disparity between Devin and Dwayne.

"It was a pick," Coach Cowan said.

Luke looked at the grass, his hands on his hips.

"Flip-flop the receivers. Dwayne you play the Z," Coach Cowan said.

The next play, Luke threw a bomb to Dwayne for a touchdown, leaving Ben in his wake.

As Dwayne pranced back to the huddle, he shook his head at Ben. "Is that the best you can do? You should just quit now, save yourself the embarrassment."

Ben looked down for a moment, then hit himself on the helmet.

Carter walked over. "Hey, you're fine. Just give him a little more cushion."

Two plays later, Dwayne caught another touchdown.

Dwayne strutted back to the huddle. As he passed Ben he said, "*Damn*, you really do suck."

Ben shook his head and again smacked himself on top of the helmet. Carter glared at Dwayne, adrenaline coursing through him.

Three plays later, Luke went to the air again. Dwayne ran a quick slant, beating Ben to the inside. Carter was playing zone coverage in the middle of the field, but he cheated over toward Ben. Luke threw a strike right between the double eights on Dwayne's chest. Dwayne thought he was gonna score again. He figured Carter would be deep in the middle of the field, and even if he wasn't it's not like he was allowed to hit him. Carter wasn't deep in the middle of the field. He was flying full speed toward Dwayne. At the exact moment the football touched his hands, Carter buried his facemask into Dwayne's sternum. A loud crack echoed across the field. Dwayne was sprawled on the ground hyperventilating, the wind knocked out of him. The practice field fell silent.

"Trainer!" Coach Cowan said.

Two athletic trainers attended to Dwayne. Zach, Luke and the rest of the first team offense stalked toward Carter. Coach Ware stepped in front and grabbed Carter by the facemask, shaking him.

"Are you color blind, boy?" Coach Ware said.

"No," Carter said, looking into the emptiness of the coach's black shades.

"Do you know what a red jersey means?"

"He should keep his mouth shut if he doesn't wanna get hit."

Coach Ware pulled Carter closer. "What did you say, boy?"

"I said he shouldn't talk trash if he doesn't wanna get hit."

"I have half a mind to throw you off this team." Coach Ware let go of Carter's facemask. "You see this chain-link fence that runs around these fields?"

Carter nodded.

"You're gonna run along this fence until *I* get tired. Now get your ass movin'!"

Carter started running. He ran until practice was over. He continued running as players left for lunch in their cars and trucks with bass pumping.

Ben walked onto the practice field, his hair still wet from the shower. He threw a hand up as Carter jogged toward him.

"Coach said you can stop," Ben said, his forehead red from his helmet.

Carter put his hands on his hips. "Thanks."

"You wanna go get some lunch? Everyone goes to Shakey's. They have a pretty good all you can eat buffet."

"Sounds good," Carter replied, his breathing heavy.

The locker room was empty. Carter hurried through his shower. Ben waited. They drove to the restaurant in Mrs. Wheeler's Toyota Camry. Ben cranked the A/C and tuned the radio to 95.5 WPGC. Carter stared out the window, the music too loud for conversation.

Ben parked in the cracking asphalt lot of the buffet. It was a cloudless day, the sun high in the sky. Carter felt the heat from the asphalt through his sneakers. Dwayne and Kevin exited the restaurant as Ben and Carter moved toward the door. Dwayne puffed up at the sight of Carter. He stalked toward Carter, with Kevin close behind.

"You tryin' to ruin my scholarship?" Dwayne said. "Fuckin' scout team hero."

"Relax, man," Kevin said with a hand on Dwayne's shoulder. Kevin was powerfully built, with tree trunks for legs.

"If you wanna talk trash," Carter said, "it's open season, red jersey or not."

"I oughtta fuck you up," Dwayne said, invading Carter's personal space.

Ben backed up a few steps. Kevin still had a hand on Dwayne's shoulder. Carter stood still, looking up at Dwayne.

"Go on then," Carter said, clenching his fists. "I got nothing to lose."

"It's not worth it," Kevin said. "Let's go."

"Punk ass bitch," Dwayne said.

Kevin pulled Dwayne back and they walked away.

Carter took a deep breath and turned to Ben. "I'm starving, let's get something to eat."

They had heaping plates as they sat in a booth across from each other. Carter took a bite of a fried chicken leg.

"Man, this is good," Carter said.

They ate as if the chicken could still run away from them. Ben pushed his plate of stripped carcasses to the side.

"I don't need you to stick up for me," Ben said, his deep set eyes still.

"I know that," Carter replied.

"Then why'd you do it?"

Carter shrugged. "He was being a dick."

"I appreciate it, but I can stand up for myself."

"Okay." Carter took a drink of sweet tea. "Thanks for waiting for me." Carter looked down. "And buying me lunch. I'll pay you back."

− 4 −

Go for the Gold

Raindrops pounded the cars and asphalt. Carter stood at his window, his fingers parting the plastic blinds. He watched the waves of water as they sluiced along the curbs and into the sewer. Bob Marley's "Redemption Song" played on his tiny tape deck, reminding him of Panama. Bob's acoustic melody was interrupted by the shouting above him.

"I can't keep doin' this," Jim Arnold said. "You spend it faster than I can make it."

"What are you making?" Grace Arnold said. "You don't have a job. I'm the only one that works in this house."

"Your part-time job doesn't even cover your fuckin' makeup. My retirement check pays the bills around here."

"It barely covers the essentials."

"No, it barely covers your shoes, and clothes, and makeup, and your dumbass tannin' bed sessions. You're not foolin' anyone. You look like a fuckin' old lady."

Carter heard the garage door open and shut, followed by light steps and three taps. He opened his door. Alyssa stood, soaked, in a tight mini-skirt and halter top. Her makeup was streaked down her face.

Carter frowned.

Alyssa stared at the white carpet, her blonde hair dark from the rain. "Can I borrow some clothes?"

Carter took a deep breath and walked to his dresser. He pulled out a T-shirt, some sweatpants and a sweatshirt. Alyssa took the clothes and went into the basement bathroom, shutting the door behind her.

"No, *you* wanted this," Jim said. "I said this area was too expensive. But like always, *you* got your fuckin' way. Oh, now you're gonna cry?"

Alyssa exited the bathroom, her face clean, her body draped in Carter's sweats. She looked like a twelve-year-old again. She held a folded towel, her tiny clothes hidden inside. She stood at Carter's doorway.

"Can I come in?" she asked.

Carter nodded. She shut the door behind her. The room was sparse, the walls white and barren. A single mattress with no bedframe sat near the window. A futon couch in front of the bed faced a twenty-four-inch TV/VCR that sat on milk crates. A paperback, *Night Train Lane,* was on a battered foot locker. Alyssa plopped down on the futon.

"Sorry, I didn't wanna go up there with them fighting," she said.

"That the only reason?" he replied with raised eyebrows.

She shrugged and took a deep breath. Her eyes were red and puffy.

Carter sat on the foot locker catty-cornered from his half-sister. "Where have you been going?"

She looked down. "Just been hanging out with some girls from the neighborhood."

"Girls don't dress like that for other girls."

She shrugged.

"You're twelve."

"I'll be thirteen next week."

"Still."

"I don't see what the big deal is."

"If it's not a big deal, why are you sneaking in and out and hiding your clothes from Mom and Dad? I should tell them what's going on."

"Who do you think bought the clothes?"

32

Carter looked hard at her. "No way."

"She did. She just told me not to let Dad see. He wouldn't under-stand."

Carter frowned.

"Go ahead and ask her."

"Just be careful, okay?"

"Yes, *Dad*." She grinned.

Carter shook his head with a smirk.

She looked around the sparse room. "What are you doing in here anyway?"

"Reading," he said, tapping the book sitting on the foot locker next to him.

She furrowed her brow, her button nose twisting. "What's a night train?"

He laughed. "It's a nickname for the greatest defensive back in NFL history. He has the record for interceptions in a season with fourteen. This is from the time when a season was only twelve games. He was also a big hitter ..."

Alyssa's eyes glazed over.

"Anyway, I was just reading."

"They didn't hook up cable down here, did they?"

"No."

"You got any good movies?"

"What do you wanna watch?"

She pulled her feet up, and sat cross-legged. "Do you have any Disney movies?"

Carter chuckled. "What do you think?"

"I know you like them." She smiled. "I wanna watch *The Little Mermaid*, but it's upstairs."

"Then go get it. You can watch it down here if you want."

She bit the inside of her cheek. "Then I'd have to go up there."

"Where is it?"

"It should be on top of the VCR."

Carter crept up the basement steps, the volume of the argument increasing with each step.

"You sit around here all day getting fat," Grace said.

He heard heavy steps.

"Let go of me!"

"You need to shut your fuckin' mouth," Jim said.

Carter stood in the kitchen, watching. His parents were in the family room, only a few feet from the VCR. His father gripped his mother's upper arms and shook her as he spoke, as if shaking her would make his words stick. Carter snuck around the kitchen counter toward them. His mother saw him first, her eyes flicking away from her husband to focus on Carter. His father followed her gaze.

The big man turned, his face a mask of barely-controlled fury. "Get your ass downstairs."

Carter ignored his father, marched to the TV, and grabbed *The Little Mermaid*. His stomach sank at the lightness of the case. He pressed the power button on the VCR.

"I said, get your ass downstairs," Jim said. Carter pressed the eject button. Jim moved within inches of Carter, his breath hot on the back of his neck. It took a moment for the machine to spit the tape out.

"Did you hear me?" Jim said.

Carter grabbed the tape as it appeared. He sidestepped his father, who glared down at him. His mother stared at the floor, avoiding Carter's eyes as he marched past.

* * *

The click of the mouse and the tapping on the keyboard put Carter on full alert. He left his bedroom and turned into the hall. The basement living room had a couch, a glass round table, wicker chairs in the corners, and a computer desk. Bright framed Panamanian molas hung from the walls. The red, orange, black, white, and yellow multi-layered fabrics were sewn together as fish, birds, and turtles.

His father turned away from the computer and glared. "You need to cut the grass."

"Can I do it later in the week?" Carter asked. "The grass is wet from the rain last night."

His dad clenched his jaw. "It's a hundred degrees out. It's dry. Do it now."

"I'm going to Ben's. Can I do it when I get back?"

The chair squeaked in protest when his dad stood up. Jim marched closer to Carter until he was within grasping distance. "I'm gonna say this once. Don't make me say it again. Get your ass outside and cut the grass."

Carter bowed his head. "Yes, sir."

He entered the garage. Boxes were piled to the ceiling. The bench press and squat rack held Olympic bars, loaded down with weight. Carter opened the garage door, and rolled out the push mower. He primed the engine, set it to choke and yanked on the cord. The motor cranked to life, and he eased the choke to run. He mowed the front and back lawns and, afterward, parked the mower back in the garage. He brushed off his calves and his knee-length mesh shorts. He shook the grass from his shoes.

Carter looked up at the sun, high and bright in the sky. The heat felt comfortable now that he was out of his football gear. He shut the garage and walked down the sidewalk towards Ben's house. He climbed the steps two at a time and pressed the doorbell. Mr. Wheeler appeared with a grin. His pointed chin, large forehead, and beady eyes made him look half alien.

"Carter, come on in," he said.

"Hey, Mr. Wheeler," Carter said, stepping inside. He slipped off his running shoes.

"That's not necessary."

"I was mowing. I don't wanna track grass on your white carpets."

"You played great in the scrimmage yesterday."

Carter shrugged. "Thanks. I'm still second string."

Mr. Wheeler patted him on the shoulder. "I don't know much about football, but from what I saw, you were better than any of those kids, first string or not."

"Thanks."

Mr. Wheeler grinned. "Your dad must be proud."

Carter looked away.

Mrs. Wheeler called out from the kitchen. "Carter, honey, could you come here for a moment?"

Carter followed Mr. Wheeler to the kitchen. It smelled like bananas and cream. Mrs. Wheeler stood behind the white laminate counter wearing an apron. A half-dozen small bowls of creamy dessert sat on the counter.

She smiled. "I need you to be my guinea pig."

Carter grinned.

"My little sister has a baby shower next weekend and I'm supposed to make the desserts. I was thinking of serving this banana caramel cream recipe that I found. I want you to try it, but you need to be brutally honest. So, if it's not good, you need to tell me."

"Okay," Carter said.

"I told her they were excellent," Mr. Wheeler said.

"You're biased," she said with a wink.

Carter took the bowl and dug a large spoonful of caramel, vanilla cream, and graham cracker crumble. "I'm with Mr. Wheeler on this. This is excellent." He devoured the dessert.

Mrs. Wheeler smiled, her blue eyes sparkling. "It's settled then." She glanced at the empty staircase beyond the kitchen. "I have one more thing I wanted your help with."

Mr. Wheeler shook his head. "Stay out of it, Jill."

Mrs. Wheeler waved him off. "Oh shush."

"You don't have to answer if you don't want to," Mr. Wheeler said as he walked away.

"Are Sarah and Ben dating?" she whispered to Carter. "I mean, I can never tell these days, it doesn't seem like anyone actually goes out on a date what with all the *hanging out* you kids do."

"I don't think so."

"Do you think Sarah likes Ben?"

Carter rubbed the back of his neck. "I think just as a friend."

She frowned. "Are you sure about that?"

Carter shrugged. "I think so, but … what do I know?"

She took a deep breath and pursed her lips. "I'm sorry. I really shouldn't be asking you these things. Please don't tell Ben, he'd be mortified."

Carter nodded and glanced at the staircase. "Is he in his room?"

"Sarah's in there. You might want to knock." She winked at Carter. "You never know."

Carter climbed the carpeted steps. Soft music spilled from Ben's room. An angelic voice sang about the chores he'd do as soon as he got home from work. Carter put his fist to the door and let it hang there for a moment. He brought his hand back down. He turned and started toward the stairs. Ben's door opened, the music instantly louder.

"Where are you going?" Sarah asked.

Carter stopped and turned around. "You two probably want some …" he paused, groping for the right word. "Time."

She strutted toward Carter. She wore a light-blue sundress with a wide red belt cinched around her waist. The dress was loose, but the belt hinted at the tight curves underneath.

Sarah laughed. "Time for what?"

Carter shrugged.

She doubled over laughing. "Oh my God, you think me and Ben?"

Carter held his hands out with his palms up.

"Hey, Ben," she called out. "Hey, Ben."

Ben appeared at his doorway, with a scowl on his face.

Sarah said, "Carter thinks we were—"

"Sarah," Carter said, shaking his head.

"What," Ben said, "hooking up?"

Sarah grinned. "Yeah, he was going to leave and give us our privacy."

Sarah grabbed Carter's hand and pulled him into Ben's room. She shut the door behind them. Ben sat in front of the television watching the Redskins with the volume muted.

"Turn that shit off," Ben said, turning up the volume on the television.

Sarah hit the power button on the stereo. She gazed at Carter. "So let's do the play-by-play. Carter comes to the door and hears Babyface on the stereo and he thinks Ben's gettin' some." She giggled.

Ben ground his teeth, pretending to focus on the preseason game.

"That's not …" Carter blushed. "I didn't know what was going on."

"But you had to have a mental picture of what you *thought* was going on," she said. "Where were we doing it?" She walked over to the bed. "Here?" She patted the bed.

Carter shook his head. "Sarah, stop."

She grinned and sauntered over to the computer chair. "How about here?" She put her hand on the back rest. She brushed her straight red hair out of her face and adjusted her glasses.

"I wasn't …"

"You weren't what?"

Carter exhaled. "You're right. I was thinking you guys were having sex on the bed, the chair, the floor, the TV, in the closet—"

"The closet." She laughed. "Isn't that for you and Ben?"

Ben frowned at Sarah.

She plopped down in the chair next to Ben. She looked up at Carter with a crooked smile, her full lips barely parting. "You get the floor as *penance* for your dirty mind."

Carter walked behind the pair and sat on the floor in front of the bed, his back resting on the wooden bed frame. He straightened his legs out in front of him. Sarah pushed the rolling office chair backwards with her bare feet as if she were Barney Rubble driving his car. She spun the chair around to face Carter. He reached forward, touching his toes.

"He's stretching again," Sarah said to Ben's back.

"Flexibility's important," Ben replied without turning his head.

"Are you first string?" Sarah asked Carter. "Have you crushed Noah's dreams of football glory yet?"

Carter looked up, his blue eyes narrowed. His brown hair was wavy and slightly disheveled, with a cowlick in front. "I'm still working on it."

"When's the first game?"

"Not this Friday, but next."

She swiveled toward Ben. "What about you, Ben? Are you first string yet?"

Ben looked over his shoulder with a scowl. "What do you care? I thought you hated football."

"I do, but you guys are obsessed with it, so I'm just trying to be a good friend. You know, be supportive. Or we could talk about journalism or the book I'm reading."

Ben exhaled. "No, I'm not starting yet. But I will next year."

Sarah frowned. "Next year? You guys haven't even played a game yet and you're already talking about next year?"

Ben shrugged. "I'm getting screwed this year at cornerback, but I should play on kickoff and punt … not that we ever punt."

"How are you getting screwed?"

Ben turned back to the television, showing his tan neck and neatly combed hair. "Ask Carter," he said without turning around.

Sarah swiveled around to Carter with raised eyebrows.

"I don't know anything," Carter said.

Sarah swiveled around to Ben. "He said he doesn't know anything."

Ben exhaled, still facing the television. "I heard him."

"Why do you think Carter would know?"

"Sarah, leave it alone," Carter said.

Sarah turned to Carter. "Leave what alone?"

Carter mimed cutting his own throat.

"You guys can't keep this from me. I thought we were friends."

"So did I," Ben said.

Sarah stood up. "What does that mean?"

"Ask Mr. Perfect over there."

Sarah narrowed her eyes at Carter.

"Ben, what are you talking about?" Carter asked, sitting up straight.

Ben stood and turned around, his eyes red, his mouth open, his overbite exposed. "Like you don't know."

"No, I don't."

Ben eyed Sarah. "Do you remember how I told you last year that the coach said I'd be first string this year?"

"I guess," Sarah said. "I don't see what that has to do with Carter."

"I was gonna get a gold jersey when Williams got injured, but they just moved a free safety to corner ahead of me. Guess who got the gold jersey." Ben crossed his arms.

Sarah looked at Carter, then back to Ben. "Correct me if I'm wrong, but it's a competition, not a personal attack."

"Fucking transfers shouldn't be allowed to play. I've been busting my ass for three years and they just waltz in and steal positions. Fucking Devin's not even that good. Coaches only like him because he's black."

Sarah threw up her hands. "Who's Devin, and what does he have to do with Carter?"

"Devin earned that starting spot," Carter said.

"You think he's better than me?" Ben asked.

"Yes," Carter replied.

"Get out of my house."

Carter exhaled and shook his head.

"I said get the fuck out!"

Carter walked out of the room and down the stairs. He stopped at the side door and slipped on his running shoes.

"Are you going home already?" Mrs. Wheeler called out from the kitchen.

"Thanks for the dessert," Carter said.

He trudged down the sidewalk, his head down. He heard the pitter-patter of quick steps behind him.

"Carter," Sarah said.

He stopped and turned around. She walked toward him, her flip-flops snapping. She pressed out her lower lip and slid her arm between his.

"Want some company?" she asked.

He nodded.

"Where are you going?"

"I don't know."

She smiled, her dimples on display. "I know just the place then."

They strolled arm in arm along the sidewalk, passing endless rows of identical townhouses.

"Nobody ever goes outside here," he said.

"Well, it is ninety degrees out."

He shrugged. "In Panama, on a weekend, the whole neighborhood would be out until dark. Granted, there was no television."

"You didn't have a TV?"

"We had a TV, but there wasn't anything good on. There was only one English station—SCN, The Southern Command Network. It was terrible. Everything was so old and they had the lamest commercials, if you could call 'em that. They were more like public service announcements."

"That's so random."

"There was this one that was like, 'You tell one lie and it leads to another. You tell two lies and then you're in trouble'."

She laughed. "Nice singing voice."

"I actually kinda liked that one. It was catchy."

Sarah pointed to a nondescript middle unit with beige siding and a bay window. "That's my house," she said.

"It's just you and your mom, right?"

She raised her eyebrows. "Stalking me?"

"Ben told me that your mom worked in a hair place?"

"It's a salon. She's a hair stylist."

"Do you guys not get along?"

41

"Did Ben tell you that we don't?"

"No, I just figured since we never go to your house."

She smiled. "Ben's house has better snacks. What about you? We don't hang out at your house either."

He nodded. "Ben's house has better snacks."

"Uh huh."

They arrived at a park with swings, a slide, and monkey bars. It was mulched with wood chips. They sat together on the swings. Sarah held onto the chains, rocking back and forth, her legs planted on the mulch. Carter did the same. Sarah turned toward Carter, the chains twisting.

"This is the first time we've been together alone, without Ben," she said.

He nodded. "Did he say anything after I left?"

She exhaled. "I don't know what his problem is."

"You didn't answer my question."

"It'll blow over. He was just mad. He's been talking about starting on varsity since we were freshmen."

Carter raised his eyebrows. "What did he say?"

"Carter."

"Seriously, what did he say?"

She took a deep breath. "He said that I should be careful around you, that you're violent, that you try to hurt people in practice. I told him that he needed to get a grip."

Carter closed his eyes for a moment and then stared at the wood chips.

"You okay?" she asked.

He didn't look up. "He's right. I do try to hurt people."

"Why?"

He shrugged and looked up at her. "I like the hitting. Before practice or a game, I feel all agitated, like I'm about to get into a fight. Then during, it's like I'm in this haze, where everything slows down."

"What does it feel like?"

"To hit someone?"

She nodded.

"Most of the time I don't feel anything, at least not right then. Sometimes I hit someone just perfectly, with the right explosion of my legs, and there's this loud crack of pads that everyone tells me about, but I never hear it when it happens. Then the guy's on the ground with the wind knocked out of him, or sometimes he's really hurt, or sometimes he pops up like it was nothing, and I'm hurt."

"Do most guys like the hitting?"

He shook his head. "They'll probably say they do, but if you watch closely, you can see the guys that recoil at the last split-second before impact, like they're bracing themselves. The coaches teach us tackling techniques, but they can't teach us to hit. Guys are hitters or they're not."

"Ben's not, huh?"

"No."

She bit the lower corner of her lip. "Why does he play then?"

He shrugged. "Maybe to wear the jersey on Friday. Maybe for popularity. Maybe to get girls. A lot of guys play for the fanfare."

"Why do you play?" She searched his face.

He smiled. "Definitely for the girls."

− 5 −

Domination

Across the field, the sideline was silent. The Arlington High School Eagles hung their heads and slouched their shoulders. The sun beat down on their necks. Carter glanced at the scoreboard. He brushed his uniform with his hand. It was crisp and clean. Twenty-eight-nil, ten minutes left in the second quarter. Coach Ware signaled plays to Luke from the sideline. They were about to add another six. Carter stood behind Coach Pitts and Coach Cowan, hoping to catch their eye.

"How long do you wanna keep the starters in?" Coach Pitts asked.

Coach Cowan took off his hat and wiped his brow. "This is a waste of our time. We get a better look in practice from the milky whites. I'd like to at least give 'em until the half." He placed his Marauders hat back on his head and pulled the brim low.

"We gotta get better preseason games," Coach Pitts said.

"Nobody wants to play us."

"I'd like to get Lynch some time with the ones."

Coach Cowan raised his eyebrows. "Who?"

"Carter Lynch."

Coach Cowan chuckled. "I thought his last name was Carter."

Coach Pitts grinned.

"Yeah, next series get him in there. Noah's complacent."

Coach Pitts turned around, looking up and down the sideline. "Carter … Carter!"

"Right here, Coach," Carter said, standing right in front of him.

Coach Pitts grinned with a toothpick in the corner of his mouth. His gray Marauders Football shirt was dark under the armpits. "Right in front of my face," he said. "If you were a snake, I'd a' been bit. Next series you're in for Noah."

Carter nodded.

Coach Pitts moved closer. He narrowed his eyes. "You know all the signals?"

"Yes."

"Just do what you been doin' every day in practice."

Carter nodded.

Coach Pitts smacked him on the shoulder pads and walked down the sideline.

"Noah!"

Noah was joking with Justin Whitehead by the water coolers. Justin was tall and well-built, with pinkish white skin and a blond crew cut. He wore number fifty-six like his hero, Lawrence Taylor.

Noah turned around with a smile. "What's up, Coach?"

"You're out. Carter's in next series."

Noah's eyes went wide. He held up his palm. "What, why?"

"I wanna see what he can do with the ones."

"This is bullshit." Noah tossed his helmet.

Coach Pitts moved with cat-like speed. He had Noah's jersey bunched up in his fist. "If I ever see you throw your helmet like that again, you'll *never* see the field."

Noah's eyes were red.

"Do I make myself clear?" Coach Pitts said.

Noah nodded.

Coach Pitts let go of his jersey. He marched back to Coach Cowan just in time to see Kevin Lewis score on an inside trap. After the extra point, the referee spotted the ball on the twenty.

"Defense," Coach Pitts called out.

Eleven kids hustled out to the field, Carter and Devin included.

Devin smacked Carter on the helmet. "It's about time," he said.

Carter read the signal from the sideline and relayed the play in the huddle. Zach scowled at Carter.

On first down the Eagles took the snap and handed the ball to the tailback. Justin Whitehead crushed the fullback at the line of scrimmage, clogging the hole. The tailback ran into his own player before being swallowed up by Zach and the rest of the defensive line.

Carter looked at Coach Pitts on the sideline. He flashed hand signals. Carter turned to the huddle and relayed the play.

The Eagles lined up with a slot back on the strong side. Justin was lined up on the back. Carter crept over, trying not to tip off the linebacker blitz. Justin glanced back at Carter, making sure he was there. The quarterback took the snap and Justin blitzed. Carter covered the back. Justin was coming fast. The quarterback threw a quick out to the slot off his back foot before being planted into the turf. Despite the pressure, it was a good pass. At the last split-second Carter stepped in front, dove, and deflected the football to the turf—incomplete.

Third and long, they're gonna throw it. This quarterback doesn't look you off. He'll tell you where he's going with his eyes.

On the snap of the football, Carter backpedaled, reading the quarterback's eyes. The inside receiver was open on a seam route. The quarterback locked onto the open receiver. Carter planted and sprinted toward the open receiver. The quarterback raised the football to his ear and threw a bullet. The receiver's head was turned, looking back for the ball as he ran downfield. He was blind to the oncoming freight train.

Carter was positioned for the knockout. He was at full speed. The receiver was helpless, unprotected, and the timing was dead on. The ball touched the receiver's hands for a microsecond before Carter rammed his facemask through the grasping hands of his opponent and crashed into the beleaguered player's head. He never heard the crack. He didn't even feel the impact. He was on the ground in a daze, the receiver next to him, still as a statue. He looked asleep. Carter saw Coach Pitts jumping up and down on the sideline. In the distance he saw Devin in the end zone with the football. Carter staggered to his feet. The receiver didn't move. The referees moved everyone away from the injured player.

Carter jogged to the sideline, shaking the cobwebs from his head. The coaches told the assembled players to take a knee and shut up. Carter took a knee next to his teammates. They looked at him with barely contained smiles.

Justin Whitehead was next to him. He leaned forward and said, "That's how you fuckin' hit someone."

Trainers attended to the player. An ambulance was positioned on the edge of the field. The player lifted his head.

"Thank God," Coach Cowan said. "That's the last thing we need."

"I think he was KO'd," Coach Pitts said.

"That boy is lethal."

The trainers helped the player up and walked him to the sideline. Both teams clapped. The head referee walked over to Coach Cowan.

"Coach Wilshire wants to call it," the ref said. "He said he already has three injured starters."

Coach Cowan rubbed the stubble on his chin. "Well I guess that's his choice."

The referee walked to the middle of the field and signaled the end of the game.

"Line up on the fifty," Coach Cowan said. "Put your helmets on and keep your mouths shut."

The opposing team queued up. The Marauders formed a line on the fifty-yard line. Carter was behind Zach and Justin.

"What the fuck," Zach said. "They're quitting? What a bunch of pussies."

Justin put his right hand down his pants and pulled it out. "They can all touch my fuckin' sweaty balls."

After they shook hands, Coach Cowan addressed the team at the near end zone. The players took a knee around the coach.

He said, "That's how Marauder Football's played. When you can make an opponent quit and beg for mercy, that's domination. And that's what we're about: domination. And that's what we have to be about, if we're gonna reach our goal of back-to-back state titles. We're gonna see better competition later in the season, but y'all should feel good this weekend, because come Monday, we're puttin' our hard hats back on and gettin' back to work. Next week, it's for real. Zach, break us down."

The team stood up, crowded together, and held their helmets high in the sky.

"Back-to-back on three," Zach said. "One, two, three."

"Back-to-back!" the team said.

Carter walked past the end zone, along an asphalt sidewalk, toward the locker room. The sun reverberated off the asphalt. Devin walked up next to him.

"Thanks for the present," Devin said.

"Did you score on that last play?" Carter asked.

Devin laughed. "You didn't see it?"

"No. I mean I saw you in the end zone, but I didn't see what happened."

"The ball popped off your helmet. It hung up in the air forever. It went right to me, and I had a clear run to the end zone."

"Pick six." Carter smiled.

"You going to the party tonight?"

Carter scowled. "Zach's a dick. I really don't wanna be at his house. Or his farm—wherever it is."

Devin laughed. "You're not exactly Mr. Nice Guy."

"What?"

Devin shook his head. "The whole offense hates you, except maybe Kevin."

"I'm not gonna ease up so guys will like me."

"I'm not saying you should. I'm just telling you. Even the defensive guys are tired of you flying up and hitting them in the back when there's a pile."

Carter took a deep breath. "What do I care? It's two years and I'm outta here."

"See, that's what I'm talking about. Can I be real with you for a minute?"

"Yeah, go ahead."

"It's a team sport. It isn't all about you. I get that you play pissed off. I'm just saying that maybe you should save that up for our opponents."

Carter nodded, his eyes on the asphalt. "Good point."

Devin grinned. "You could start being a team player by coming to the party tonight. Dwayne told me it's the best party of the year. The only guys invited are football players. He said there's twice as many girls as guys. Last year it got busted by the cops. That's why they moved it to Zach's farm. Two hundred girls in the middle of nowhere, no supervision—that doesn't sound fun to you?"

"I'll think about it."

Carter and Devin entered the locker room. Raucous laughter and voices hung in the air. Justin stood in his tighty whities, straddling a broomstick. He held his hand out as if he was grabbing onto an imaginary ass and started thrusting. His face contorted. "Oh yeah, Amber, you like it like that." He mimed spanking as he thrust his pelvis. "Oh yeah, smack that ass."

Much of the team laughed and egged him on. Noah sat on the bench quietly, his head down. Ben stood at his locker, his uniform spotless, laughing at Justin's antics. He didn't look at Carter.

Coach Cowan walked into the room. He stood in the doorway with his arms crossed, scowling at Justin. The laughter slowed and gradually ceased as, one by one, each player spotted their coach. Justin was in mid-thrust when he saw Coach Cowan. His imaginary erection deflated as he pulled the broomstick from between his legs.

Coach Cowan shook his head at Justin. "Boy, you got some

problems." He turned to Carter. "I need to see you in my office." He looked at Noah. "You too."

Carter and Noah followed the coach. As soon as they left the locker room, laughter erupted. Coach Cowan stopped at the door to his office.

"Wait here," Coach Cowan said to Carter.

Noah and the coach entered the office. The door shut. Ten minutes later, Noah emerged with red eyes and slumped shoulders. Coach Cowan stuck his head out.

"Carter, come in here," he said. "Shut the door behind you."

Coach Cowan walked behind the oak desk and eased into the leather chair. Behind him were shelves loaded with trophies and plaques and signed footballs.

"Have a seat," Coach said, motioning to the two wooden chairs in front of his desk.

Carter sat down. He still wore his socks, football pants, and sleeveless undershirt. Eye black was smudged under his eyes. Coach Cowan's dark hair was matted down from the hat that sat on his desk.

"You're a transfer, right?" Coach asked.

"Yes, sir," Carter said.

"Where you comin' from?"

"Panama. Central America, not Florida."

"That's a long way."

Carter nodded.

"Coach Pitts and I like what you been doin' in practice and in the scrimmages."

"Thank you, sir."

"I'm movin' you up to the first team. This is a big responsibility. Do you understand that?"

"Yes, sir."

"I mean we already got a proven commodity with Noah. And I don't like benchin' a senior, especially one that's pretty damn good. But dammit, boy, you sure are hard to ignore."

Carter stared, blank-faced.

Coach Cowan chuckled. "What I'm tryin' to say is you keep doin' what you been doin', you'll be just fine. If you slack off even one bit, Noah will be there nippin' at your heels. You get what I'm tryin' to tell you?"

"I think I understand, Coach."

Cowan scowled. "You think? There ain't no time for thinkin' in this game, you gotta know."

Carter stared at his coach, his eyes unblinking. "*I know* I'll be the best defensive back you've ever coached."

Coach Cowan nodded his head with a grin. "You know what all the best defensive backs have in common?"

"No, sir."

"Confidence."

– 6 –

Initiation

The sun was orange and low in the sky. Devin steered the compact car uphill on a gravel road. Carter read the photocopied directions.

"Is this right?" Devin asked.

"According to the directions," Carter said.

"There's nothing out here but farms."

"I think that's the point."

At the crest of the hill, they heard the faint sound of music and a cacophony of voices.

"That's gotta be it," Devin said.

Midway down the hill, close to a hundred cars and trucks were parked haphazardly on the pasture in front of a stone farmhouse. Devin pulled into an open spot just off the road. They stepped from the car. Carter and Devin walked down the road, the volume increasing with each step. Devin's hair was freshly cut, his fade slanted, with three lines shaved into the side of his head. Carter wore a pair of baggy jeans and a white T-shirt that said *Operation Just Cause* across the front. He walked with his hands in his pockets.

They passed a couple making out in the back seat of a Buick. Devin slowed down to catch a peek. He glanced at the back of Carter's shirt as he caught up to his friend.

"Is that a pineapple on your shirt or a man?" he asked, laughing.

Carter grinned, his teeth white and straight. "Both. It's ol' pineapple face, Manuel Noriega."

Zach's farmhouse had a front porch that spanned the entire length of the building. The metal roof was rusting. A group of teenage girls clustered around a swinging chair attached to the porch roof. They laughed and talked. A few turned their heads toward them. Devin blushed and gave them a wave. They giggled.

Devin looked down and scowled at his dusty white Nikes. "Got my new kicks dirty already."

"Should we knock?" Carter asked.

Devin looked up from his shoes. "I don't know." His nose was long, his cheekbones high, his brown skin had a tinge of red.

A girl from the group sauntered over, her hips rocking back and forth, her cowboy boots clomping on the wooden porch. She held a bottle of Corona with a lime wedge inside. The girl wore short jean shorts and a tank top. She smiled at the boys through perfect teeth.

"Carter and Devin," she said.

They widened their eyes. "How'd you know that?" Devin asked.

"You're the two transfers everyone's been talking about. I saw you guys at the scrimmage. You came to the right place." She smiled and bit the corner of her lower lip.

"For the party or the school?" Carter asked.

She giggled. "Both. I'm Amber by the way."

Amber had big, round, green eyes, and a thin nose.

Carter stood, staring. "It's nice to meet you."

Devin looked at the pair with his head cocked.

"Why don't you two walk around, enjoy the party," she said. She opened the front door and stepped aside. Voices and music flooded the air.

Devin stepped inside. As Carter moved to follow, Amber grabbed his hand. He stopped and turned.

She raked her teeth over her bottom lip. "Why don't you come find me later?" she said.

Partygoers were scattered everywhere. The house had a rustic feel. Exposed wooden beams crisscrossed the ceiling, and a generous stone fireplace was set into the wall. Deer heads and football memorabilia were mounted on the walls. To their right, guys were crowded on a couch watching college football. Voices and music drowned out the commentary. Beyond the television was a staircase going up. Girls stood together, red plastic cups in hand, laughing and telling secrets. To the left a group of girls and guys bounced quarters into shot glasses on the dining room table. Carter followed Devin straight ahead, down a short hallway to the kitchen. Zach, Justin, and Noah sat around a square kitchen table, casually drinking, a half-dozen girls around them. In front of the kitchen counter, three kegs were submerged in trash cans filled with ice. Dwayne and Luke pumped piss-colored liquid into red cups held out by underage girls like it was communion wine.

"It's the army boys," Zach said, raising his cup. His crew cut was gelled, his button-down pressed.

Carter and Devin turned toward the table.

Noah glowered at Carter. "Hey, douchebag, you're not keepin' my position."

A strawberry blonde sitting next to Noah giggled, baring a mouth full of metal.

Carter smiled. "It's a lot easier to keep it than to get it."

Justin stood up, stretching his six-foot-two frame. His fresh crew-cut was turned into a tight Mohawk. "It's a party, boys. Tonight ain't about football. It's about fuckin' and gettin' fucked up."

A handful of guys raised their cups. "Yeah, buddy!"

Justin stepped between Carter and Devin and put his arms around them. He walked them to the kegs.

"Hey, Dwayne, you know these two boys," Justin said with a crooked grin.

Dwayne looked at Carter with a scowl. Large diamond studs punctured both his earlobes.

"What's wrong, Dwayne? You want your red jersey?" Justin laughed.

Dwayne handed his drink to the girl next to him. "I'm gonna fuck you up."

Justin had a shit-eating grin.

Luke jumped between them, wrapping Dwayne up in a bear hug. "Relax, he's just fucking with you," he said.

Dwayne backed off, moving back to the keg. He glared at Justin.

"Quit being a dick," Luke said to Justin.

"I'm just tryin' to be a mediator here," Justin said, trying to contain his smile. "Gettin' defensive backs and receivers to call a truce. Maybe y'all can kiss and make up."

"Fuck you," Dwayne said.

"Well at least get my boys here some beer."

Dwayne motioned to Devin and handed him a beer in a red cup. Luke handed Carter a beer. Dwayne gave Devin a crash course in how best to secure female companionship.

Carter opened the sliding glass door and walked onto the deck. It was packed with groups of guys and girls talking and drinking. Everyone had an orange tinge from the last bit of sun as it dropped below the horizon. A handful of girls smoked. He guzzled his beer. A tall girl in heavy makeup and a tight shirt took a drag from her cigarette. She dropped her hand to her side, burning Carter's forearm. He yanked his arm back.

"Hey, watch it," he said with a scowl. "You burned my arm."

"Then move out the way," she said, matching his scowl and placing her cigarette back to her lips.

In the blink of an eye, he snatched the cigarette from her hand and tossed it over the edge of the railing. She stood dumbfounded. He turned away from her and walked down the deck steps to the back yard. A mixed group of kids sat around a fire pit, mesmerized by the flames. Most of the boys were backup defensive backs, Ben included. The girls looked young, probably tenth grade.

"What's up, guys," Carter said as he approached.

"Hey, Carter," one of the guys said—a skinny kid with patchwork facial hair. "What are you doing slumming it out here?"

Ben stared into the fire, his back to Carter.

"Didn't y'all hear?" the skinny kid continued. "Carter's the new starting free safety."

"Good for you," another kid said, raising his red cup.

Carter gulped the rest of his beer. The girls, previously uninterested, eyed Carter with curiosity. The boys made no attempt to continue the conversation or to make room for him around the fire, so he walked past toward the barn. A single lightbulb shined above the barn door. The wooden building was dilapidated, its red paint peeling. A metal trash can stood to the right of the open door. He dumped the plastic cup in the can. He glanced inside the door. It was empty except for an old motorboat on a trailer. It was a cruiser, but the engines were long gone. The upper deck was open air. Portholes along the hull signified lower deck sleeping quarters.

He hiked past the barn, stopping at the top of a bluff. Down the hill was a pond about half the size of a football field. Bulrushes and cattails sprang up from the water edge. The middle was still and blue. He moved down to the edge and stood listening to the frogs, his hands in his pockets.

"There you are," a female voice said.

Carter turned around. Amber stood with her hands on her hips and a smile on her face.

"Hey," Carter said.

She strutted down to the water, bumping him with her hip. "I thought you were gonna come find me?" She pulled the hair tie from her ponytail and shook her head, letting her dirty blonde hair settle on her shoulders.

He blushed. "I was just looking around."

"Are you shy?" she asked, interlacing her hand in his.

He looked at the water.

She slid in front of him, her chest brushing against him, her hand still intertwined in his. "Do you like me?" she asked.

"We've known each other for thirty minutes."

She frowned. "I didn't say love. You should know if you like some-one right when you see them."

"Are you asking if I think you're pretty?"

She nodded, her bottom lip pushed out. "Am I?"

"You look beautiful, there's no doubt about that."

"Aww, aren't you just the sweetest?"

She stepped closer, pressed against him, and slid her hands around his lower back, just below ol' pineapple face. He pressed his lips to hers. Her mouth parted, her tongue stirring against his. After a moment they separated.

"I like you," she said. "I'm sure now. A kiss can tell a girl everything she needs to know about a guy."

Carter narrowed his eyes. "All that from a kiss?"

She giggled. "So … if you happen to find yourself in the basement later, I want you to come down here to the barn. Nobody will be here. It'll be easier."

Carter raised his eyebrows. "Easier for what?"

"You'll see."

"I'm actually thinking about getting outta here."

She frowned. "You just got here. The party just started. It's gonna get good, you'll see."

"All right."

"You hungry? I saw some pizza somewhere."

"Yeah, I could eat."

They strolled arm in arm up the hill, past the barn, to the fire pit. Only the girls remained from the group. Carter glanced up at the deck, and again only girls. They stared at Carter as if he didn't belong.

"What's going on?" Carter asked Amber. "Where is everyone?"

The corners of Amber's mouth quivered. "Not sure. Let's go inside and see."

They wandered through the crowd of girls on the deck, opened the sliding glass door and entered the kitchen. A couple of girls squirted wine from a box into their cups. The same girls from earlier still sat at the kitchen table. Zach and Justin stood in the hallway across from a closed door. They leaned against the wall, their arms crossed. Amber looked up at them and motioned with her eyes. Justin moved first, stepping in front of Amber and Carter to open the door. Zach wrapped up Carter in a bear hug, using his mass to push him toward the open door. Carter saw the stairs leading down. He thrashed, pushing back, not giving ground.

"Relax," Amber said. "It's okay."

"Just go down there, damn," Justin said. "It's for your own good."

Carter continued to struggle. Zach had control of Carter's upper body. Justin grabbed Carter's legs and they carried him downstairs. Amber closed the door. Zach and Justin carried him through a crowd of his teammates to the middle of the room.

"I knew he'd be a dick," Zach said as they dropped him.

Carter looked around. The light was low, the ceiling was low, the wooden joists visible. It was musty but cool. The floor was gravel. Sixty or seventy football players crowded around the edge of the room. A dozen or so of Carter's teammates stood with him in the middle, stuck in a similar position. Ben and Devin were included in this group. He stood up and dusted off his jeans.

"What the hell is this?" Carter said.

"Initiation, bitch," Noah replied. He stood with his arms crossed, his biceps bulging. A cardboard box filled with cucumbers sat at his feet.

Carter glanced around for an exit. "I don't give a fuck about your initiation. Let me out."

"It ain't my initiation, it's yours," Noah replied.

Carter walked toward the stairs. Zach and Justin stood at the bottom of the steps, almost five hundred pounds of muscle blocking the way.

Zach shook his head. "No way you're getting out of this."

Carter turned around and saw another set of stairs on the opposite wall. He marched across the room. Eight guys blocked the exit, Dwayne and Luke in front.

"Relax man," Luke said. "It's not that bad. It's actually pretty awesome. So quit being a dick."

Carter took a deep breath and shook his head. "This is bullshit." He walked back to the middle of the room. He stood alongside Devin.

"Chill," Devin said. "Team player, remember."

"All right," Zach said, stomping to the middle of the room with his captives. "Now that everyone's here and accounted for we can begin." Zach glowered at the players standing in the middle of the room. His beefy arms were sunburnt, his cheeks red. "Everyone who plays varsity football for the North Potomac Marauders has to pass the initiation test. A lot of you guys fresh off the J.V. squad already passed at the party during spring camp, but we still have a few bitches left."

Carter crossed his arms, eyeing Zach.

"There are only two rules for initiation." He turned, his arms aloft like an actor addressing an audience. "Rule number one: no two initiations can ever be the same. Rule number two: the seniors decide what the little bitches have to do." Zach looked at the uninitiated players with a smirk. "We thought this time we'd be nice and give you a choice of three different tests. Don't y'all bitches think that's nice of us?" Most of the hostages stared at the gravel floor. "I asked y'all a fucking question!"

A few guys nodded their heads. A few spoke the affirmative.

"So here's the deal. Option number one is, in my opinion, the easiest. This is what I'd do if I were in your shoes." Justin and Noah suppressed grins. "Option one is quick and painless. All you have to do is get on your knees, and let Justin smack you in the face with his dick." Zach chuckled.

Eyes widened among the captives.

"Don't worry," Justin said. "I'll be gentle."

"Come on y'all—that's not so bad," Zach said. "It won't hurt and it'll be over in a split second."

Carter stood expressionless.

Zach continued. "Now option number two is called the jubie. Noah over there has a box of cucumbers." Noah picked up a penis-sized cucumber and held it in front of his crotch. Justin and several others laughed. "All you have to do is hold the cucumber in your ass-crack for ten seconds." Zach looked at the assembled neophytes. "I'll give y'all a hint on getting that cucumber to hold. If you want it to stay in place, you gotta stick up in there just a little bit."

"Just the tip," Justin blurted out.

Everyone in the room laughed except for the thirteen kids in the middle.

"Now option three," Zach said, "is by far the most difficult and most embarrassing of the three tests. If you choose this, you're fucking insane. For option three, you have to strip down and leave all your clothes, wallet, and keys down here, where we'll keep them until you've completed the test. You'll exit the basement up those steps over by Luke and Dwayne." Zach pointed across the room to the star quarterback and receiver. They stepped aside revealing concrete steps. "Now once you get outside, you have one goal: find a girl to fuck." Zach laughed. "She's gonna know you're ready to fuck because, well, you'll be butt ass naked." A spattering of laughter ensued. "And because we're all about safety here, Luke will give you each a condom."

Luke stepped forward and held up a box of condoms as if it were a game show prize.

Zach continued. "Once you get some pussy, you can get your clothes back. This last one is fucking hard. You're gonna be outside naked in front of two hundred girls trying to get laid. If you can't do it, you'll just have to sleep outside with your dick blowing in the wind. So, what's it gonna be, faggots?"

The captives glanced at each other, waiting for someone to choose.

Zach exhaled and tapped an imaginary wristwatch. "Let's go, I don't have all night." He glared at Ben. "What about you, little Wheeler? You got the stones to be the first one to make a choice?"

Ben stared at the gravel. "I'll do the first one," he said.

"What was that?" Zach asked. "Speak up."

"The first one."

Much of the room laughed. Zach's eyes widened. He glanced at Justin and Noah. Justin shrugged.

"What about you, Carter?" Zach said. "You're such a tough guy. Think you can hold a cucumber in your ass?"

Carter took a deep breath and rubbed his temples. "Y'all are gonna pay for this shit. Every last one of you."

"Is that your choice?" Zach said with a crooked smirk. "You want the jubie?"

Carter shook his head. "Let me out of here. If I have to leave my clothes ... fine."

Carter marched to the Bilco doors, where Luke and Dwayne stood. He took off his T-shirt, slipped off his running shoes, and pulled down his jeans. The eleven undecided players followed him. They stripped down to their boxers and socks. Ben stood alone, fully clothed in the middle of the room.

"Can I change my choice?" Ben asked. "I'll go out naked."

Zach shook his head. "On Friday night, can you change a decision, or do you just have to deal with the results? What do you guys think, should we let little Wheeler change his decision?"

"Dick-slap the little faggot," someone from the audience said to laughter and applause.

Carter looked across the room at Ben. His head was down, his shoulders slumped. He glanced at Devin.

Devin shook his head and mouthed, "This is messed up."

"Sorry little buddy," Zach said. "Now get on your knees and take your medicine."

Ben bent down in his jean shorts, his knees digging into the gravel, tiny shards creating indents in his skin. His eyes were closed. Justin sauntered in front of him. He pulled his zipper down. Ben's chin trembled. Noah handed Justin a cucumber. Justin put it up to his crotch, turned his hips and smacked the vegetable across Ben's face. The room erupted in laughter. Ben opened his eyes. The cucumber still dangled in front of his face. Ben staggered to his feet, little bits of gravel sticking to his knees.

Zach scowled at Ben. "Go on back upstairs, *you're done.*"

Ben trudged up the basement steps. His teammates stepped aside like he was infected with some horrible disease.

As the door shut someone shouted, "Cocksucker!" The room erupted in laughter once again.

Zach moved toward the dozen guys that stood by the concrete steps in their underwear. The crowd closed in.

"Let us out," Carter said.

Zach laughed. "Not like that." He shook his enormous head. "That's not naked. Y'all better get them drawers off."

Carter took a deep breath. The guys looked at each other with wide eyes and downturned mouths.

"I'll tell you what," Zach said. "Y'all can wear your socks and shoes, but the drawers stay here."

Carter bit the inside of his cheek. He pulled down his boxer shorts, stepped out of them, and slipped on his running shoes. The others followed suit.

"Don't forget your condoms," Zach said. "I wouldn't be raw dogging with some of those hoes out there."

Carter glared at Luke and Dwayne. "Move out of my fucking way."

They stepped aside. Carter snatched the condom from Luke and climbed the concrete steps. He pushed the Bilco doors open. A crowd of girls were massed outside. Camera flashes blinded him. Shouting, laughter, and catcalls pierced the humid air. He blinked, trying to focus through the bright lights. He saw cameras and smiles, girls holding up trench coats and blankets.

"He has a nice body for a white boy," a girl shouted.

"Do you want a coat?" another girl asked.

Carter pushed his way through the crowd and sprinted toward

the barn, the single light beckoning. The crowd cheered as he ran. He swung the door open and slammed it behind him. The barn was dark except for a flickering yellow light coming from the portholes of the boat. Close to the door, he was concealed by darkness, but if he moved any closer, he'd be illuminated.

"Amber?" he said.

After a moment she popped her head out on the upper deck of the boat. Her body cast a long shadow in the dim light. She held a beach towel.

"Look at you," she said with a wide smile. "Why don't you step closer so I can get a good look?"

He stood still in the dark shadows.

"You *are* shy," she said laughing. "Don't you trust me?"

"Can you please bring me that towel?"

"Aww, you seem upset. It was just a joke."

She put the towel over her shoulder and climbed down the metal ladder that hung off the back of the boat. She strutted toward him with a bright smile, her teeth glowing in the dim light. She stopped at the edge of the shadows, some ten feet away.

"Why don't you meet me halfway," she said. "I don't bite."

"Come on Amber, this isn't cool," he said.

She pressed out her lower lip. "There's not a guy at school that wouldn't love to be naked and alone with me. What's wrong?"

"You lied."

She frowned. "It was gonna happen either way. I thought you liked me."

He was still and silent.

"How about we make a deal? I'll take off my top if you come over here into the light." She waited for a response.

He said nothing.

"I'll take that as a yes," she said.

She folded the towel, and placed it between her legs to hold it in place. She slipped her pink tank top over her head. Her stomach was tan and toned, her breasts mashed together in a white lace pushup bra. She reached behind her back and unclasped. She crossed her arms and slid the straps and the bra down. Her breasts were tan and firm. She bit her lip. He stepped forward into the light. She gasped, her eyes on his erection.

"You do like me," she said with a smirk.

He reached for her crotch, grabbing the beach towel from between her legs. He unfolded it and wrapped it around his waist, his erection pitching a tent.

She pressed out her lower lip. "Hey, I was enjoying the view." She glanced at the square plastic packet in his hand and giggled. "What do you think you're gonna do with that?"

He stepped forward and pressed his chest to hers. She tilted her head back and they kissed, slowly and softly. She pulled away.

"I have a surprise for you," she said as she strutted to the boat, her bra and tank top in hand. She looked over her shoulder and mimed a kiss his way. "Come on."

He followed, the bright beach towel wrapped around his waist. He stood underneath her as she climbed the boat ladder. Carter saw a flash of white under her jean shorts as she climbed. He scaled the ladder to the top deck. She was gone. He followed the flickering light down the steps into the cabin below, entering the first room to his right. A single bed filled most of the small space, and a candle flickered on a built-in bedside table. Amber was on her side, her head propped up by her hand, her slender body wrapped in a flannel comforter. Jean shorts, a white bra, a pink tank top, and white panties were piled in a heap in front of the bed.

Carter felt faint. He placed the condom on the bedside table and sat on the edge of the bed as he slipped off his shoes and socks. He gazed at her, his face hot.

"Are you okay?" she asked, her lips curled.

"Yeah. I guess I didn't expect this to happen. I'm not really prepared."

She smiled, laughing. "Prepared? We're not taking the SAT's."

He frowned. "Please don't laugh."

She stopped laughing, her mouth turned down. "Carter, I'm sorry. I didn't mean anything by it. I really like you. I thought you'd like this."

"I do," he said, looking down at the towel wrapped around him. "I just don't know what I'm doing."

She smiled. "You certainly know how to kiss, and that's a lot of it right there. Why don't you just get in with me, and we'll see what happens. We can just lay here if you want."

Carter tugged the towel off his waist and dropped it on the floor. She opened the flannel comforter. He slid in next to her on his side, one arm propping himself up, the other draped over her lower back. She pressed her body and her lips against his. His erection stiffened against the coarse hairs of her pubic area. She grabbed his penis and pulled it down between her legs. She rubbed his erection back and forth over her clitoris, moaning, moisture building. She leaned into his ear.

"Do you want to?" she asked through heavy breaths.

He turned toward the bedside table and grabbed the condom. He fumbled with the wrapper, his heart racing.

"Give it to me," she whispered. "Lay on your back."

He handed her the wrapper and lay on his back. She sat up and straddled his thighs, ripping the condom wrapper as she did so. She took the rubber disc and rolled it down his erection. Amber, still straddling him, lowered herself onto his penis, gasping as he entered.

His hands found their way to her hips. She braced her hands against his muscular chest. He moved his pelvis in rhythm with hers for a few minutes. Her eyes were closed. Her lips were swollen, her mouth open.

"Wait," he said.

But she moved faster, pushing him past the point of no return. He groaned as he climaxed. She moaned and exhaled, her eyes shut tight. Eventually she shuddered, her breath coming out in one smooth motion. She opened her eyes and smiled before collapsing against him. Carter turned to face her as she nuzzled against him, her arm and leg draped over his body.

"I'm sorry," he said.

She propped herself up on her elbow and raised her eyebrows. "Why?"

"I don't think that was very good."

She frowned at him. "You didn't like it?"

He propped himself up toward her. "No, it's not like that. I mean for you. I think maybe I was too fast."

She smiled, her pink lips glistening in the candlelight. "I thought it was very good."

"Did you ... you know."

She laughed. "Did I what?"

"You know."

"Have an orgasm?"

"Yeah."

"That's why I got on top." She grinned. "That way I can push my own buttons."

He looked down, then back at her. "Have you ever done this before?"

She scowled. "I'm almost eighteen, what do you think?"

He shook his head. "I'm sorry, that's not what I meant. I mean this initiation thing." He pursed his lips. "If you don't wanna tell me, it's okay."

She grinned and pecked him on the lips. "Let's just say it was a first for both of us."

"Is this what the initiation's supposed to be? We're all supposed to have sex?"

"Every initiation's different."

He narrowed his blue eyes. "I'm asking about this one."

She shrugged. "I doubt all the guys are gonna have sex. Probably only a couple of them." She winked at Carter. "Only the really hot ones."

"So everyone else is gonna sleep outside naked?"

She giggled. "No, the girls are just gonna tell Zach and Justin that they had sex with the guys so they can get their stuff back. They're gonna make out, and some guys might get a blowjob."

Carter nodded. "The girls knew, didn't they?"

She smiled. "That's why I was telling you to relax when they took you down to the basement. It did turn out pretty great, don't you think?"

He smiled for a second then his mouth went flat. "What about guys that nobody likes?"

"We didn't have a problem finding at least one girl to hook up with each guy. I don't wanna give you too much of a big head, but a bunch of girls asked about you." She grinned. "I told those little hoes that you were mine."

"So we run out of the basement naked thinking that we have to convince some girl to sleep with us, when really the girls are there ready to wrap us up in a jacket or blanket or whatever and take us some place to hook up?"

"Pretty awesome, huh?"

"Shit."

"What."

Carter squirmed out from under her. "I gotta go check on Ben."

"Who?" she said, sitting up.

"Ben Wheeler."

She frowned. "Why?"

"He fucked it up. He didn't run out with the rest of us."

Amber put her hand over her mouth, concealing a grin. "Oh my God, he didn't choose one of the other tests?"

Carter nodded. "I just let them do it to him."

She shook her head, still smiling. "This is crazy. Nobody thought anybody would choose the first two. What did they do to him?"

"They acted like Justin was gonna hit him in the face with his penis, but he did it with a cucumber. Afterward they told him to go back upstairs and everybody kind of looked at him like he was nothing."

She shrugged. "Maybe he's a faggot."

He scowled. "Don't say that."

"Is he your friend?"

"He was my first friend here."

"Was or is?"

"He hasn't been talking to me lately."

She held her palms up. "Well then he doesn't sound like a friend to me. I don't know why you care. He made the choice, not you."

Carter shrugged.

"He's probably gone anyway."

Carter nodded. "I guess so."

"So why don't you take that thing off and grab another one from my purse."

− 7 −

One Lie Leads to Another

Carter stood at the kitchen counter slathering peanut butter on wheat bread. He gulped down a glass of milk. Alyssa sat next to him with sleepy eyes, slurping the milk from her sugary cereal. Their mom trudged down the stairs in a long silk robe tied at her waist. Her hair was disheveled. Without makeup, her face showed crease lines around her mouth.

"Do you need a ride?" Grace asked Carter. "I'm taking Alyssa at eight."

"It's okay, Mom. We start at seven-thirty anyway. I'm just gonna walk."

Grace inspected Carter with a frown. "Sweetheart, do you think maybe you should wear something a little nicer for the first day of school?"

Carter glanced down at his baggy jeans and gray T-shirt.

"And that hat's seen better days."

Carter pulled the brim of his baseball cap low over his eyes. "I gotta go, Mom." He shoved the bread back into the refrigerator and placed the peanut butter in the pantry. "No time to change now."

She shook her head, turning away.

He swiped the sandwich and his backpack, and marched to the door. "See you guys later," he said.

The birds chirped and the late summer sun shone through a cloudless sky. He ate his sandwich as he walked alongside the townhouses, the peanut butter sticking to the roof of his mouth. As he approached the main road through his neighborhood, he saw Sarah ahead of him. He jogged to catch up. She wore red sequined flats like Dorothy from Oz and a blue sundress with white polka dots. She glanced over her shoulder as he gained ground.

"What up, beyotch?" she said with a smile. She flipped her pink satchel to her outside hip to give Carter more room on the sidewalk. It was adorned with a cartoon fairy. Her hair was brushed to the side, a few strands hanging over her glasses. Her face was flawless without makeup, her lips full without lip gloss.

"Not much," Carter said. He held up his half-eaten sandwich. "You want some?"

"What is that, peanut butter? No jelly?"

"Yeah."

"That's gross."

He took another bite. "Tastes good to me," he said, his mouth full. After swallowing, he glanced down at her hands. "What's with the gloves?"

She held up a hand encased in a long white glove that went halfway up her forearm. "It makes me feel like I'm living in a different time. You know, like when people wore top hats and addressed each other as sir and madam, not dude and man."

"Excuse me, Madam, may I escort you to your destination?" Carter said in his best stuffy voice. "It is improper for a young lady to be unescorted on a public street." Carter held his arm out like a chicken wing.

She laughed and slid her arm through. "Did you see Ben over the weekend?"

"Saturday at the scrimmage," Carter said as they walked.

She took a deep breath. "Last I talked to him he said he was going to the big football party at some farmhouse." She pursed her lips.

He glanced at her. "Why, what's wrong?"

"I don't know. I went over to his house Sunday, but his mom said he was sick. And then today, I didn't see him. Last year he waited on the corner for me every day. I'm assuming you went to the party."

"Yeah."

"Did you see him there?"

"Just the back of his head. He doesn't talk to me, remember."

She frowned. "Did something happen there?"

He bit the inside of his cheek. "Where?"

"The party, where do you think?"

He sucked in his bottom lip and pressed it out. "Maybe. Like I said, I didn't see him much."

"I know the football team has initiations. Two years ago, a kid went to the ER for alcohol poisoning."

"What happened?"

"Nothing as far as I know. He still plays."

Carter raised his eyebrows. "Who?"

She ignored his question. They watched the red hand on the traffic light across the street. Cars and trucks zipped past, the smell of exhaust in the air.

She turned to Carter. "Did they force you to drink?"

"No."

She nodded.

"Who was the kid that got alcohol poisoning? You said he still plays."

"Your boy, Noah. Congrats by the way, I heard you took his position."

The light flashed *walk* in green. They picked up their pace as they moved across the four-lane road. Carter glanced at the cars, the front ends lurching forward as the three-thousand-pound machines ground to a halt in front of the crosswalk.

"It's not *his* position," Carter said.

She glanced at him, her mouth flat. "You're right, it's yours. You're a man of your word, Carter Lynch. You said you'd take his position and you did."

"You say that like I did something wrong. Didn't you say it was a competition, not personal? I worked hard. The coaches didn't give me anything."

She pursed her lips. "You're right, I'm sorry. I'm happy for you. I tend to be cranky in the a.m."

Carter exhaled. "I don't think anyone wanted me to have this position."

She stopped and turned to Carter. He stopped, their arms still interlocked. "I'm sorry for being a bitch. You don't deserve it." She shook her head and exhaled, her eyes searching his. "I hate football. Ben's mad at you over it, putting me in the middle of you guys. Kids get hurt on and off the field. You know, Noah was a nice kid in middle school. It's like they get on varsity and turn into varsity assholes."

They continued down the sidewalk, the sprawling brick school looming large in the background.

"Is that what you think is gonna happen to me?" Carter asked.

She smiled briefly. "I like you despite your head-ramming fetish, not because of it."

* * *

The lunchroom was filled with the buzz of voices, clanging trays, and stomping feet. Carter pushed his tray along the metal counter. Justin nudged in front and dumped his empty tray on the counter.

He turned to Carter. "What's up man, let me get in line with you."

They grabbed plates of pulled pork, corn, and fries from the lunch lady and placed the heaped platters on their trays.

Justin smirked at Carter. A large M was shaved into the side of his pale head. "I heard *you* had fun on Saturday."

Carter was blank-faced. "It was all right."

"All right?" Justin said with a frown. "I heard you fucked Amber all night."

"It's none of your business."

Justin cackled. "Did she keep those cowboy boots on?"

Carter shook his head, his mouth turned down.

"That body's bangin' too, all tan and shit."

"You're holding the line, young man," the elderly cashier said.

Justin turned toward the cashier and closed the gap. He paid for his meal, took his tray off the counter, and moved behind her. The elderly woman took Carter's money while Justin mimed having sex with her from behind. Laughter broke out among the kids behind Carter. She turned around and found Justin standing still.

She narrowed her eyes. "What are you doing?"

Justin gave her a bright white smile. "Just waitin' for my friend, ma'am."

"Go sit down," she said.

Justin left as Carter took his change. Carter scanned the hall for potential dining places. Dwayne, Kevin Lewis, Michael Townsend and a few other black football players sat together, with a handful of black girls interspersed. A table of white football players was on the opposite side of the cafeteria. Zach, Noah, and Luke sat among them, with white girls interspersed. There was a table of boys with black clothing and studded belts, with chains slung from their belt loops to their pockets. There were tables of girls ranked in terms of attractiveness. There were tables with Asian girls, Latino boys, and every other racial, ethnic, and gender divide imaginable. *I wish Devin was in my lunch period.*

One person sat by herself. Sarah was in a corner, a brown paper bag in front of her. She sipped from her thermos with one hand, the other holding open a paperback. Despite the differences between the cliques and cultures, most of the kids were similar in their dress, their speech, and their mannerisms. Sarah was the outlier. She looked like she belonged in a café, drinking coffee in some famous European city.

Carter balanced his tray and paced over.

"May I join you, Madam?" he said in his portentous voice.

She glanced up from her book. "Why yes, my good sir."

Carter placed his tray in front of her and sat down.

She scrunched up her face. "How can you eat that crap?"

Carter shrugged, picked up a fry, and shoved it into his mouth. "What are you reading?" he mumbled, his mouth full.

She flipped the cover of the tattered text. "*All The President's Men* by Bernstein and Woodward."

"What's that about?"

"You don't know who Bob Woodward and Carl Bernstein are?"

"Should I?"

"Well of course. They were the Washington Post journalists that broke the Watergate scandal. You think football requires courage. Politicians are snakes."

A hand touched Carter's shoulder. He turned around to Amber's pouting face. "I thought we were gonna have lunch together," she said.

Carter raised his eyebrows. "You never said—"

"You don't mind if I borrow my *boyfriend*, do you?" Amber said to Sarah, her smile dripping with artificial sweetener. Carter's eyes widened at the word "boyfriend".

"By all means," Sarah said.

"Come on, sweetie," Amber said, tugging on his T-shirt.

Carter stood and grabbed his tray. "I'll see you later?"

Sarah smirked. "I don't know, are you allowed?"

* * *

Carter and The North Potomac Marauders took a knee on the dusty practice field in front of Coach Cowan. The players had their helmets off exposing their young faces, some marked with acne, many more with red marks on their foreheads. They had disheveled hair that was wet with sweat. Coach Cowan took off his hat and wiped his brow. His eyes were red, his face stubbly. He placed his hat back on his head.

He glanced around at the players in front of him. "I don't like what I been seein' this week." His jaw was set tight. "On Monday and Tuesday we looked just plain flat. And today, y'all figured out a way to look even worse. If y'all think Washington Heights is just gonna lay down, you got another thing comin'. These guys are the real deal. We might be seein' them again in the playoffs. If you come out flat on Friday, these guys will eat your lunch. As of right now, I'm puttin' this entire team on notice. If you're not givin' me the type of effort that I expect, I'll find someone else. Don't think I can't do it. We got damn near a hundred kids. If you think you're somethin' because you got that black jersey ..." he shook his head. "Well, I'm here to tell you that you're wrong. *Dead wrong.* You're only as good as your last play. I can replace anybody on this team. And I do mean *anybody.* I don't care how good the paper says you are." Coach Cowan paused for effect. "You know what separates the state champions from everyone else?"

"Hard work," Justin blurted out.

Coach Cowan shook his head. "You gotta work hard, but lots of teams work hard. Most of 'em don't amount to a hill o' beans. It ain't just about workin' hard. It's about attention to detail and doin' all the little things. I expect wide receivers to get those blocks downfield, to come off the ball just as hard on runnin' plays as they do on pass plays. I expect lineman to play to the whistle. I see too many fat linemen takin' plays off." Coach eyed Michael Townsend and his gut. "If you're so fat that you have to take plays off, you won't play for me—*period.* I expect running backs to run north and south and finish runs by lowering their shoulders. I see too much goddamn dancin'. I expect linebackers to make plays at the line of scrimmage. I see too many arm tackles. I expect defensive backs to lock down those receivers. You should take it as a personal insult if your man catches a single pass. We're givin' up too much.

"The bottom line is we're not playin' state championship quality football. If this was the best we could do, fine. But it's not, and y'all know it and I'm not gonna stand around while y'all piss it away."

He glanced at Coach Ware. "What do you think, Coach?"

Coach Ware stood with his arms crossed, his face shielded by dark shades. He shook his head. "They think they can just show up and teams are gonna roll over."

Coach Cowan put his hands on his hips. "I think it's even worse than that. We got a couple guys that think they don't even have to show up. Luke, what is our attendance policy?"

"If we miss three practices—"

"Stand up, Luke," Coach Cowan said.

Luke stood up in front of his teammates. "If we miss three practices without an excuse provided by phone or parents' note we'll be kicked off the team."

"And here we are, not even to our first game yet and we already got two players with three unexcused absences. They're done. So, if you see Keith Howard or Ben Wheeler, you tell 'em they better turn their stuff in or their parents are gonna get a big bill. These rules apply to everyone. I'm a tell you right now, don't test me. Tomorrow I expect to see state champions." Coach Cowan looked at his quarterback. "Luke, break us down."

* * *

Mrs. Wheeler stood in the doorway, bags under her eyes. She forced a smile.

"Carter honey, I'm glad you're here," she said. "Come in."

Carter stepped inside, the setting sun behind him.

"I really need to talk to you," she said.

They walked into the kitchen. Carter sat on a stool at the counter, his hair still wet from the shower. Mrs. Wheeler stood opposite.

"I just stopped by to see how Ben's doing." Carter said.

She rubbed her temples. "To be honest, I really don't know. But something's really wrong. I know Ben, and …" she trailed off. "Well, I just know something's really wrong."

Carter bit the inside of his cheek. "Is he sick?"

She exhaled, shaking her head. "I wish it were that simple. He won't go to school or practice. He won't even leave his room. Since he started playing football, he's never missed a single practice. I think something happened, but he won't talk to me."

Carter looked down at the counter.

"You used to come over here every day and then I stopped seeing you."

Carter looked up, his eyes wide. "I didn't do anything."

"I didn't think you did. I'm just trying to understand what's going on with my son. What happened between you two?"

Carter shrugged. "He was mad at me and told me to leave, so I did." He looked back to the counter.

"Why, honey? I won't be mad, I promise. I'm just trying to understand."

"He really wanted to start this year. He's upset that's he's still on the scout team, and he thinks I'm partly to blame for that."

Her shoulders slumped. "How is that your fault?"

Carter shook his head. "The first team right corner tore his ACL the second week of camp, but they didn't move Ben up. They moved the safety that was ahead of me to corner ahead of Ben. So, I moved up at safety instead. Then they moved Devin from the left side to the right to start over Ben."

"I don't understand. Who's this Devin person, and how are you involved?"

"Devin's a transfer like me. Ben thinks it's unfair that we're both starting but we haven't been with the team for very long. I'm really sorry."

She frowned. "No, honey, you have nothing to be sorry for."

Carter rubbed the back of his neck.

"He was grumpy when you guys were practicing all day," she said.

"Are they called two practice days?"

"Two-a-days."

"He was upset then, and was probably mad about not playing, but I think this is different. It's much worse. Do you have any idea what might've happened?" Her eyes searched Carter's.

"I'm not sure." He glanced away.

"Can you talk to him? See if you can find out?"

"I can try."

She had tears in her eyes. "Thank you, Carter."

"Is it okay if I go upstairs?" he asked.

"Of course."

Carter knocked on Ben's bedroom door. No response. He knocked harder. Nothing.

"Hey, Ben, it's me," Carter said through the door. "I just wanted to see how you're doing. I'm gonna come in, okay?" Carter put his hand on the door knob and turned.

"Go away," Ben said.

Carter released the knob. "Can I come in and talk to you?"

"When I told you to get the fuck out of my house, I meant it."

Carter took a deep breath. "Coach Cowan said you violated the attendance policy. He's kicking you off the team." There was a long pause. "Ben?"

"What difference does it make? It's not like they would've ever given me a chance."

"That's not true. You were on the kickoff team."

"That doesn't matter now, does it?"

"You just need to have your mom and dad talk to Coach Cowan. He'll let you back on."

"Maybe I don't wanna be back on. You know, Sarah was right. Football is a stupid ass game."

"It wasn't your fault," Carter said through the door. "You didn't do anything wrong at the initiation." There was silence. "Ben?"

"Amber's been with half the football team. She's a whore."

Carter didn't respond.

"Sarah told me you two were boyfriend and girlfriend," Ben said. "I wouldn't touch that skank with a ten-foot-pole."

Carter didn't respond.

Ben laughed. "You still there, or did you run off for an HIV test? Hey, douchebag, you still there?"

Carter clenched his fists. "If it wasn't for what happened on Saturday, I'd punch you in your fucking face."

Ben laughed. "There he is, the real Carter Lynch."

Carter walked away.

− 8 −

The Unraveling

Ben and Sarah sat across from one another at a back-corner table. Carter stood balancing his tray of hot dogs and French fries. He trudged to his own peer-assigned lunch spot. Amber greeted him with a smile.

"Hey, you," she said, patting the space next to her.

Carter stepped into the bench seat. Zach, Noah, Justin and Luke were talking and laughing with their favorite groupies. Carter took a deep breath and loaded a fry into his mouth. Amber ate a salad from a clear plastic container.

She nudged Carter with her hip. "Look at those little sluts," she said, gesturing with a nod of her head. "The camel toe crew."

"Camel toe crew?"

She giggled. "You don't know what camel toe is?"

Carter shook his head.

"It's when girls wear really tight pants and you can see the lips of their vag. It looks like a camel's toe. Not that I've ever actually seen a real one, like, on a camel."

Carter frowned.

She cackled. "What? That's funny and you know it. I can't believe how sheltered you are sometimes."

"I thought they were your friends?" Carter asked.

"They are. Doesn't mean they're not a bunch of little sluts."

Carter glanced at the camel toe crew. "They're just talking."

"You don't see what they're really doing."

"What are they doing?"

"Look at Lilly," she said.

Lilly had long wavy strawberry blonde hair, wide set blue eyes, and a thin figure. Her smile was expansive, bright, and shiny from her braces.

Carter thought of Alyssa as he watched Lilly giggle at Noah. "What about her?" he asked.

"See the exaggerated way she flipped her hair back. It's so sexual. She's so fucking giggly all the time. It's like this annoying background noise you can't get away from."

"She seems nice enough."

Amber scowled. "And Riley's the biggest slut. She blew like five guys at the initiation party. She looks like a Spanish hooker. I can see those dark nipples from here. It's so fucking gross."

Riley had thick, dark, wavy hair that hung just beneath her shoulders. Her face was symmetrical, her features round and soft. In the bright fluorescent light of the lunch room, Carter could see the darkness of her nipples through her white tank top and bra. She was laughing at Justin, who had his hot dog at his crotch.

"I doubt she did that," Carter said. "Everybody talks so much shit around here."

Amber smirked. "She was the one bragging about it."

"Whatever, it's none of my business. Don't you have anything nice to say about your friends?"

"Molly's okay," she said. "She has some wicked thigh spread though."

Molly was tall and curvy, with red hair, and freckles. She sat next to Zach, his hand on her leg.

"Do I even wanna know what thigh spread is?" Carter asked.

She laughed. "You know, when you sit down and your thighs spread out."

Carter shook his head. "I'd hate to hear what you say about me when I'm not around." He took a bite of his hot dog.

"I tell everyone what a big dick you have." She giggled.

He choked and swallowed. "Funny."

"Chloe's the only one I actually don't like."

Chloe had long straight blonde hair to the middle of her back. She had a bright smile and a girl-next-door kind of face. She and Luke shared a lunch. He occasionally touched her hand. It was like they were in their own little world together.

"I think Luke really likes her," Carter said.

"She walks around like she thinks she's better than everyone," Amber replied. "She's such a little bitch."

Carter rubbed his temples.

"Everybody, look at Justin," Riley said from across the table.

Amber nudged Carter. He looked up. Everyone watched Justin sneak over to a back corner table carrying a bunless hot dog. Carter's stomach churned. *Come on, Justin, just throw it away.* Justin crept behind Ben.

"Hey, Ben," Justin said.

Ben turned around, and Justin smacked him in the face with the hot dog that he dangled from his crotch. The kids sitting with Carter exploded with laughter and pounded on the table. Most of the kids sitting nearby laughed and pointed. Ben turned around and hung his head.

Sarah stood up, glaring at Justin, the lunch table separating them. "What the fuck is your problem?" she said.

"You want some of my hot dog too?" Justin asked as he thrust his pelvis, flopping his imaginary penis up and down. A crowd of onlookers laughed.

Sarah narrowed her eyes. "You're sick. People who do stuff like this are fucking deviants. They usually have real sexual problems. What's yours?"

Justin grinned. "Whatever, bitch." As he turned to walk away, he tossed the hot dog up in the air. It landed on Ben's lunch tray. Ben flinched and the crowd got one final laugh at his expense.

* * *

"Come on, we'll be quick," Amber said.

"I'll never make it," Carter said, sliding into the back seat of the Chevy Suburban SUV.

Amber was already climbing over the back seat into the third row. Her tight black mini-skirt was hiked to mid-thigh as she climbed over. He caught a glimpse of her black thong.

"Hurry up, we're wasting time," she said.

He climbed over the seat. She reached under her mini-skirt and slid her thong down her legs.

"We're not going anywhere?" he asked.

"You don't have much time, right?"

Carter glanced at the windows. "People can see in."

She smiled. "Isn't that part of the fun?"

"Seriously."

"The back windows are tinted," she said. "Quit being a baby."

Sitting next to him on the seat, she turned, leaned over, and undid his belt. She shoved her hand down his pants. He placed his hand between her legs, touching her clitoris.

Clothes came off as if they were in a race. He kicked off his shoes and pulled his boxer briefs, jeans, and socks off in one fell swoop. She removed her blouse and unclasped her bra, sliding it down her arms. He yanked his T-shirt over his head. She hiked her skirt and lay back across the seat with her legs open. He thought of Justin's comment. *That body's bangin' too, all tan and shit.*

He stopped, his eyes glazing over.

"What's wrong?" she asked.

He snapped from his fog and refocused on her naked form spread-eagled in front of him. He grabbed his jeans from the floor and retrieved a condom from the front pocket. She looked up at him in anticipation, as he slid the condom on, her lower lip sucked into her mouth. Her face was flushed, her green eyes wide and dilated. He hovered over her, his hands next to her shoulders, propping himself up. She pressed her fingertips into the flesh of his chest, leaving little pink marks. Her hands slid down his V-shaped torso. She stopped at his obliques and pulled him toward her. She held her breath as he pushed inside. Her head was held back, her mouth open, her eyes closed. He stirred slowly at first, the moisture increasing with each movement. Then they moved together in a stronger rhythm.

Amber held her head up and opened her eyes, gazing into his. She smiled, her lips parting, her teeth bright white—perfect.

"It feels good," she said. "Keep going."

And he did. Their hips ground with a steadily increasing power and rhythm. She pressed her lips to his, their mouths open, their tongues twisting. Amber detached her mouth from his, breathing heavily into his ear.

"Harder," she said, digging her nails into his back.

He responded to the pain with deep powerful thrusts. Her heavy breathing turned to moans. Her vaginal walls contracted and pulsed. She let out a long slow breath. Her body went limp; her head lolled to the side.

After a moment, she looked up. "Did you?"

"I'm close," he said.

"You're running outta time, loverboy." She giggled. "Don't worry, I know just the thing."

Amber slipped out from under him. He sat up. She stood in front of him hunched over, her head just beneath the SUV's ceiling. She turned around, her mini-skirt hiked and bunched above her hips. Her ass was tan and round, her hips flared before curving inward at her waist.

"Move forward," she said, "to the edge of the seat."

Carter scooched to the edge, moving his knees outside of hers. She bent forward at her torso. He grabbed her hips and guided her onto his penis as she sat in his lap. She used her legs to push against him, moving hard and fast. He groaned as he watched himself slide in and out of her. He climaxed shortly thereafter.

She turned around with a grin. His well-defined chest moved up and down with his diaphragm, his breathing audible. His face felt hot. His back stung. She sat down next to him. When she moved from his view, he saw the school through the front windshield.

"Shit," he said, "what time is it?"

She shrugged and giggled.

"I'm sorry, I gotta go." He grabbed his clothes, pulling his underwear from his jeans. His clothes went back on almost as fast as they came off.

"Oh my God," she said. "Your back ... I'm so sorry."

"It's no big deal," he said, pulling his shirt over his wounds.

She pressed out her lower lip. "You're just gonna leave me here ... naked?"

He exhaled with a frown. "If I'm late, I won't play tomorrow."

"Get that cute butt of yours moving then. You can make it up to me later."

He slipped on his running shoes, pecked Amber on the lips and climbed over the rear seat. He exited the SUV and slammed the door behind him. The student parking lot was empty. He sprinted across the asphalt, his shoes barely touching the surface. He saw players walking toward the practice field. He bumped into Dwayne as he squeezed through the door.

"You better hurry up, white boy." He laughed. "No time for that Jane Fonda shit today."

Carter burst into the locker room. It was empty, except for Zach and Justin who walked toward the door. Carter turned his padlock three full turns, landing on 13.

"Where you been?" Justin said. He leaned in toward Carter and sniffed. "You smell like pussy."

Zach and Justin cackled.

Carter turned and glared at the pair. "Back the *fuck* up." He turned the padlock to the left, going through the zero. He stopped at 27 then went back to the right stopping at 4. He yanked on the lock. It didn't budge. "Shit," Carter said, restarting the combination sequence.

"Aren't y'all army boys supposed to be early for everything?" Justin said.

"If you're not fifteen minutes early, you're late," Zach said with a chuckle.

Justin looked at the clock. "You got about four minutes, and you ain't even in your locker yet."

The lock finally released. Carter yanked it open and pulled off his T-shirt, tossing it on the top shelf.

"Holy shit," Justin said.

"What the fuck happened to your back?" Zach said, laughing. "What'd you do, fuck a werewolf?"

Carter ran to the bathroom. The toilets were open, no stalls, only short three-foot-tall dividers. He undid his pants and pulled the condom from his penis, throwing it in the toilet. Zach and Justin marched up behind him, their cleats click-clacking against the tile. Carter pushed his penis back into his boxer briefs and held up his pants.

"Now he's getting rid of the evidence," Zach said.

Carter kicked the lever, flushing the condom.

"It's so sad to see this happen." Justin cackled. "They get some pussy and then they just can't control themselves. They become, like, pussy addicts. We're gonna have to have one of those meetin' things …"

"An intervention," Zach said.

Carter sprinted past his hecklers, back to his locker.

Zach and Justin followed.

"We'd help you, but we gotta get goin'," Justin said. "Shit, we're almost late."

Zach was already jogging gingerly out of the locker room, careful not to slip in his cleats. Justin ambled after.

Carter pulled his pants over his girdle and put his cleats on. He threw his shoulder pads and jersey over his head. He plopped his helmet on and ran from the locker room, his cleats sliding on the tile. Outside, he reached under his jersey, grabbing a shoulder pad strap as he ran. He secured it to the front of his pads. Just beyond, The Marauders were lined up for stretch. He buckled his chin strap and sprinted across the black top, his mouth piece dangling from his facemask. He continued across the dirt and grass practice field toward the team. His teammates spelled Marauders with their jumping jacks. Carter slipped into the back of the line as his teammates finished the letter "S." He breathed a sigh of relief as he bent over and touched his toes on a ten count with the rest of the team.

If he still wore a white jersey, nobody would've noticed. The back of the line was a sea of white. His black jersey stuck out like a sore thumb. Coach Ware stomped toward him. Carter stood and clapped one time along with everyone else at the conclusion of the hamstring stretch. Coach Ware grabbed him by his facemask.

"Why are you late?" he said.

Because I was having sex in the school parking lot. "No excuse, sir," Carter replied.

Ware shook his head with a smirk. Carter's reflection was caught in his black shades.

"What did Coach Cowan say yesterday at the end of practice?" Ware said.

"He wanted to see state championship football today," Carter replied.

"Do you think state champions show up late to practice?"

"No, sir."

Coach Cowan marched over. Coach Ware glanced at him.

"Here we are, a day away from the first game of the season," Coach Ware said to Cowan, "and our starting free safety feels like he can show up whenever he wants."

Coach Cowan shook his head, his eyes narrowed. "What did I tell you in my office after the scrimmage?"

"You told me not to slack off," Carter said.

Coach Cowan took his hat off and wiped his brow. He was clean-shaven except for his bushy mustache. "God dammit, Carter. I just told y'all yesterday about not testin' me with the rules. And now you go and do this. You got a good excuse?"

Carter looked down. "No, sir."

He exhaled and shook his head. "I'm startin' Noah tomorrow."

– 9 –

Back in Black

Carter stood on the corner two streets up from Sarah in his black and gold number 20 jersey. He stepped off the sidewalk into the grass as a handful of freshmen walked by. They leaned forward, their backs heavy with books. He moved back on the sidewalk, his running shoes wet with dew. He smiled as Sarah turned from her cul-de-sac to the main road. She trudged along the sidewalk with her head down, holding the strap of her pink satchel. She glanced up. He caught her eye. She glared back at him, her mouth shut tight.

"Good morrow to you, Madam," Carter said in his portentous voice.

She scowled and continued past without a word.

Carter turned and walked next to her. Sarah hogged the sidewalk, forcing Carter to walk in the grass median strip.

"What's wrong?" he asked.

"What do you care?"

"If this is about Ben, he's the one being an asshole."

She stopped and turned toward Carter. "You really disappoint me. I thought you were different."

Carter held out his palms. "Different from what?"

She continued walking.

He followed. "Seriously, different from what?"

"Everyone else."

Carter exhaled. "I don't know what you want from me."

She shook her head. "I don't want anything from you."

The dew seeped into his socks. "I thought we were friends."

"So did I," she said.

"So what's the problem then?"

"It's my fault really. I just have a higher standard for my friends."

Carter frowned. "What the hell does that mean?"

She sighed. "It means I'm not friends with people that do nothing when my friends and I are being abused."

His face felt hot. "You mean the cafeteria?"

"Was there another incident when you were a coward?"

"That's bullshit, I'm not afraid of anybody." He tightened his jaw.

"Then why didn't you stick up for Ben?"

"Why should I!"

She flinched. "Because he's your friend."

"He was never my friend." He shook his head. "Without you as the bridge between us, we would've never even started hanging out."

"How about doing the right thing then? Or how about standing up for me?" She placed her hand on her chest as if she were saying the pledge of allegiance.

"Why am I held to some higher standard than everyone else? I didn't see Ben standing up for you. He was right there. I was across the room."

She glared, her eyes wet. "Ben's not capable of standing up to Justin, but you are, aren't you?"

He looked down at his feet.

"Leave me alone," she said.

She turned and ran toward the traffic light. The light flashed from *walk* to the number 20 in red. She sprinted across the street, her skirt floating around her as the number on the sign ticked down to 0. As the cars accelerated past, Carter watched Sarah's form disappear on the other side of the road.

* * *

They marched two by two on the asphalt sidewalk adjacent to the parking lot. Their black helmets were on, chin straps buckled. They wore black pants and black jerseys with gold trim. The stadium loomed large in the distance. The lights were on, barely visible in the late-afternoon sun. It was muggy and hot, silent except for the click-clack of cleats on the black top. In the distance the scoreboard was lit with 88:49 counting down on the clock. Occasionally a car or truck honked from the parking lot, followed by shouts of encouragement. The lot was mostly full. An eight-foot-tall chain-link fence surrounded the stadium. Fans dressed in black and gold poured in at the open gate, where volunteers took their tickets or their money.

At the end of the asphalt sidewalk, a single gate was open. An old man sat guard just inside on a folding chair. The North Potomac Marauders sauntered onto their field, clustering at the nearby goalpost. Zach was in the middle.

"Hey, y'all," Zach said. "I've never lost a single game in this stadium, and I don't intend to start now. We play fast, we play aggressive, and we don't let up ... ever. Remember, this is our house. You hear me? This is our *fucking* house! Back-to-back on three. One, two, three."

"Back-to-back!" ninety-six kids said in unison.

They lined up in perfect rows and columns and went through their stretch routine. Carter bent over, touching his toes. He turned his head to the right and was blinded by the sun hanging low in the sky. *That glare's gonna suck in the first quarter.* He pulled his leg, touching his heel to his butt. A handful of guys hopped around to maintain balance. Fifty yards in front of him, eighty guys in white jerseys, silver pants, and blue trim hit their pads to a beat between each stretch.

After stretch and warmup, Carter ran to the corner of the end zone with Devin, Noah, and the rest of the defensive backs. Coach Pitts stood in khakis and a black polo with an M and crossed swords stitched into the upper left corner. His sleeves barely contained his biceps. He had a toothpick in the corner of his mouth and a resolute smile on his face. Carter and his teammates backpedaled, turned, planted, and sprinted as Coach Pitts whipped the football at them. They jumped and caught the ball at the highest point.

Coach Pitts said, "Bring it in."

The defensive backs crowded around the coach.

"These guys can play," Coach Pitts said. "But if we play our game like I know we're capable of, we'll be fine. We play fast, we play aggressive, and we don't give 'em anything easy. And remember, if they do happen to catch a pass, I expect them to pay for it."

Coach Cowan yelled, "Down at the goal line."

The scout team defense lined up against the first team offense. The offense scored each time with minimal resistance. A line of players, Carter included, stood behind the offense to conceal their plays from their opponent. They clapped with each practice touchdown.

Carter snuck peeks over his shoulder at their opponent, watching the receivers. They were fluid, graceful, and fast. The quarterback could scramble and he had a decent arm, but he was erratic. *If you get in, don't bite on the play fake. You won't have the speed to catch up to these guys if you fall behind. If he scrambles, you gotta stick with your man until he crosses the line of scrimmage. And like Coach Pitts said, if they catch anything, they pay for it.*

After Coach Ware was satisfied, the first team defense trotted out to face the scout offense. Each play ended with negative yards and some third string running back being pummeled in the backfield.

The Marauders exited the field two-by-two, just like they came in. In the locker room, some guys banged on lockers and pads and bragged about what they were going to do. Some guys were in the bathroom adjusting their uniforms. A couple of guys purged their nerves in the toilets. Some guys joked around. Some looked like they'd been drafted to fight a war they didn't want to be in. Carter hung his helmet in his locker and sat in front. Devin sat next to him. His eyes were red, his lids droopy. He had Riddell squares stamped into his fade.

"Are you all right?" Carter asked.

Devin shook his head. "I don't think I slept at all. I was tossing and turning all night."

"You'll be fine. That first hit'll wake you up."

"I watched a bunch of film. I think these guys are good. Especially number two, Scooter Brooks. You know his uncle plays for the Redskins."

Carter laughed. "You think that's his real name?"

Devin frowned. "Hell if I know, but he might be the best receiver in the state. He might even be better than Dwayne."

"I wouldn't worry about him if I were you. They're gonna put him inside, and try to get a mismatch on Noah. And even if they don't, you got the speed to stick with anybody."

"You should be starting."

"It's my own fault." Carter shook his head. "At least I'm still on kickoff and punt."

Coach Cowan stepped into the locker room. "Bring it in," he said.

Justin stuck his head into the bathroom. "Get in here. Y'all are worse than a bunch a girls."

The team took a knee on the tile in front of Coach Cowan. The coach said the Lord's Prayer to bowed heads. At the conclusion of the prayer, the players looked up with their eyes focused.

Coach Cowan looked them over. "It's not gonna cool off much tonight, but that's why we practice in the heat all summer. Make sure y'all are drinkin' plenty of fluids. I don't want guys crampin' up." He paused. "I'm not gonna stand up here and lie to you. We're gonna be in a dogfight tonight. These guys are big and fast and they'll hit you right in the mouth. This might be the best team we'll see until playoffs. Hell, we'll probably see them again *in* the playoffs. I know some of you guys are feelin' nervous and scared. I'm a tell you right now that it's good that you're nervous. It's good that you're scared. It shows me that you care, that you don't wanna let your teammates down. The truly courageous aren't guys that have no fears. The truly courageous are guys that are scared to death, but they go anyway. I can promise you one thing. If you come out and use that nervous energy, channel it into a fury, you'll do things on this football field you never thought possible. Let's be focused, aggressive, and remember: *this is our house.* We have a fifty-somethin' home winning streak to defend. I'd like to keep that goin'."

"It's sixty-three, Coach," Justin said.

Coach Cowan chuckled. "All right then, Justin, break 'em down on sixty-four."

It was still light out as they marched back to the stadium. The parking lot was packed, cars now spilling into the grassy overflow. The Marauders walked through the single gate, the old man still guarding entry. They queued up at the goal post. In front of them was a machine blowing smoke. The cheerleaders, the dance team, and the pep squad girls lined up on both sides beyond the smoke, forming a human tunnel.

A loud drumbeat and an electric guitar riff boomed from the loudspeakers. Zach burst through the smoke as the first lyric pounded the air. *Back in black.* Ninety-five guys followed. The music shook the stadium as girls in short black and gold skirts shook pom-poms with bright smiles and glittery makeup.

Carter lined up on the thirty-five-yard line for the kickoff. He was close to the sideline, second to the last man on the end. Carter watched the kicker. His hand was high in the air. He dropped it suddenly and Carter began to run in lockstep with the kicker. He was at full speed when the kicker boomed the ball high and deep into the fading afternoon sun. Carter sprinted downfield, blowing past the big kids in the first wave. Blockers came from left to right trying to set up a wall down the sideline. The kickoff returner caught the ball a yard deep in the end zone. He hesitated, glancing down at his feet before sprinting toward the human wall at the sideline. Carter squeezed in, cutting his angle down. He was fifteen yards away. Five yards, still unblocked. He slammed into the returner's rib cage, tackling him at the ten-yard line.

Carter stood on the sideline as Noah, Devin, Justin and the rest of the defense trotted out. The first two plays were much like the warmups with the running back being smothered in the backfield. On third and twelve, the Marauders blitzed, but Washington Heights kept their running backs in to pass block. Noah was one-on-one with their slot receiver, Scooter Brooks. The receiver sprinted up field fourteen yards and broke outside on the out. Noah was three steps behind. Scooter caught the pass for the first down. Noah dove at his feet, making a touchdown-saving tackle.

Coach Pitts yelled from the sideline, "Don't let him get you turned the wrong way. Watch his belt buckle."

The Washington Heights Warriors ran the ball on first and second down for short gains. On third and seven, the quarterback faked the handoff. Noah bit on the play fake. The quarterback launched a rocket downfield to Scooter on a corner route. Noah trailed by five yards, but the ball sailed beyond the receiver's outstretched arms.

The Warriors punted on fourth down. Coach Pitts scowled at Noah as he jogged off the field.

"What the hell are you doin'?" Coach Pitts said. "How the hell do you bite on a play fake on third and long? Get it together."

Kevin Lewis ate up big chunks of yardage slashing inside and outside. Luke capped off the drive with a touchdown pass to Dwayne in the back corner of the end zone.

It was late in the third quarter, and the sun had long disappeared, replaced by the artificial glow of the stadium lights. The Warriors and Marauders were in a defensive stalemate until Scooter Brooks ran a double move—a hitch and go. Noah bit hard on the hitch. The receiver was wide open on the go for a forty-yard touchdown. After the extra point, the game was tied, seven-seven.

"God dammit," Coach Cowan said, tossing his clipboard. He turned to Coach Pitts. "Noah's gettin' torched. Get Carter in next series. They'll keep comin' back to number two until we shut him down."

Luke and the offense answered with a fifty-yard pass to Dwayne. The referee threw the yellow flag as Dwayne caught the ball over his shoulder with a defender still draped over his back. Three plays later Kevin scored on a sweep as the last few seconds ticked off the third quarter. The extra point was blocked. The score was thirteen-seven.

After the kickoff, Carter stayed on the field. Devin gave him a nod. On first down, the Warriors ran inside. The running back was swallowed up by Zach and the defensive line—no gain. On second and long, Carter was locked up man-to-man with Scooter. *Coming your way, they're gonna test you.* The quarterback faked the run and threw deep. Carter was stride for stride with the receiver as the ball sailed over their heads: incomplete. On third and ten, Scooter sprinted downfield, and turned around at the first down marker. The quarterback threw a bullet. The receiver reached to catch the ball over his head, his eyes tracking it through the sky. As the ball touched his hands, Carter planted his facemask in the middle of Scooter's back, the whiplash jarring the ball loose.

After the punt, the Marauders' offense went three and out. When the Warriors lined up for that first down play midway through the fourth quarter, they hadn't thrown on first down that entire game, and they hadn't thrown a single pass at the Marauders' skinny five-foot-eight cornerback, Devin. Past events don't necessarily predict future events. The Warriors quarterback took the snap, and a three-step drop. He let loose a bomb, high and deep, a tight spiral. Devin was hip to hip with the six-foot-one receiver, sprinting downfield, focused on the ball sailing toward him. He pressed the receiver toward the sideline with his backside, as if he was boxing him out for a rebound. Devin leaped and snagged the football, his vertical jump making up for his lack of height.

Later, on the sideline, Devin couldn't wipe the smile off his face.

Carter, standing next to him, grinned. "I'm glad you stayed awake for that one."

Devin laughed. "I hadn't seen any action the whole game, but I had a feeling it was coming my way."

"That was a great play."

Kevin Lewis popped a fifty-yard run to take the Marauders deep into Warrior territory. It was first and goal from the nine-yard line with four and a half minutes left in the game.

"They're done," Carter said to Devin.

Kevin Lewis went in motion. On the snap, Luke turned and tossed the football to Kevin. The Warriors' outside linebacker came on a blitz. He rammed his helmet into the ball and it squirted from Kevin's hands. The Warriors' safety scooped it up with nothing but green in front of him. The safety raced down the Marauders' sideline, eighty-five guys watching, stunned. Dwayne took a deep angle from the opposite side of the field, catching the kid from behind at the nineteen-yard line. The score was still thirteen-seven, Marauders on top.

"Defense!" Coach Cowan called out, his face red.

On first down, the Warriors' quarterback rolled out, looking for a receiver. Everyone was covered, so he ran it, getting out of bounds after six yards. On second down, Carter was man-to-man on Scooter. He ran a bubble route behind the line of scrimmage. The quarterback threw the ball into the dirt a few yards behind the receiver. Everyone stopped on the incompletion except for Carter. The ball was live. Carter scooped it up and sprinted downfield, five yards ahead of the nearest player, before the Warriors realized and gave chase. It felt like slow motion, the ball skipping on the ground and bouncing into his arms as he caught it in stride and motored down the field, the end zone getting closer, the sound on mute. As he crossed the goal line, sound burst back into his consciousness. The fans stomped on the aluminum stands, cheering. The announcer called out his name. He tossed the football to the referee and was mobbed by the defense, all ten of them making the eighty-yard jaunt down the field. They threw a flag for excessive celebration.

* * *

Carter stood in his black Marauder sweatpants and a T-shirt. He slammed his locker shut. Zach and Justin strolled by dressed in their street clothes.

Zach lifted his chin to Carter. "Good game."

Carter nodded, throwing his duffel bag over his shoulder.

"You're comin' to the party, right?" Justin said.

"It's at my house," Zach added.

"I'll see you guys there," Carter replied.

Carter stopped at the locker room door and glanced around the empty room. Used athletic tape, paper Gatorade cups, and clods of turf littered the floor. He walked into the hallway. Coach Cowan locked his office door with a briefcase in hand. His face was haggard, his eyes red.

"I expect you'll be on time for films tomorrow," he said with a smile.

"Yes, sir," Carter replied.

"Were your parents at the game tonight?"

"No, sir."

"We're at home again next week. You should tell 'em to come, because we're on the road for three weeks after that."

"Yes, sir."

Coach Cowan and Carter walked out of the locker room together. The parking lot was empty except for a Chevy Suburban and Cowan's pickup truck.

"Need a ride?" Coach asked.

Carter looked over Cowan's shoulder. Amber stood in a short sundress, cowboy boots, and a grin. Coach Cowan glanced back then turned to Carter.

"Don't do anything stupid tonight," he said.

– 10 –

Sociology Sucks

The garage door was open, the afternoon sun high in the sky. The makeshift weight room was cramped, but orderly. Carter picked up a metal Olympic bar and set it on the bench press. Forty-five-pound metal plates leaned against the rack. He grabbed onto the lip of a plate and heaved it onto the bar, sliding it into place before repeating the ritual on the opposite side. He lay down on the bench, his feet still planted on the concrete. Easing the barbell off the rack, he lowered the weight to his chest and pushed. After ten repetitions, he set the barbell back on the rack. He stood up and stretched his upper body. He added another forty-five-pound plate to each side.

With everything in place, Carter entered the basement through the garage. His dad sat in front of the computer, entranced by the tiny pixels on the screen. Carter passed him quietly and walked up the basement steps, taking two at a time. His mother was in the kitchen placing a casserole in the oven. She wore sandals and tight designer jeans that hugged her thin legs and hips. Her dark hair was streaked with auburn highlights.

"Hey, Mom, can you spot me for like five minutes?" Carter asked.

Grace shut the oven door and turned toward her son with a smile. "Sure, sweetheart. I just need to take the casserole out in twenty minutes." She took off her oven mitts and set them on the counter. She followed Carter down the basement steps.

Jim peeled his eyes from the computer screen to glare at Carter and Grace as they descended.

"What are you doin'?" Jim said to Grace.

"Helping Carter," she said as she passed, not making eye contact.

In the garage, Carter sat on the bench. His mother stood behind with her hands on the bar. He glanced back.

"I probably won't need help on this one," Carter said. "So don't touch the bar unless I say help."

Carter pressed the bar off the rack. His upper body bulged, his veins popping on his arms as he moved the weight up and down. He exhaled as he pushed and inhaled as he lowered. After eight repetitions he placed the bar back on the rack.

"I might need your help on the next one," he said as he stood.

He picked up a twenty-five-pound circular plate from a neat stack along the wall.

"I still can't believe how good you're doing," Grace said. "You should've heard how the other parents were talking about you in the stands. I'm so proud of you, sweetheart."

Carter's face felt hot. "Thanks, Mom. It's only been four games. We've got a long way to go." Carter slammed the weight on the bar and grabbed another from the stack.

She smiled, showing crow's feet in the corners of her small blue eyes. "Still, you should be very proud of all your accomplishments."

Carter slammed the weight on the opposite side of the bar. "Thanks."

The basement door opened and Jim's mammoth pale frame squeezed through. He eyed the weight on the bench press before frowning at Grace's feet. "You shouldn't be out here in sandals."

Grace glanced at her shoes then to her husband. "Oh, it's fine. Carter knows what he's doing."

Jim nodded, his jaw set tight. "He does, does he?" He glared at Carter. "How much you got on there?"

"Two seventy-five," Carter said.

Jim crossed his meaty forearms and chuckled, exposing his gap. "You can lift that much? What do you weigh, like a buck fifty?"

"One sixty-seven." Carter waved his arms back and forth.

"Step back," Jim said to Grace. "You're not gonna be able to pull this thing up when it crushes his chest."

Carter frowned. Grace stepped aside.

"Don't touch it," Carter said to Jim, "unless I say help."

Jim had a crooked grin. "How many you doin'?"

"Two." Carter stretched his arm across his body.

"You gonna do this, or you just gonna stand there?"

Carter sat down on the bench and took a deep breath. He lay back and reached up, spacing his hands evenly on the bar. Carter took three rapid breaths and pushed the bar off the rack, the full brunt of the weight bearing down on his torso. He inhaled as he lowered the weight to his chest. As it touched him, he exhaled and pressed upward, his entire body taut. The bar moved slowly upward, stopping at the top. He took three rapid breaths and eased the bar back down again, this time bouncing the bar off his chest before pushing it upward. The bar made slow progress. Carter's back arched, his face glowing red. Jim put his hands under the bar, but didn't touch it until Carter slammed it back onto the rack. Carter sat up, the red draining from his face.

Grace clapped, smiling.

Jim scowled at his wife. "He bounced that second one. That doesn't count."

Carter rolled his eyes.

"You just continue to amaze me," Grace said to Carter. She turned to Jim. "You know Carter was in the paper again today. They called him a superstar transfer."

"What I don't understand," Jim said, "is why other teams don't run at you more. As small as you are, that's what I'd do."

Carter took a deep breath. "I play in the middle of the field. They run at me all the time."

"If it were me, I'd send a big tight end right at you, one of those big basketball players. He could just push you out of the way and grab the football like a rebound."

"That would be offensive pass interference."

Jim shrugged. "If I were playin', there's no way I'd let someone your size tackle me."

Carter clenched his fists. "Maybe you should talk to the Alexandria Central coach, give 'em some pointers, since you know so much."

Jim glowered at his stepson. "Watch your tone."

"He doesn't look smaller than the other kids," Grace said.

Jim smirked. "Come on Grace, they got a three-hundred-pound lineman."

"I don't play on the line," Carter said.

"I'm just surprised your coach wouldn't want some kid that was my size playin' in the middle."

Carter exhaled. "You think size is all you need to be a good football player? You have no idea what you're talking about."

"Watch it."

"No, I won't watch it. We got plenty of big kids that sit the bench, because they suck."

Jim dropped his arms and clenched his fists. "You will watch it."

Carter ignored him. "They might be big, but they're slow, they're weak, and they don't wanna hit anyone."

"When I played, I was big, strong, and I hit everything that moved. I hope you don't run into anyone like me." He chuckled.

"Jim, nobody cares about your J.V. football career," Grace said.

Carter stifled a laugh.

Jim narrowed his eyes at Grace, then at Carter. "I didn't have time for football. I had to work. I wasn't born with a goddamn silver spoon in my mouth."

"You wouldn't even make the scout team here," Carter said. "I could probably run the forty backwards faster than you can run it forward."

"Carter, stop it," Grace said.

"Let him keep talkin' shit," Jim said. "Let's see him back it up in the real world." Jim stomped from the garage, down the driveway, and into the street. He motioned for Carter. "Come on, tough guy. Put your money where your mouth is."

"Jim, stop this," Grace said. "This is getting out of hand."

"Come on out here too," Jim said to Grace. "You can judge the winner."

Carter and Grace walked into the street.

"We'll start here," Jim said, pointing to the long crack in the asphalt in front of them, "and we'll go to the end of the last townhouse on our row. That looks close to forty yards."

Carter shook his head. "More like thirty, but it doesn't matter what the distance is."

"Go stand across from the last townhouse," Jim said to Grace. "Hold your hands up and we'll go when you drop them."

"This is ridiculous," Grace said as she walked down the street.

Carter bent over and touched his toes. He lined up on the crack beside Jim, one foot forward, one foot back.

"What are you doin'?" Jim said. "I thought you could beat me runnin' backwards?"

Carter turned around, his back toward the finish line. "How am I supposed to see Mom drop her arms?"

"You shoulda thought of that before talkin' all that shit."

Carter placed his right foot forward, pigeon-toed, his left foot back, and his knees bent. Jim put one foot forward, his toes over the line. Carter turned his head to the left, watching his dad. As soon as Jim's calf flexed, Carter pushed his right foot into the asphalt before sprinting backwards with a fluid stride, his arms pumping back and forth. Jim's heavy footfalls were a yard in front. Halfway to the finish line, he passed the bulky sergeant. Carter smiled at his father as he passed the finish line a few yards ahead of him.

"God dammit, Arnold," Jim said to himself.

Carter and Grace laughed and walked toward the garage.

"He got you," Grace said to Jim.

Jim tightened his jaw as he followed. "Doesn't mean I couldn't just run him over in a game."

"Why don't you put *your* money where *your* mouth is," Carter said with a smirk. "Since you're so big and strong, you should be able to lift more than me." Carter motioned toward the bench in the garage.

"Oh shoot," Grace said. "I've got to get my casserole. You boys play nice." She ran into the house.

Jim stood in front of the bench, eyeing the bending bar on the rack.

"You gonna do this, or you just gonna stand there?" Carter said.

Jim sat down. Carter moved behind the bench.

"Do you want a spot?" Carter asked.

"I got it," he said.

"All right," Carter said, his hands up.

Jim rolled his neck, lay back, and put his hands on the bar. He pushed the bar off the rack. It plummeted straight down onto his chest, bouncing a few inches in the air before pinning him to the bench. His face was beet red. He squirmed under the pressure.

"Help," he said.

Carter stepped forward, grabbing the bar with a reverse grip. He pulled upward with all his might. The bar dropped onto the rack with a dull thud.

Carter cackled. "I guess playing video games doesn't make you very fast or strong."

Jim sat up, shaking his head. "Weight room strength ain't the same as real world strength. I can still beat your ass."

Carter stood silent.

Jim stood up, his nostrils flaring. "Ain't got nothin' to say about that?"

Carter stared at the concrete floor.

"Let's see how tough you really are." He grabbed Carter by the throat and squeezed.

Carter looked up, his eyes wide, his breath stifled. Jim let go, and

Carter wheezed for breath. Jim pushed him into the front yard. Carter stood, his hands by his side, staring at the grass. Jim stomped in front of him, his stance wide.

"You think you're so fuckin' tough," Jim said. "Why don't you hit me? Take a shot. Come on, tough guy. Come on, *hit me.*"

Carter's head was down, his hands open. He never saw Jim swing, but he felt the impact on his cheek. He hit the ground hard.

"Come on, get up, tough guy," Jim said.

Carter pushed himself off the turf, turned and sprinted down the sidewalk, away from his stepdad. The townhouses flashed by in a blur as if he was in a car. High on adrenaline, he felt like he could run forever. He turned down a cul-de-sac, the playground in the distance. At the playground, he stopped and bent over with his hands on his knees. Oxygen coursed through his lungs as his shoulders heaved. Despite the mild weather, the park was empty. Carter wandered into the playground and sat on a park bench, his back to the road. He put his head in his hands, rubbing his temples. The empty swings loomed ahead of him.

The sun, high in the sky, crept down, and turned a dim orange. The streetlamps flickered on even though it was still light out. Something touched him on the shoulder. Carter shot upright, his eyes red and puffy.

Sarah stood with her mouth open and eyes wide, staring at his cheek. "What happened?"

"It doesn't matter." He turned around and sat on the bench, looking down at the playground's wood chips.

She moved around the bench, her gray corduroys swooshing. "It does matter." She bent down and put her hand under his chin, raising his gaze to meet hers. "It does matter."

He grabbed her hand and removed it from his chin. He shook his head, staring at the ground. She sat down next to him.

"What are you doing here?" she asked.

He shrugged.

"How long have you been here?"

He shrugged.

"Do you want to come to my house for some ice?"

"I don't know what I'm doing," he said. A few tears slid down his face.

"We don't have to talk about it. I'll just sit here with you."

She scooched closer, her thigh touching his. She grasped his hand, their fingers interlaced. Her hands were small and soft. She smelled faintly like strawberries. He didn't look up but breathed her in, clutching her hand as if her mere touch and scent could heal him. They sat like this until the sun vanished beneath the horizon.

He gazed at her, illuminated by the street light. Her features were soft and round, her pale skin flawless. "I'm sorry," he said.

She shook her head. "Don't."

"No, you were right. I should've stood up for you in the cafeteria. The truth is I'm a coward."

She squeezed his hand and leaned back with a smile. "Everybody at school says how tough you are."

"I'm a coward when it counts. I didn't stand up for you or Ben. I didn't stand up for my mother. I couldn't even stand up for myself today."

"What happened?"

"Same thing that always happens." He took a deep breath. "My dad."

"I'm sorry," she said.

"Don't be."

"It's getting really dark." She peered at the bruise on his face. "Why don't you come with me for some ice? That bruise isn't getting any smaller."

"Okay."

They stood and strolled down the sidewalk hand in hand.

"Does he hit your sister?" she asked.

He shook his head, his eyes downcast.

"If you don't want to talk about it."

"No, it's fine," he said. "He doesn't hit my sister. Sometimes he gets rough with my mom, but I've never seen him punch her in the face."

She squeezed his hand. "Then why does he do it to you?"

He shrugged. "Maybe it's because I'm not his kid—biologically."

Sarah gaped at Carter.

"You never noticed that our last names are different?"

"It's not Lynch?" she asked.

"Mine is, but theirs is Arnold."

"Why didn't you tell me that?"

"I don't know. I guess it never came up. I call him Dad, and he raised me, so I do think of him as my father." Carter looked at Sarah. "Granted, he is a dick."

She smiled for a split second. "How old were you when your parents split and your mom got remarried?"

"I was three or four. It all kind of happened at the same time, in Fort Bragg, North Carolina. According to my biological father, my mother and stepfather had an affair while he was away in the field."

She winced.

"Supposedly, it was quite the scandal. Bio-Dad said he could've ruined his career – hit him with an article 134 or something."

"Do you remember it?"

"Not really. I do remember her getting caught, because my mom got pregnant with my sister. I guess Bio-Dad and my mom weren't having sex."

She frowned, her pink lips turning down. "I'm surprised she didn't have an abortion."

"My mom's Catholic. Not that she ever goes to church."

"Maybe it was a way out of the marriage," Sarah said.

"Maybe."

They walked up the steps to the front door of Sarah's townhouse. Her house had mold growing on the beige siding. It was a middle unit with a bay window in front and no garage. She pulled a key from her pocket and turned the deadbolt. They entered the kitchen immediately to the left. It was cozy, with a small round wooden table in front of the bay window. A white refrigerator hummed in the background. She opened the freezer and fished out a bag of frozen peas.

"Here," she said, "put this on your face."

He held the peas to his cheek. "Thank you."

"Sit down." She motioned to the kitchen table. He sat down. "Do you want something to drink?"

"Maybe after my face stops being numb," he said.

She sat across from him at the table. She took off her glasses and swept her red hair from her eyes.

"Can you see me?" he asked.

"You're blurry." She smiled. "Do you ever see him?"

"Who, Bio-Dad?"

She nodded.

"Not for six or seven years. I think I was like nine the last time I saw him. He was remarried with a baby girl. It was a disaster. I didn't wanna be there. I don't think he wanted me there. I don't think his wife wanted me there. I didn't feel anything for him then, and even less now. I mean, how can you have a bond with some guy you haven't spent any time with?"

"I don't know that you can. Not unless you build something."

"That's the thing. He's not even someone that I wanna be around. It's like he looks at me and sees the affair. He wanted my stepfather to adopt me so he wouldn't have to pay child support. We haven't spoken since. Maybe I'll change my name entirely when I turn eighteen."

She was quiet for a moment. "He's missing out."

"I doubt he sees it that way. I'm sure he blames everyone but himself."

He exhaled. "What about you?"

She shrugged. "What about me?"

"Where's your dad?"

She stared down at the table.

"I'm sorry," he said. "Please tell me he's still alive."

She looked up with a smirk. "He's very much alive ... unfortunately. My father's a professor at George Washington University. He teaches sociology. What a stupid ass subject."

"What kind of job can you get with a sociology degree?"

She laughed. "Sociology professor."

He chuckled, the ice packet still on his face. "Sounds like digging holes and filling 'em back in again."

"Exactly."

"So you don't see him?"

She shook her head. "Never. When he met my mother, he was her professor and was married with kids. Still is, as far as I know. Anyway, when he got my mom pregnant, she dropped out of school and never told anyone because he agreed to pay for me. She knew that if she told, he would get divorced, fired, and there wouldn't be any money."

He put the peas on the table. One side of his face was red. "Sarah, I ..." He shook his head. "Talk about missing out. I think you're really great."

She smiled. He put the peas back on his face.

"The money's been like a curse," she said.

He raised his eyebrows. "How so?"

"It's like my mom never had to really grow up and be responsible because she always had the money to keep us afloat. But it's only been just enough to get by. There's no college fund for me, that's for sure. I don't know what she's going to do when I turn eighteen."

"I thought she worked as a hair cutter?"

Car headlights flashed into the bay window, then cut off.

She giggled. "You mean stylist? I doubt she even works twenty hours a week. It's basically her partying money."

There was the sound of hurried steps on the concrete outside. The front door opened.

Sarah shook her head. "Speak of the devil."

Her mother barreled into the kitchen breathless, wearing a tight maroon skirt, her keys jingling in her hand. She looked more like Sarah's older sister than her mother. She grinned at Carter, showing a glimpse of white teeth.

Carter took the peas off his face.

"Who's this cutie?" she asked Sarah.

Sarah rolled her eyes. "This is my friend Carter. Carter, this is my mother."

Her face was round. Her skin was pale and flawless, much like Sarah's. She was curvy and thin in all the right places.

He stood up and offered his hand. "It's nice to meet you, Mrs. Cunningham."

She smiled, her lips full and glossy, her blue eyes shrouded in eyeliner. "Please, call me Julie." She took Carter's hand for a split second and pulled away. "Your hand's frozen."

"Sorry," he said picking up the peas from the table. "It's from holding this."

She craned her neck to look at the side of his face. "Oh my God, what happened to you?"

He shrugged. "Nothing, it was just an accident."

She giggled. "Did you try to kiss Sarah?"

"Mom," Sarah said, "we're friends."

Carter sat back down at the table.

Julie narrowed her eyes at Sarah. "You sure about that? Look at him, he's so freaking adorable." She grinned. "If I were you, I'd sprinkle sugar on him and just eat him up."

Carter's face went hot.

A car horn blared from outside.

"Oh, that's for me," she said. "I've got to get going." She looked at Sarah. "Have you seen my purse?"

"No," Sarah replied.

Julie glanced at the counters then marched to the staircase beyond the kitchen. Her heels smacked against the wood as she climbed the staircase.

Sarah looked at Carter with a smirk. "That's my mother."

"She seems nice," Carter said.

Sarah frowned. "She's selfish and childish."

The front door opened and heavy steps pounded the linoleum. A tall, muscled man in jeans and a tight black T-shirt peered into the kitchen. His hair was dark and gelled, his face handsome. His strong cologne wafted into the kitchen.

He glanced at Sarah. "Where'd your mom go?"

"Upstairs."

He stomped to the stairwell. "Babe, we gotta go," he called out. "Come on, let's go."

He appeared in the kitchen. "How long can it take to get a purse?" he said to no one in particular.

"Depends on how close it is to a mirror," Sarah said.

Light footfalls slapped the wooden steps. The man turned.

"It's about time," he said. "We're never gonna make it."

"The opening acts are lame anyway," she said.

He grunted. "My friends are the opening act."

"Let's go then."

As they marched past, Julie stuck her head in the kitchen. "I'll be home late," she said to Sarah. "Be good, and definitely don't do anything to that boy that I'd do." Her giggle lingered in the air.

"Is that your mother's boyfriend?" Carter asked.

She nodded with her mouth turned down. "His name's Lincoln. He's a big dumbass. Says he's some kind of fighter, calls it mixed martial arts. He says it's going to be bigger than boxing."

"How long have they been together?"

Sarah laughed. "If my mother dates someone for more than a month, it's a miracle." She stood up, grabbing the peas from the table and stashing them back in the freezer. She smirked at Carter. "I try not to get attached."

"How's Ben doing?"

Sarah exhaled and sat back down at the table. "He's not much better, but at least he's going to school, and at least people are leaving him alone."

Carter nodded. "That's good."

"So. What are you doing tonight?" he asked.

"I don't know. What about you?"

"I'm supposed to go to the movies with …"

"Amber," she said with a frown.

Carter glanced down, avoiding her eyes. "Yeah. Sorry."

"I don't know what you're apologizing for," she said.

He looked up. "Do you wanna go? We're seeing *Freddy's Dead*."

She smiled, but her eyes were still. "I'd rather not play the third wheel. You'll have your hands full with Amber. I'm sure she'll be all over you during the scary parts."

– 11 –

Forty Ounce to Freedom

The air was crisp and cool—perfect football weather. Fans dressed in black and gold, filled the stadium seats. The lights illuminated the field and the stands. The cheerleaders had been doing pushups every time the North Potomac Marauders scored. They started with strict military pushups, but slipped into knee-pushups as the score ballooned into the fifties. A handful of booster club men counted hooded sweatshirts boasting the inevitable district championship.

"You guys are out," Coach Pitts said.

The first team defense groaned.

"We've still got half the third quarter left," Justin said.

Coach Pitts frowned. "Cheer on your teammates."

Carter stood next to Devin on the sideline. They watched the second team defense stuff the Washington and Lee Lancers. He thought about Ben. *He could be playing right now.*

Carter turned to Devin. "There's a party at Molly's tonight. It's just a handful of guys—mostly girls. You wanna go?"

"I got a date with Tasha."

"Come after, bring her. District championship tonight, we gotta celebrate."

"Molly is Zach's girl, right?"

"Yeah."

"You're my boy, Carter, but I can't be hanging around them. And I sure as hell can't have my girl around their bullshit. I don't know how you can stand it."

Carter looked away. "Amber's friends with their girlfriends. They're not that bad."

Devin shrugged, put his hands in his armpits, and turned back to the game.

* * *

Carter sat on a stained brown couch wearing a black hooded sweatshirt emblazoned with *District Champs 1991*. Zach snored in the recliner adjacent to him. A half-full forty-ounce was nestled in the crook of his arm like a baby. Carter placed his own bottle on the coffee table in front of him. A quarter-inch of warm malt liquor floated at the bottom. Amber and her friends laughed in the kitchen. Carter stood up, woozy, and staggered toward their voices. Amber, Lilly, and Molly passed around a bottle of booze and play-fought over who was the biggest whore.

"I'm not a whore, I only fuck Carter," Amber said with a grin.

"What's he like?" Lilly asked. Her eyes and mouth drooped. A piece of lettuce stuck in her upper braces. She leaned on Molly.

Carter scowled.

"I can't look at that shit anymore," Amber said. "It was funny an hour ago. Now it's just gross."

Molly cackled.

"What?" Lilly asked.

"Come here," Amber said. Lilly stumbled over. "Open your mouth." Amber pulled the green lettuce leaf from her upper braces and held it up to Lilly. "This shit was in your braces."

Lilly scrunched her face. "Eww, you guys. Why'd you let me walk around like that?"

Molly took a swig from the strawberry booze bottle, her red lipstick

114

leaving a stain. She was tall and curvy, with black velvet pants and a low-cut red sweater that would've been obscene were it not for her long red hair hanging over her breasts.

"You didn't answer Lilly's question?" Molly said to Amber. "What *is* he like?" Molly glanced at Carter with a grin.

Carter held out his palms. "I'm right here."

The girls giggled.

"At least we're not talking about you behind your back," Amber said.

"I think I'd prefer it that way." Carter walked back into the living room and sat on the couch.

"His body's rock hard, just like his dick," Amber said. The girls laughed.

"How big is it?" Lilly asked.

There was a pause then more laughter.

"Have you ever had an orgasm?" Molly asked.

"You mean orgasms?" Amber emphasized the 's'.

They cackled.

"What about Zach?" Amber asked.

There was a pause.

"What?" Amber said.

"How do you tell a guy to slow down?" Molly asked. "I mean he's like a jack hammer that breaks down after thirty seconds."

Amber and Lilly laughed.

"I'm serious, it's not funny," Molly said.

They stopped laughing.

"I swear everything he does must come from porn," Molly said.

"You just have to tell him," Amber said.

"He'll be so mad. I can't."

"Yes, you can," Lilly said. "He's not gonna find anyone hotter than you."

"He will when he's playing football at Virginia Tech next year," Molly replied with a sniffle.

"Aww, it's gonna to be okay," Lilly said.

Justin emerged from the hallway with a shit-eating grin. He sauntered over to the couch and sat next to Carter. Zach still snored in the recliner. Riley staggered down the hall shortly thereafter. Her dark hair was disheveled, her lip stick smudged. She went into the kitchen. Her friends said she looked like she'd just fallen out of a Mexican whorehouse. They all giggled.

"I love drunk chicks," Justin said as he leaned back on the couch.

Carter didn't respond. This didn't stop Justin.

"You know why?"

Carter glanced at him. His Mohawk was freshly cut, his blue eyes bright and alert.

"Because when they're wasted, they'll let you do whatever you want to 'em. I did some shit to Riley ..." Justin cackled. "When she gets married—I mean how is she ever gonna explain that shit to her husband?" Justin shook his head. "She'll always have my stench on her."

Carter stood up and ambled to the kitchen.

"Where you goin'?" Justin said.

Carter ignored him.

"Hey, fuck face, wake up," Justin said to Zach.

Amber, Lilly, Molly, and Riley sat at the dining room table, slurring nonsense at each other, still passing the strawberry booze water.

"Could I talk to you for a minute?" Carter said to Amber from the edge of the kitchen.

Amber stumbled from the dining room to Carter. Despite her alcohol-induced sloppiness, she still exuded raw sexuality.

She gave him a sloppy kiss. "I was so proud of you tonight," Amber said.

"We should get going," Carter said.

She pressed out her lower lip. "What, why?"

"You're wasted and it's getting late. It's already past one. I have films tomorrow morning."

"I'm staying here tonight. My mom knows I'm sleeping over."

"I should get going then. My dad would kill me if he knew I had my mom's car out this late."

She grabbed his hand, stroking his palm with her thumb. "I'm sorry, sweetie, that's my fault. My mom freaked when she got my grades. She never stays mad. I'll probably get the truck back next week."

Carter shook his head. "It's fine. I just can't get the car very often."

Lilly shuffled toward them. She looked at Carter. "Have you seen Noah?"

"He was playing video games in the TV room a few hours ago, but I haven't seen him since."

Lilly stumbled down the hall.

Carter glared at Amber. "By the way, I don't like you telling your friends private stuff about me."

She grinned. "Oh, come on, it's all good stuff. They probably wanna fuck you now."

Carter took a deep breath. "I'm gonna get going."

"Don't go," she said wrapping her arms around his waist and whispering in his ear. "Pretty please with a cherry on top. I'll make it worth your while."

"An hour."

She let go, grinning. "Why don't you come back to Molly's mom's room with me? I have a present for you." Amber turned, looking at the curvy redhead. "Hey, Molly, is it okay if Carter and I go back to your mom's room?"

"Go ahead," Molly said, smiling. "Does Carter know the rule?"

"Don't worry," Amber said with a giggle. "Every drop will be inside me."

Carter and Amber strolled down the hall to the master bedroom. They heard Lilly arguing with Noah through a closed door.

"Calm down," Noah said. "It's not a big deal."

Amber put her ear to the door.

Carter shook his head. "Don't. Leave 'em alone."

She flashed her pouty face. "You're no fun."

They continued to the master bedroom. Amber opened the door without knocking, flipping the overhead light on as she did so.

"So bright," she said.

She adjusted the dimmer switch, turning the light from bright white to dim yellow. Carter closed and locked the door behind them. A king-sized bed took up most of the room. A dresser sat along the wall next to the door.

Amber unzipped her boots and kicked them off. She sprawled on the bed as if she were making a snow angel. Carter slipped off his running shoes and climbed on the bed next to her.

Noah and Lilly continued to argue down the hall, their voices penetrating the bedroom.

Amber gaped up at the motionless ceiling fan. "The room's spinning," she said.

"You okay?" Carter lay on his side, his head propped up with his arm.

"I think I drank too much. Gonna rest my eyes." Her speech was slurred and fading.

"You want me to tuck you in and let you sleep?"

She shook her head, her eyes closed. "I'm 'posed sleep … Molly's room."

"Why don't I go see if they're done in there?"

She moaned. "No, don't go. Have to give … you something."

"Give it to me tomorrow. I should get home anyway."

She shook her head. "No … don't go."

She pulled her tight sweater over her head and dropped it on the bed. Her black bra had a front clasp. She undid it, freeing her breasts, the bra straps still looped round her shoulders. She fumbled with the top button on her jeans.

"You do it," she said.

He reached over, undid the button and pulled the zipper down. A few pubic hairs poked through her lacy black thong. She lifted her butt off of the bed and pushed her jeans and thong down her legs. She stopped at her knees, breathless. She was fully exposed, her jeans and underwear bunched around her knees.

"You take them off," she said.

He pursed his lips. "Amber, you're wasted. You can't even move. Why don't we do this tomorrow?"

"Just do anything you want."

He grabbed onto her pants and underwear and tried to slide them back up her legs. He stopped at her upper thighs. Her butt was firmly planted on the bed.

"No," she said. "It's okay. You can have me."

He took a deep breath. "Amber, I can't. I mean I can—"

"Wanna know a secret?"

"Sure."

Carter heard a pounding sound coming from the front living room.

Her eyes were sealed shut. She breathed heavily as if she were sleeping. "My brother."

"What about him?"

"He did stuff to me."

Carter sat up and gripped her hand, his eyes wide. "What kind of stuff?"

She was silent. Carter heard gruff voices through the walls.

"Amber, wake up." He shook her body. "What kind of stuff?"

He heard heavy footsteps in the hall.

She smirked, her eyes still shut. "Bad stuff … he—"

The banging on the door jolted Carter upright.

"Open up, it's the police."

Shit.

He grabbed Amber's pants and yanked them over her butt. He snatched her sweater off the bed and pulled it over her head.

He spoke into her ear. "Amber, get up." He shook her body, the mattress squeaking. "We gotta go."

There was another loud knock that almost took the door off the hinges.

"Open this door now, it's the police." the officer said. "You have ten seconds to open this door or I'm gonna kick it in!"

Carter slipped his running shoes on and pushed the dresser in front of the door. He hurried to the window, unlocked it and pushed, but it wouldn't budge. It was painted shut. He pushed again with all his strength. The paint cracked and the window opened. He rolled Amber to the edge of the bed. She laughed as her world rotated. He slammed her boots over her wool socks and zipped them up. Grunting, Carter heaved her over his shoulder. She giggled. The adrenaline had wiped away any tipsiness he'd been feeling. He carried Amber to the window.

The police officer kicked the door, breaking the lock, but he was blocked by the dresser. The racket jolted Amber from her stupor. Carter helped her through the ground floor window. The officer slammed into the door, pushing the dresser enough to slip into the room. Carter dove through the window head first. He tucked his head and landed with a thud.

"Stop right there," the officer said, shining his flashlight at the couple.

Carter stood and helped Amber to her feet. They ran to the parking lot, Carter pulling her by the arm.

"Shit," Carter said. "It was right here."

Carter looked around. Two police cars with flashing lights were parked near the entrance to Molly's apartment. Beyond the housing complex was a small copse of dark trees.

"Let's go," he said, yanking Amber toward the woods.

The going wasn't easy: Amber kept stumbling, complaining that she was going to throw up. He hoisted her over his shoulder and continued toward the tree line. Amber bounced up and down, her face green. He ran down an embankment, stepped over a concrete gutter and disappeared into the dark trees. Safe within the brush and bark, he set Amber down. She dropped to her knees and heaved. Hot liquid splashed on dead leaves. He kneeled with her, rubbing her back as she emptied a night of strawberry alcopop. She groaned as he helped her to her feet.

"You okay?" he asked.

She nodded, wiping her mouth on her sweater sleeve.

"The car's gone," he said.

"They probably towed it," she said, reaching under her sweater and clasping her bra.

"What do you mean *they* towed it? Who's they?"

She spat bile on the ground. "The apartment people, I guess. They tow after midnight if you don't have a pass."

He glared at her. "Are you fucking serious?"

"What?"

He clenched his jaw. "You don't think you should've told me this?"

She sighed. "You said you were gonna leave at like eleven."

"Christ, Amber." He exhaled, shaking his head. "Why didn't you tell me when it started to get late?"

"Stop yelling at me. I'm wasted. How am I supposed to remember that?"

Carter peered at the apartment complex through the trees. "Who is that behind the bushes over there?"

"Where?" Amber asked.

Carter pointed. "That first building on the left, right next to the front door. I see two people."

"I don't see anyone."

"It's Noah, and I think that's Lilly. I should go get them. Noah's probably trying to find his car." He took a deep breath and pulled his hood over his head. "Wait here."

Carter ran from the woods, hopped over the drain pipe and climbed the embankment. Toward the top of the hill, he stopped and dropped flat onto his stomach. He squinted, gazing across the road. There were no cops in sight. He sprinted for the bushes across the street. Noah and Lilly argued, the holly hedges concealing half of their bodies. They hushed as soon as they heard Carter approaching, their eyes wide.

"You scared the shit out of me," Noah said.

"The cars were towed," Carter said.

"Zach's Jeep is still here, and Justin's Explorer."

"They must've had parking passes."

Noah clenched his jaw. "Fuck, Lilly. My dad's gonna kill me. Your fuckin' friend's payin' for this."

Lilly's wavy light brown locks hung past her slight shoulders. She wore a thick sweater and corduroys. Her face was tear-streaked, her eyes puffy. "Molly doesn't have any money. And I told you about the pass last week. You told me to remind you."

Noah clenched his fists, his biceps bulging beneath his flannel. "Then why didn't you remind me?"

"Maybe I was too focused on you wanting to have a *threesome*." Lilly crossed her arms over her chest.

Noah's pale face went red. He hung his head, revealing a swirling light brown cowlick. "I'm sorry, okay. Every guy thinks about it. I'm just the only one stupid enough to say it."

Carter stared at the sticker on the front door. *Unauthorized Vehicles Will Be Towed At Owner's Expense*. There was an address and company name underneath: *Glenn's Towing*.

"Guys, we gotta go," Carter said. "The cops can see us from here."

"How do you know that?" Noah asked.

"I saw you, didn't I?"

Carter led Noah and Lilly across the road, down the embankment, and into the woods where Amber waited. Lilly hugged her friend.

"What happened?" Carter asked. "Who called the cops?"

Lilly blushed.

Noah shrugged. "Lilly was yellin' at me."

"Where's everyone else?" Carter asked.

Noah scratched the back of his head. "Don't know. As soon as I heard that bangin' on the front door, I knew it was the cops. No normal person knocks like that. We went out the window."

"So did we," Amber said.

"We think everyone else got busted," Lilly said.

"Zach's dad'll take care of it," Noah said. "He's a lawyer."

"So, what do we do now?" Amber asked.

"Let's go get the cars," Carter said. "The sticker on the front door said the tow lot's on Fremont Avenue. Does anyone know where that is?"

"I do," Noah said. "It's not that far from here."

"Does anyone have any money?" Carter asked.

Noah opened his wallet, the Velcro tearing. "Thirty-five bucks, you?"

"I have twenty-two," Carter replied.

"My purse is at Molly's," Amber said.

"Mine too," Lilly said.

"We could wait for the cops to leave and go grab the purses," Noah said.

"It won't help," Amber said. "I only have like ten bucks."

"I spent all my money on party food," Lilly said.

"Shit," Carter said, "I guarantee you it's at least a hundred bucks to get a car out."

"Let's go down there and check it out," Noah said. "What do we have to lose? It's only a fifteen-minute walk."

"I'm cold," Amber said, her arms wrapped around herself.

"You want my sweatshirt?" Carter asked.

She shook her head. "No, I'll be fine once we get moving."

The quartet cut through the woods and across a few streets. They walked along Calvert Street until they reached Fremont Avenue. The street was home to a couple of construction companies, a landscaper, a junk yard, a trucking company, and a tow yard. One side of the street was left wooded so that those living in the nice neighborhood on the other side didn't have to look at *Sanford and Son* across the way. They crept along the edge of the woods.

"How'd you know about this road?" Carter asked Noah.

"My dad used to work for a landscapin' company that has their yard here," he replied.

Glenn's Towing appeared to be open. There was a small office next to the front gate. It was well lit, and an old man sat inside behind a cramped desk. The gate was shut. It was an eight-foot-tall chain-link fence with barbed wire on top. They could see their cars with the back bumpers facing the gate.

"Someone's comin'," Noah said.

They backed up into the woods, waiting and watching. A tow truck lumbered down the road. It slowed before stopping at the gate. The driver beeped his horn. The old man stood up and hit a button on the wall inside the office. The gate with wheels opened, propelled by a chain and an electric motor. The driver pulled in and parked the tow truck off to the side, leaving the gate wide open. The driver climbed out of the truck and went into the office with a clipboard. The old man greeted him, and they stood talking over the paperwork.

"Now's our chance," Carter said.

"What the hell are you talkin' about?" Noah said.

"Let's run up there, get the cars and drive 'em out before they shut the gate."

"Are you fuckin' crazy?"

"That's dumb," Amber said to Carter.

"It's not dumb," Carter said. "That gate moves really slow. I counted like twenty-five seconds from the time the old man hit the button and the gate finished opening. We just need to get to the cars without them noticing. When we start the engines, we should have at least twenty seconds to get out before the gate shuts."

"That's dumb. The cars are facing the wrong way," Amber said with a frown. "You'd have to turn the cars around, and it's too crowded in there. It would be like a twelve-point turn."

Carter grinned. "We're gonna back straight out."

"You are crazy," Noah said with a crooked smile. "But it could work."

"You guys are so fucking retarded," Amber said. "You're gonna get arrested. Carter just started driving like two weeks ago." She shook her head. "Let's go back and try to find Zach or Justin. They'll give you guys the money."

"I agree," Lilly said, "let's go back. Zach or Justin will help."

Noah shook his head. "No, we're not askin' for shit."

"Let's hurry then," Carter said to Noah. "I'll let you pull out first, but you gotta pick up Amber and Lilly because I might not have time to stop."

Lilly looked like she was going to be sick. "Don't do it, Noah."

"They're not gonna do it," Amber said.

"Just be ready to jump in Noah's car," Carter said.

Carter and Noah crept up to the tow lot. The darkness covered their approach but the gate was bathed in yellow light. The men still talked. Gravel crunched under their shoes as they ran past the gate to their cars. Carter opened the door to his mom's powder-blue Buick Skyhawk. Noah slipped inside his dad's Nissan Sentra and started the engine. Carter fired up his own engine a split second afterward. Alerted by the noise, the men in the office ran out to check the lot. Noah sped toward the gate in reverse, Carter right behind him. He was moving quickly but carefully, keeping the vehicle under control. The old man smacked the button on the wall, and the gate started to move. It looked like Noah was going to clip the gate, but he made it through unscathed. Carter was three car-lengths behind him, gunning the engine of the old Buick wagon. The tow truck driver waved his arms. Carter blew past him, squeezing through as the gate shut on the front passenger quarter panel, scratching the car and knocking off a hubcap. He turned, the tires screeching as he backed onto Fremont Ave. He slammed on the brakes. Amber and Lilly jumped into Noah's car with wide smiles. Carter jammed the automatic transmission into drive and spun the front wheel as he floored it.

They drove seven miles down Route 1 to the North Potomac Denny's. They parked in back behind the dumpsters. Noah climbed from the driver's seat, grinning from ear to ear. Lilly pressed her body and her lips against him. Amber jumped on Carter, hugging him with her legs wrapped around him. After a moment the couples disengaged and the group reunited.

"That was bad ass," Noah said to Carter. "I used to think you were an asshole, but you're all right, man."

"I could say the same about you," Carter replied with a grin.

"We almost didn't make it. I think the gate closed faster than you said it would."

Carter laughed. "It seemed that way, didn't it?"

Noah shook his head with a smirk. "You fucker. You had no idea how long it was gonna take for that gate to shut."

"I had an idea, but it was more of an estimate than an exact time. I'm starving, let's get something to eat. I could kill for an omelet."

"Oh my God, look at your mom's car," Amber said with her hand over her mouth. "What are you gonna do? Your dad's gonna kill you."

Carter moved next to Amber. Noah and Lilly followed. He nodded his head, his mouth turned down, inspecting the damage. He looked at Amber, his jaw set tight. "You know what? My dad can go fuck himself." Carter kicked the driver's side door, adding a size ten-and-a-half dent. "I'll tell 'em somebody sideswiped me while I was parked. This car is a piece of shit anyway."

− 12 −

What's Done Is Done

Police sirens intruded on Carter's REM sleep. His eyes fluttered. Lights flashed round and round, piercing his blinds. His head pounded. *Shit, they got my license plate number. I'm so dumb. I should've listened to Amber.* His stomach sank. He popped out of bed, naked except for boxers. He parted the blinds and peered out his bedroom window. Two fire trucks, a fire chief SUV, and half-a-dozen marked and unmarked police cars were parked on his block. They were clustered near the Wheeler's townhouse.

He dressed quickly and exited through the garage. He glanced at his mom's station wagon. The scratches were deeper than he remembered—down to the metal. He shook his head at the dent on the door. *What the fuck was I thinking?* Mr. and Mrs. Wheeler stood across the street by an unmarked police car. Mrs. Wheeler leaned on her husband, her face buried in his neck. Two detectives in dark suits spoke with the couple. An ambulance was in their driveway. The garage door was open. Fire fighters roused the Wheeler's next door neighbor. An older couple was escorted outside in their pajamas and robes. Fire fighters entered their home, staring at yellow handheld devices.

Carter walked down the sidewalk toward the commotion. A burly police officer stood on the sidewalk blocking his way.

"What happened?" Carter asked.

He shook his head. "Sorry, sir, I'm not at liberty to say. Please stand back from the scene." He used the magic word but it came out more like a command.

Carter walked back toward his house. A few neighbors stood on their front stoops in pajamas and sweats, watching the scene. He glanced across the street at the Wheelers. Mrs. Wheeler wailed and tried to push her way back to her home. Mr. Wheeler restrained her. Carter turned around, looking at the ambulance. He saw a gurney covered in a white sheet being loaded inside. The paramedics wore respirators. There were audible thuds as the ambulance doors were slammed shut. His stomach twisted in knots. *Ben.*

The ambulance pulled out of the driveway slowly, lights flashing. There were no sirens. The officers and fire fighters were subdued, talking in low tones and whispers. Mrs. Wheeler's sobbing cut through the quiet. The Wheelers were whisked away in an unmarked police car, following close behind the ambulance. The elderly couple was led back into their home by a fire fighter.

* * *

Carter lay in the dark, the streetlight casting slivers of light through the blinds. Raindrops pelted his window. His eye throbbed. He thought about Ben. *Was that him on that gurney? It had to be, and you know why.* There were five quick taps on his window, a pause, then five more. He groaned. His ribs ached when he moved. He staggered to the window, splitting the blinds with his fingers. Sarah stood in a dark raincoat, her hood up and her face pressed against the window. He mouthed, *hold on.* He crept into the garage, turned the light on and eased up the garage door, careful of the noise. Sarah bent down and squeezed under the door. She yanked the hood off her head and hugged Carter, the moisture from her raincoat seeping into his T-shirt and boxer shorts. She buried her face into the crook of his neck and sobbed. They stayed that way for several minutes.

She raised her head from his neck and stepped back. Her eyes were wet and puffy. "He's gone, and I think it might be my fault."

Carter shook his head. "No. It's not."

"He told me that he loved me and I …" She placed her head in her hands. Her chest heaved with sobs. "I didn't know what to say. I wanted to explain, but how do you explain to someone that loves you that you don't love them back?"

"I don't know," Carter replied.

"He just got mad and yelled at me and told me to leave. That was the last time we talked."

"I'm sorry, Sarah."

She was silent, staring at the concrete.

"You can't put this on yourself. You were a good friend to him."

She looked at Carter, her eyes wide. Her lower lip quivered and new tears flowed down her cheeks. "Your face."

"It looks worse than it feels."

"What happened?"

"I put a dent on my mom's car and my dad put a dent on my face."

"He can't keep doing this to you. We could talk to Mrs. Little at school. She'd know what to do. She's really nice—"

"Sarah, no. It's not important right now. Let's go inside."

Carter put his hand on her upper back and guided her into his room. He glanced at his alarm clock: *1:23 a.m.* She unzipped her jacket. Carter took it and set it on the edge of the futon. She plopped down on the couch. Her face was red and blotchy. Carter slipped on sweatpants and sat in front of her on the army footlocker that doubled as a coffee table.

"I'm sorry it's so late," she said. "I came by earlier, but your dad said you weren't allowed out."

"I'm glad you're here," he replied.

She took a deep breath. "I went by to see Ben this afternoon. His mom answered the door. She was a wreck. She told me that Ben ran her car in the garage. It was carbon monoxide poisoning." Sarah shook her head. "I should have seen it coming."

Carter grasped her hand, cradling it in both of his. "Sarah … you couldn't have. Nobody did."

She swallowed the lump in her throat. "I wish I could do it over. I knew he was hurt, but I just walked away."

"If I tell you something, will you promise not to tell anyone?"

Her eyes were wide, her eyebrows raised. "It depends on what it is."

"You have to promise me, or I can't."

She frowned. "You're scaring me."

He pursed his lips. "It's bad. Please don't say anything."

"Okay." She nodded.

"It was the initiation at Zach's farmhouse. He was never the same after that."

She glared and snatched her hand from his. "I asked you about it then. You told me you didn't know what was wrong with him."

"I'm sorry. I thought it would blow over. And Ben and I weren't exactly friends."

Her face was red. "Don't you make excuses, not now."

He stared at the carpet. "You're right." He nodded and looked up. "We were shoved in the basement of the farmhouse. It was Ben and me and Devin and ten other guys that had to go through the initiation. All the other guys were around the room, blocking the exits. They gave us three choices. We could allow Justin to smack us in the face with his penis. We could hold a cucumber in our ass for a certain amount of time or we could go back to the party naked."

She shook her head. "Let me guess. Zach and Justin were running the show."

"It gets worse. They told us that we had to sleep with someone at the party, or we would sleep outside with no clothes on."

She tightened her jaw. "Amber."

Carter's face was hot. "I'm sorry."

She scowled. "No, it's fine. Go on."

"Zach made it seem like running out into the party naked to try to sleep with some girl was the worst option."

"Jesus."

"He convinced Ben to make a decision first, and Ben chose to let Justin smack him in the face with his penis."

"Please tell me he didn't do it."

Carter shook his head. "He didn't. Ben closed his eyes, and Justin smacked him in the face with a cucumber."

"Just like at lunch."

"Yes."

"Did that happen to anyone else?"

Carter pursed his lips. "That's the problem. The whole thing was a test. Everyone else picked to go outside and sleep with a girl. He chose to be smacked in the face with Justin's penis. Everybody looked at him like he had some disease. He was totally humiliated."

She glared at Carter. "So, then the rest of you guys ran out naked and slept with some skank."

"No, it wasn't like that. We ran out naked, but there was some girl right outside to cover us up, and a lot of the girls lied, told Zach and Justin that they slept with the guy even when they didn't so they could get their stuff back."

She narrowed her eyes, searching his face. "Is that what happened with you and Amber? Did she wrap you up in a blanket and give you a peck on the cheek?"

He rubbed the back of his neck. "Not exactly."

She stood up and grabbed her jacket, shoving her arms through the sleeves. "I thought so."

"Sarah, it's not like we're together."

"That's for sure." She zipped up her jacket. "You need to tell your coach what happened. And you need to tell Mrs. Wheeler."

"A lot of people could get into serious trouble. I'd be a snitch. Who knows, they might cancel the season."

"You're an asshole."

She stormed out of his room into the garage. He followed.

"He's gone, Sarah. There's nothing that can be done about it now."

She stopped at the garage door and glowered at Carter. "If that's what you think, you're not who I thought you were."

And then she was gone, into the rain, into the night.

* * *

Carter slung his duffel bag over his shoulder. A handful of guys dressed in the locker room. He walked to the hall and stopped at Coach Cowan's office. The door was open. He stuck his head inside. Cowan sat on the couch, a remote in hand, watching game film. Carter tapped his knuckles on the open door. The coach glanced at Carter and paused the clip. His speckled hair was matted to his head in the form of his hat. His mustache widened with his smile.

"What can I do for you, Carter?" he asked.

"Can I talk to you for a minute?"

"Come on in."

Carter stepped into his office, dressed like his coach in black Marauder sweats.

"Grab one of those chairs," Coach Cowan said, motioning to the chairs in front of his desk.

Carter picked up a chair and set it down across from the couch. He placed his duffel bag on the floor and sat down. He gnawed on the inside of his cheek. Coach Cowan narrowed his eyes at Carter's shiner.

"You look like you got somethin' important on your mind," the coach said.

Carter nodded. "This is difficult to say."

"Does this have somethin' to do with your eye?"

Carter looked down. "No, sir. It has to do with hazing and Ben Wheeler."

Coach Cowan stood, marched to his door, and closed it. He returned to his seat on the couch. "Go on," he said.

Carter went on to tell his coach in detail about the hazing that Ben endured that night at Zach's farmhouse.

There was a long silence. "I just think if we didn't have that initiation, he'd still be here today," Carter said.

Coach Cowan took a deep breath, shaking his head. "It's a damn tragedy. I wish I'd known what was goin' on. I'm glad you came to me with this. I know it took a lot of courage to come forward. And don't worry, we'll keep this conversation between us."

Carter nodded. "What do we do now?"

"Son, this is no longer your responsibility. I'll handle it from here. You just need to concentrate on playin' football. It's playoff time. We gotta turn it up a notch."

"Are you gonna talk to Ben's parents?"

"Uh, yeah, I'll need to do that, but I'd rather not get into all that with you. This is a private matter. You have to remember we're dealin' with grievin' parents. We have to be extra careful that embarrassin' things about their son don't come out. Do you understand what I'm tryin' to tell you?"

"I think so."

"Listen, Carter, you can't tell *anyone* about this. You start spreadin' this stuff, a lot of people bound to get hurt. The Wheelers especially. Do you understand?"

"Yes, sir."

"Will you keep it under wraps and let me handle this?"

"Yes, sir."

Coach Cowan nodded. "I'm proud of you, son."

– 13 –

The Two Minute Drill

The Marauder stadium was packed. It was mostly adults on the cold aluminum stands, their hot chocolates and coffees in hand. Some stood, shivering, their hands buried in their pockets. The students fought for standing room along the fence that separated the fans from the cheerleaders and football players. The students rarely watched the games; they were usually blowouts. It was more of a social event for them. With the cheerleaders covered up in their winter gear and the scoreboard tight, the focus was on the game.

Coach Ware shook his head, his hands on his hips, as he watched the third down pass to Dwayne fall incomplete. He was decked out in a Marauders track suit and a knit cap. Condensation spilled from his mouth as he said, "Punt team." He tossed his clipboard toward the bench.

Carter lined up on the punt team, split out like a wide receiver. He signaled to the referee that he was on the line. He turned his head to the left, concentrating on the football in the long snapper's hands. A Washington Heights defender stood in front of Carter, his hands at chest height. When the ball moved, Carter sprinted downfield, the defender a yard behind and losing ground. He heard the thud of the football booming off the punter's foot. He didn't look up as the football sailed over his head, instead focusing on one thing: the return man.

The Washington Heights Warriors punt returner was small but shifty. Carter expected to veer off course and give the returner space for the fair catch. The punt returner looked up at the football swirling high over his head. His hands were held out in front of him like a basket. *No fair catch.* The ball fell from the sky into the returner's gloved hands. Carter didn't have to break stride. He blasted through the returner, his shoulder and facemask planted in the middle of the eight and two. Number eighty-two was sprawled on the ground, the wind knocked out of him. He still clutched the football in both hands.

The referees took an injury timeout. They spotted the ball on the Washington Heights thirty-three-yard line. The Marauders nickel defense huddled near the sideline, Coach Cowan in front. Carter glanced at the scoreboard. The Marauders were on top Twenty to fourteen, with 1:36 left on the clock.

Coach Cowan said, "Hey, let's be smart. They got a minute and a half left and one timeout. That's plenty of time for them, but they got a long field. Defensive ends, don't let that quarterback get outside of you. Defensive backs, don't give 'em anything deep, and keep them in bounds. And when you tackle someone, don't get off the pile, make the refs pull you off."

The clock ticked down as the Warriors battled their way to the Marauders' thirty-one-yard line with pinpoint passing, shifty scrambling, and a running back draw.

The Warriors lined up in an empty formation, three receivers on the left and two on the right. The quarterback was in the shotgun, alone in the backfield. The Marauders had three down linemen and a middle linebacker. Five defensive backs played press man-to-man on the five wide receivers. Noah and Carter were twelve yards deep on the hashes with explicit instructions not to let anyone behind them. Justin tapped the left hip of the nose guard in front of him. On the snap, the nose guard shot in the gap to the left of the center. The center moved with the nose, creating a crease on the right that Justin barreled through untouched. He planted the quarterback on the turf.

The result: a loss of seven. The Warriors burned their final timeout.

Second down and seventeen.

Ball on the Marauders' thirty-eight-yard line.

Thirty-seven seconds on the clock.

The Warriors were in the spread. The quarterback fired a frozen rope to the outside receiver on a hitch. The receiver gained seven yards before being tackled inbounds. The clock was moving. The warriors hurried to the line, the quarterback shouting the play. The inside receiver, Scooter Brooks, ran a slant, beating the rover. The quarterback hit the receiver in stride. Carter tackled him after a ten-yard gain. The clock stopped on the first down, but promptly restarted after the referee spotted the ball. Again, the Warriors hurried to the line, this time with a running back in the backfield. The center snapped the football. Justin and the defensive line raced into the backfield unscathed. The running back slipped behind them and the quarterback looped a screen pass over their heads. The running back caught the football and raced up the middle of the field, until Noah and Carter buried him into the turf. It was a gain of ten and another first down.

The Warriors' quarterback shouted, "Kill, kill!"

The Warriors' offense was already set as the referee spotted the ball. They snapped the football as soon as it was spotted. The quarterback spiked the ball in front of him, stopping the clock.

Second down and ten.

Ball on the Marauders' eleven-yard line.

Seven seconds on the clock.

On second down, the Warrior's quarterback lofted the football into the back corner of the end zone. Scooter had the corner beat by a step. Noah was out of position. The stands were silent as the perfect pass fell from the sky into Scooter's outstretched hands. The receiver dragged his foot but was a few inches beyond the end line, out of bounds. There was a collective gasp, followed by cheering from the fans, after the referee ruled the pass incomplete. Coach Cowan called his final timeout.

Third down and ten.

Ball on the Marauders' eleven-yard line.

Three seconds on the clock.

Coach Cowan trotted onto the field. The defense huddled around him.

"This is it, guys," Coach Cowan said, his face red. "We gotta have this one." He eyed each of his players. "They won't have time to run another one, so they'll try to get it to the end zone. I think they'll come back to that fade route to number two. We're gonna go Nickel, Double two. Carter, I want you to go to whichever side number two's on and double cover him. Noah, you go opposite." Coach Cowan grabbed Carter by the facemask. "Son, you got one job. Do not let that kid score."

The Warriors were spread out with four receivers to the left and one to the right. Number two, Scooter Brooks, was all alone on the right side, near the sideline. The Marauders' cornerback lined up directly in front of him, in press man-to-man coverage. Carter was eight yards behind on his inside shoulder. *Look at his alignment. He's too close to the sideline. He's not running a fade. He's gotta come inside. Slant maybe, skinny post.*

Carter moved to the inside a couple of yards. Coaches on both side-lines screamed last-second instructions, but they were drowned out by the crowd noise. Carter focused on the star receiver's belt buckle. He backpedaled as Scooter sprinted forward, beating the press, leaving the cornerback in the dust. After five yards, the receiver cut inside at a sixty-degree angle. The quarterback fired a bullet. Carter planted and exploded forward. Scooter caught the ball at the two-yard line. As soon as the ball touched his hands, Carter leveled him, the ball squirt-ing to the turf. Another Warriors' receiver picked up the ball and dove into the end zone. Carter lay on the grass in a daze as the Warriors celebrated around him. A referee stepped into the melee waving his arms back and forth, signaling an incompletion, not a fumble. The clock said 0:00, the score still twenty to fourteen.

The Marauder sideline charged the field, jumping up and down in a frenzy, followed by the students and parents. Number two held out his hand. Carter took it, and Scooter hoisted him to his feet.

"Good game," he said, his face rigid.

"Thanks, you too."

* * *

The locker room was raucous with talk of parties, recaps of the game, and *going to state*. Carter sat on the bench in front of his locker. He had his head in his hands, massaging his temples.

"Hey, man, you all right?" Devin asked as he zipped up his Redskins starter jacket.

Carter looked up. "I'm fine, I just have a headache."

Devin patted him on the shoulder, laughing. "You need to stop using your head as a battering ram."

"You're probably right."

"I'll check you later."

"See ya, Devin."

Carter stood like an octogenarian. He grabbed the sweatshirt hanging in his locker and pulled it over his head. He picked up his duffel bag and staggered into the hall. Coach Cowan and Coach Ware laughed in Cowan's office. Carter stood in the hall waiting. He caught Coach Ware's eye.

"Lynch, what are you doin' out there?"

"I just need to talk to Coach Cowan for a minute."

"I'll see you in films tomorrow," Coach Ware said to Cowan.

"Bright and early," Cowan said.

"Don't forget the doughnuts."

Coach Cowan laughed. "I won't."

Coach Ware smacked Carter on the back as he walked by. "Nice game, two-zero."

"Thanks, Coach."

Coach Cowan invited Carter into his office and shut the door behind them. He stood in the middle of his office with his arms crossed. He didn't offer Carter a seat.

"What do you need?" Coach Cowan asked.

"I just wanted to see what was happening with the Ben Wheeler situation," Carter said.

"And I told you before that I was handlin' it."

"That was like three weeks ago, and I haven't seen anything happen."

Coach Cowan exhaled and put his hands on his hips. "And you prob'ly won't see anything happen. Son, this is a private matter. A *delicate*, private matter. And this is the last time I'm a tell you. It's handled. Leave it alone."

"Did you talk to the Wheelers?"

"Yes, I did, and the last thing they want is this bullshit tarnishin' their good name."

"What about Zach and Justin? Are they gonna get in trouble for the hazing?"

Coach Cowan's nostrils flared, his eyes narrowed. "And what would you have me do to 'em? It seems to me that the whole team was there. Every single one of you was prob'ly drinkin'. Would you have me bring the cops in and arrest every last one of you? Boy, we just won a huge game. We're one win away from back-to-back state championships and you wanna talk about some dumb shit that happened in August. What the hell's wrong with you?"

Carter stared at the floor.

"You're like a goddamn pit bull with a bone. Now get outta my office."

* * *

Carter paced on the sidewalk in front of the Wheelers' townhouse. The afternoon sun was waning in the sky. His hands were in the front pocket of his hooded sweatshirt. Their side door opened. Carter turned quickly and marched back toward his house.

"Carter," Mrs. Wheeler called out.

He stopped and turned around. "Hi, Mrs. Wheeler."

She walked toward Carter. Her face was pale and haggard. Her brown hair was stringy. She had dark circles under her eyes.

"You were out here for a long time," she said. "Did you want to come up? You know you can still come and visit."

Carter pursed his lips. "I don't know. I mean …"

Mrs. Wheeler crossed her arms over her sweater. "Honey, it's cold. Why don't you come up? I'll make you some hot chocolate."

Carter slipped his running shoes off at the door and followed Mrs. Wheeler into the kitchen. She pulled a carton of milk from the refrigerator, glancing at the date.

She sighed. "It used to be I couldn't keep milk in this house. Now I have to check dates." She poured the milk into a Pyrex measuring cup and placed the cup in the microwave. "The key to good hot cocoa is to use milk instead of water."

Carter sat on a stool against the counter. "I've never had hot chocolate with milk."

She smiled, her eyes still. "You're in for a treat then."

Carter glanced around the room. The shades were drawn. The couch in the family room looked rumpled as if someone had been sleeping there. Dishes filled the sink. She stood facing him on the other side of the counter, her hands hanging onto the edge. Her knuckles were white.

"So, how's everything going?" she asked.

Carter shrugged. "I don't know …"

The microwave beeped. She grabbed the Pyrex cup from the microwave and set it on the counter.

"I saw in the paper that you guys are going to the state championship." She opened a cabinet and picked up a mug that read *Supermom*. She frowned. "I hope you don't mind this old mug. I need to do the dishes."

Carter swallowed. "It's fine."

Mrs. Wheeler poured the milk into the mug. She opened the drawer and pulled out a spoon. She emptied a packet of cocoa into the warm milk and stirred.

"I'm sorry that I haven't been by to see you and Mr. Wheeler," Carter said.

"Oh, honey, you are certainly welcome anytime, but it's not your responsibility."

Carter nodded, his eyes downcast.

She set the spoon in the sink and pushed the hot cocoa across the counter to Carter. "The milk isn't too hot. You should be able to drink it right away."

Carter took a sip from the mug and set it on the counter. "That's really good."

"I'm glad you like it. I used to make this for Ben and Sarah all the time in the winter. You know it's funny. The first time I made this for Sarah, she said the same thing as you, that she'd never had it with milk."

Carter sipped the hot cocoa.

"How is Sarah doing these days?" Mrs. Wheeler asked.

"I haven't seen her much," Carter replied.

She frowned. "That's too bad. I always thought you two got along so well."

"She's mad at me."

"I can't imagine what for. You know, of all of Ben's friends, you were always the most polite."

Carter gazed at the Supermom mug. His eyes filled with tears. He blinked, a few tears slid down his face.

"Carter, honey, it's okay." She moved around the counter. She bent over and wrapped her arms around him.

"I'm so sorry," he said, his words barely audible.

She rocked him back and forth like a child. "It's okay. There's nothing to be sorry for."

"There is," he said, his voice clearer, his tears drying.

Mrs. Wheeler let go and sat next to him on a stool. "Honey, no, you can't do this to yourself. I'm no fool. I saw how Ben treated you. He was a good boy, but he wasn't comfortable in his own skin yet. That made him jealous. Do you understand what I'm trying to tell you?"

"Did Coach Cowan talk to you and Mr. Wheeler?"

She furrowed her brow. "Should he have?"

Carter went on to tell Mrs. Wheeler in detail what happened to her son at the initiation. After, she wiped the tears from her eyes with her thumb and index finger.

"I'm so sorry, Mrs. Wheeler. I should've told you before. I was afraid to admit that I didn't help Ben. I was there and I just let it happen."

She sniffled, took a deep breath, and sat up straight, her shoulders back. "Now, Carter, you listen to me, and you listen good."

Carter searched her face, waiting for his punishment.

She said, "You will *not* put even one single ounce of this weight on your shoulders. Do you hear me?"

Carter nodded, his eyes glassy. "Do you want me to go with you to the school?"

She shook her head. "I don't want you getting embroiled in this. You have to promise me that you will not tell anyone that you told me."

"Okay."

"As a teacher in the district, I've been to the school board meetings, and I know what these people are like. I don't want to scare you, honey, but they'll sacrifice *you* if that means saving the reputation of the football program."

"What are you gonna do?"

"I don't want this to happen again. The hazing has to stop."

– 14 –

Going to State?

Like soldiers going off to war, the North Potomac Marauders said their final goodbyes to family, friends, and girlfriends. The low afternoon sun dropped behind the school. Carter stood in the shade, leaning against the brick school near the locker room door. His black knit cap was pulled low over his eyebrows. His gear was in an oversized mesh bag at his feet. Amber stood in his personal space, her hands warming in the front pocket of his hooded sweatshirt. Her lips were full and shiny with lip gloss. Her green eyes searched his face.

"What's wrong?" she asked.

Carter exhaled. "I don't know."

"I've never seen a guy that wasn't happy about playin' for the state championship. You get to stay in a hotel tonight. You're gonna be playin' at UVA."

"I can't seem to shake it. You know, what happened to Ben."

"Why are you so obsessed with this? I think what he did is just … creepy."

"I think the initiation killed Ben."

She frowned. "What are you talkin' about? He was perfectly fine. Nobody hurt him."

"You don't understand. Zach and Justin humiliated him in front of the whole team. And he wanted to be accepted more than anyone. It crushed him."

"Why would you bring this up now?"

He rubbed his temples and looked at Amber. "Because nobody cares. Coach Cowan told me he was gonna do something about it. He's a liar."

Cowan stood in front of two idling school buses. The buses were half-full, with players immersed in their headphones or socializing with the kids around them. Players queued up at the doors, their equipment bags slung over their shoulders.

"Let's go everyone. Buses are leavin'," Cowan called out.

Amber removed her hands from Carter's pocket, stepped back and crossed her arms. "And what's your coach supposed to do? Ben's dead. He's not comin' back."

"He could stop the initiation."

"This is stupid. It's not like he was even there."

Carter shook his head. "If he told everyone that they'd be kicked off the team if they participated in any hazing, it would stop. I guarantee it."

She narrowed her eyes. "I don't understand you. Ben didn't even like you. You said so yourself."

"Carter, move it," Coach Cowan called out.

Carter glanced at his coach, then back to Amber. "That doesn't matter. It could've just as easily been me in his shoes. Shit, Noah almost died from alcohol poisoning a couple years ago."

"You know what, Ben was a little bitch. It's nobody's fault but his own."

"I said move it, Carter," Cowan called out.

Carter pushed off the wall, grabbed his bag and slung it over his shoulder. He glared at Amber. "No. You're a little bitch."

Amber's eyes went wide. She slapped Carter across the face. Onlookers from the crowd and the bus snickered, laughed, and heckled. Carter held his glare for a moment. He turned and marched toward the bus.

Justin hung out the bus window with a wide smile. "Damn, Carter, she hits harder than you." The bus erupted in laughter.

Cowan was beet red, his jaw tight, his fists clenched. Carter ignored his gaze as he moved to the bus door. "Don't you step on my bus," Coach said.

Carter stopped and turned toward the coach. He was close enough that Carter could smell the coffee on his breath. Carter glanced at Cowan's clenched fists at his side.

"What the hell's your problem, boy?"

Carter stared at the asphalt beneath his feet.

"*Look at me* when I'm talkin' to you," Coach Cowan said.

Carter looked up.

"You gotta be the most selfish goddamn kid I know. We're about to play for the state championship and you're holdin' up my buses. We got a hundred guys on this team, and they're all *waitin'* on you." Cowan shook his head. "Then you're gonna bring your *goddamn girlfriend problems* too. This is football, son, not *Days of Our Lives*. I oughta send your ass home now. Is that what you want?"

Carter stared at the coach's clenched fists and white knuckles.

"I said look at me!"

Carter blinked and stared at the coach. He dropped his equipment bag on the asphalt.

"What the hell do you think you're doin' boy?"

Carter started to walk past, but the coach grabbed him by the upper arm. Carter stopped and looked at the tight grip around his arm. He turned slowly, looking Coach Cowan in the eye.

"Get your *fucking* hands off me," Carter said.

Coach Pitts appeared from the bus. "Coach, let me talk to him."

Coach Cowan let go. "You're done. You're off this team!"

Carter walked away.

"You can forget about next year too," Coach Cowan called out.

"Do you really think this is necessary?" Coach Pitts asked. "Let me talk to him. I can work it out."

"He's done," Coach Cowan said. "Let's go, we gotta state championship to win."

Carter pulled his hood over his head, slid his hands into the front pocket of his sweatshirt and walked past the assembled families and friends of his former teammates. The crowd was silent as he moved past.

A young boy yelled out in a high pitched voice, "Quitter."

A few kids giggled. Their parents shushed them.

Carter shuffled home, his eyes focused on the concrete sidewalk. He breathed a sigh of relief at the sight of the empty parking spot in front of his parents' townhouse. He pushed the garage door open and slipped inside, shutting the door behind him. He locked his bedroom door, stripped down to his boxer briefs and crawled into bed. He pulled the comforter tight over his body. He lay on his side, his knees pulled to his chest. He was silent as the tears ran across his face.

* * *

Carter's stomach growled. His whole body was sore, as if he'd been fighting while he slept. Sunlight punctured his blinds. He smelled bacon and coffee. He glanced at his alarm clock: *10:11 a.m.* He picked up his jeans and hooded sweatshirt from the floor and dressed. He used the bathroom and brushed his teeth. Steeling himself, he trudged up the basement steps to the kitchen. His parents and younger sister sat on stools at the counter eating breakfast. They were still in their pajamas. They looked at him with wide eyes and arched eyebrows.

Jim set his fork down with a clang. "What the hell are you doin' here?"

"Aren't you supposed to be with the team?" Grace asked.

"I quit," Carter said.

Jim shook his head, a smirk on his face. "Why?"

Carter shrugged. "The coach …"

Jim chuckled. "The quitter's mantra. It's always someone else's fault." Jim spoke in a mocking girlish voice. "The coach was mean to me. He was always yellin'. It hurt my feelin's."

"Jim." Grace shook her head. "That's not necessary."

"This is so embarrassing," Alyssa said. A piece of bacon was stuck between her braces. "Do you know what a nightmare this is going to be for me?"

Carter glared at his sister. "Shut up, this isn't about you."

Jim stood up, his fists clenched. "You will *not* talk to your sister that way."

"Why do you care if I play football or not?" Carter said to Jim. "I'm too small, remember? I'm just taking your wise advice."

Jim shook his head and marched around the counter, closer to Carter. "You're not puttin' your cowardice on me. So damn sensitive. I offer some constructive criticism and you just fall apart. If you're gonna get anywhere in this world, you best develop a thick skin."

"Your dad's right," Grace said. "You can't go quitting when things are hard."

"I could care less if you play football," Jim said. "But you're not gonna sit around here after school and not contribute. From now on, if you want somethin', you're gonna have to buy it yourself. No more free rides."

Carter's mouth was a flat line. "When I turn eighteen, you'll never see me again."

Jim pounced on Carter, his meaty hands wrenching Carter's neck. Carter's eyes dimmed, his breath stymied.

"You think you can make threats in my house?" Jim said.

Jim let go. Carter coughed and sucked in oxygen. He stood straight, glaring at his father, his fists clenched. He stood there for a moment then turned and marched down the basement steps. He grabbed his knit cap, opened the garage door and left. He pulled his cap over his head and started jogging, the cold wind biting his face. He continued running until he was outside of his neighborhood, along the main highway. He slowed to a walk along the concrete sidewalk. Steam spilled from his mouth with each breath. He shoved his hands in his front pocket and leaned into the headwind.

After a few miles, his feet were frozen, his face numb. He hiked into the parking lot of the public library. Two cars were parked in a lot that could hold a hundred. He took off his hat as he entered the heated building. Immediately to his right was a long desk with an elderly woman sitting behind a fat computer monitor. She glanced up from her bifocals.

"Can I help you find something?" she asked.

"No thank you," Carter said, "I'm just looking."

Carter strolled through every bookshelf, glancing at the titles. Past the shelves he browsed through the magazines and newspapers. The front cover of the *Alexandria Gazette* read *The Marauders Plan to Pillage Another State Title*. He grabbed a copy of *Sports Illustrated* and ambled to a cluster of tables and chairs. He read the magazine cover to cover. After, he read another one. He continued like that until the elderly woman told him that they were closing.

A gust of wind smacked him in the face as soon as he stepped out of the library. He felt faint, his stomach rumbling. He jogged on the sidewalk, the wind swirling, his eyes watering, and his face numb. Cars zipped by, leaving their exhaust hanging in the air. His feet smacked the sidewalk, but he could barely feel them. A few miles later, he turned into his neighborhood. He slowed to a walk and put his hands on his hips, sucking in the bitter air.

He heard a few polite beeps behind him. He turned to see a red Honda Coupe stop along the sidewalk. The window powered down.

"Carter," Sarah said from the passenger's seat.

Carter turned and jogged from the sidewalk to the street where the car was parked along the curb.

"I've been looking everywhere for you," Sarah said.

Julie leaned over from the driver's seat with a smile.

"Hi, Mrs. Cunningham," Carter said.

She frowned. "Stop with the Mrs. Cunningham, and get in before you turn into a Popsicle."

Sarah opened the door and stepped from the car. She pushed the seat forward and climbed into the miniscule back seat. "Get in," she said.

Carter sat in front and shut the door.

"Are you okay?" Sarah asked.

"I'm fine," Carter said, "I just went to the library."

Julie pulled into her driveway. She was dressed in black tights, a short skirt, and tall boots. The car idled, the headlights still on.

"You're not coming?" Sarah asked.

Julie frowned. "You know I'm supposed to meet Lincoln."

"Whatever."

Carter opened the car door. "Thank you for the ride Mrs.—I mean, Julie."

She winked. "You're welcome, cutie pie."

Sarah pushed the front seat forward and stepped from the car. Sarah and Carter strolled up the steps to the front door. Julie was already gone. Sarah fished for her key, cranked the deadbolt, and pushed inside. She flipped on the lights. Carter pulled his knit cap off, his short brown hair matted to his head. Sarah took off her jacket and hung it in the hall closet.

She frowned at Carter's sweatshirt. "Where's your coat, Panama boy?"

"I left it at home."

"You want something to eat? I was going to make spaghetti for dinner."

"I thought you were mad at me," Carter said.

She stepped forward and kissed him on the cheek, her warm lips lingering on his cold face. "I'm not."

"Do you mind if I sit down? I feel a little faint. I haven't eaten since breakfast … yesterday."

Sarah's eyes widened. "Why don't you lay down in the living room? I'll heat you up some bread to tide you over until dinner."

"I'll just sit here," he said, sitting at the kitchen table by the bay window. "I wanted to talk to you."

"You look pale," she said walking closer to him. She put the back of her hand to his head. "You don't feel hot."

He smirked. "How could I? I was freezing my ass off."

She moved over to the counter, picking up the tea pot. "I'll put some tea on."

Carter rubbed his temples. "Thank you."

She flashed him a grin.

"Why were you looking for me?" he asked.

"My friend Megan was at school yesterday for the big farewell." Sarah took a deep breath. "She told me what happened."

"That's what I wanted to talk to you about."

"After dinner," she said. "You look like frozen death."

Carter sipped herbal tea and devoured warm bread slathered in butter. Sarah simultaneously tended a pot of pasta and a pot of bolognaise on the stovetop. She glanced over her shoulder at Carter before fishing a piece of spaghetti from the pot and tossing it against the wall. It stuck in place.

"I think we're about ready," she said.

They ate in silence. Carter inhaled his heaping plate of pasta. Sarah watched him, her eyebrows raised. He wiped his face with his napkin and washed the last of his spaghetti down with water.

"This is the best food I've ever had," he said.

She laughed. "You were starving—literally. I could've fed you crackers and you would've said that."

"Thank you."

She grinned. "You look better. There's color in your face."

He exhaled, his smile fading. "I quit football."

She nodded. "I figured. It was interesting timing, though. The state championship and all."

He frowned.

"I'm not criticizing. I'm just worried about you."

"I thought you'd be happy. I thought you hated football."

She reached across the table and squeezed his hand. "It doesn't

150

matter what I think. This is about you. Why'd you do it? I thought you loved football."

"I didn't plan to quit." He shook his head. "It all happened so fast."

"Start from the beginning."

"I guess I was mad at Coach Cowan. I told him about what happened to Ben like a month ago. Then I asked him about it and he lied to me. He said he was gonna talk to the Wheelers but he never did."

"Did you tell them?"

He nodded. "I told Mrs. Wheeler."

Her eyes were wide. "What did she say?"

"She said I should keep quiet about it, that she's gonna handle it."

Sarah smiled for a second. "I'm sorry, I interrupted you."

"It's okay. So, right before the buses were supposed to leave, I was talking to Amber about Ben, and she said he was a little bitch."

"She's a little bitch."

"That's what I said."

Sarah laughed. "How'd that go over?"

He smirked. "She slapped me."

Sarah put up her fists like a boxer. "Do you want me to kick her ass?"

He chuckled. "Then Coach Cowan started yelling at me because I was holding up the buses. I dropped my bag and started to leave and Coach Cowan grabbed me by the arm. I told him to get his fucking hands off me."

She sighed. "I'm sorry. I don't know what to say."

"I don't even understand it myself. It's not like I'm not used to being yelled at. I don't know. It was like I hit a breaking point. I just snapped."

"What happened after that?"

"I went home and slept. The next morning, my dad was being an asshole. He grabbed me by the throat."

Sarah winced. "Those red marks on your neck."

He nodded. "You know, for the first time in my life, I wasn't afraid. I remember looking at his face and thinking about bashing it in with my fists. I left because I could feel myself getting all amped up." He rubbed the back of his neck. "I didn't have anywhere to go, so I walked to the library. You and your mom picked me up when I was walking back."

She bit the bottom corner of her lower lip. Her blue eyes searched his face. "You can always come here."

"Okay."

"What are you going to do now?"

He looked down at his empty plate, then back to Sarah. "I gotta get out of my house. I can't be there anymore. I'm gonna get a job and save up so I can leave on my eighteenth birthday. It's fourteen months from today."

"What about football?"

"It's over. Cowan said I can't come back next year."

She pursed her lips. "I'm sorry."

He glanced at the sink, pushed his chair out and stood. He picked up his plate. "We should clean this up," he said, taking her plate and placing it on top of his.

She stood, sucking in her plump lower lip before pressing it back out. He placed the plates in the sink; she brought the glasses. They stood by the sink, facing each other. She looked up at him through her oversized specs.

He pulled his sleeves up his forearms. "I'll wash," he said.

She was unresponsive.

He gazed down at her. She nibbled on her lower lip. He removed her glasses and placed them on the counter. Her skin was a perfect porcelain with a hint of strawberry in her cheeks. He brushed her hair from her blue eyes and pressed his lips to hers. She reciprocated with more force, their lips parting, their tongues touching. He slid his arms around her waist and pulled her close, her chest against his. She squeezed her arms around him. After a moment she pulled back with a grin, her lips swollen.

"I really like you, Carter Lynch."

– 15 –

Porta Potty

Carter and Sarah walked arm in arm along the sidewalk to the high school. A banner hung at the school entrance: *Back-to-Back Varsity Football State Champions!* Sarah was bundled in her red pea coat and gray scarf. Her hair spilled from her blue wool cap. Carter looked like a disgruntled veteran, with an old army jacket and his black knit cap pulled low over his eyebrows. A few parents and kids hurried into the school. Inside, the high school was an ocean of linoleum. To their left, adults and teens congregated in front of the auditorium.

The stadium seating in the auditorium was nearly filled. The adults spoke in hushed whispers. The majority of the football team was positioned front and center. They were boisterous and comfortable on their home turf. The Wheelers were also in front, but on the left hand side. Carter and Sarah snagged two empty seats toward the back. There was a single wooden podium with a microphone attached in the center aisle facing the stage. Four police officers stood in front, two on each side. A long table was set up onstage with a microphone in front of each VIP. Carter recognized two of the ten serious figures seated at the table. Coach Cowan looked innocent with his fresh shave, neatly combed hair, and dark suit. Walter Sullivan, the diminutive principal, joked with Cowan. The coach didn't look amused.

"What's up with the police officers?" Carter asked Sarah.

"A few years ago, some kids were having sex in the janitor's closet," Sarah said. "One of the girls got pregnant. The girl's father blamed the school for lack of supervision. He came after the superintendent at a school board meeting."

"That's crazy."

Sarah nodded.

"Do you know the people on stage?" Carter asked Sarah.

"There's Principal Sullivan and of course Coach Cowan, but you know them."

Carter nodded.

"The guy next to Principal Sullivan with the hairy neck and the scrunched up face, that's the superintendent, the one that was attacked, Dr. Richard Perry. The woman on the far right is Mrs. Little. She's one of the junior class counselors. I just love her. And the guy with the white hair next to her is Mr. Shepherd. He's one of the senior class counselors. I don't know much about him. The five old dudes on the left are all school board members."

Coach Cowan stomped to the center of the stage and told the football players to sit down and be quiet. He returned to his seat.

Dr. Perry tapped on the mic in front of him. "Can I have your attention please? We're about to start."

The auditorium quietened. Latecomers stood lining the back wall. Dr. Perry led the audience in the pledge of allegiance. Sarah pulled out her handheld tape recorder and pressed record.

Dr. Perry cleared his throat. "This emergency school board meeting has been called to address the possible problem of hazing and bullying by members of the varsity football team." A couple of random boos erupted from the audience.

Dr. Perry continued, "It was brought to my attention two weeks ago that new football players *may* have been subjected to an initiation where they were bullied. I've dedicated every ounce of my energy to get to the bottom of this serious allegation. Here at North Potomac High School we have a no-tolerance policy for bullying. Coach Cowan interviewed every single active member of the football team, including the seniors. I believe we have ninety-five student athletes on the football team." He turned to Coach Cowan and smiled.

"Yep, ninety-five," Coach Cowan said. "The kids told some funny stories, but nothin' that was bullyin' or hazin'. Football's an intense game and these kids are under mountains of pressure and expectations. It's important that we allow them to have some fun and even do a little razzin', provided they don't stray too far. Havin' said all that, I'm still deeply concerned about the possibility of this problem. To be frank, if a single young person is hurt on my watch because of bullyin', it's one too many. Even though I feel that our state champion football team—"

A few hoots and hollers emanated from the audience.

Coach Cowan smiled and restarted. "Even though I feel that our *state champion football team* isn't guilty of hazin' or bullyin', I *am* open to Dr. Perry's recommendations to make sure we don't run into these problems in the future." Coach Cowan turned from the audience to Dr. Perry.

"This is total bullshit," Carter said to Sarah.

Dr. Perry said, "I've elected to have Coach Cowan put the entire team through an hour of sensitivity training each season to make sure these things don't happen here. To take it a step further and to make sure that we're not unfairly singling out the football team, all sports will be required to complete the training. As educators, our goal is to provide a safe environment to learn. I'll continue to make this a top priority. We'll maintain, as always, a zero-tolerance policy on bullying.

"We'll now open up this meeting for comments from the public. Anyone who wants to speak, please line up behind the podium. Our regular school board meeting rules apply. If you use bad language, or conduct yourself in a rude or threatening manner, you will be removed from the premises. Furthermore, we have a one-minute time limit on each speaker. Please be respectful and don't monopolize the microphone."

Sarah leaned over to Carter. "That's funny coming from him."

A handful of football players and adult men lined up behind the podium. Mr. and Mrs. Wheeler were toward the back. The audience clapped each time a football player spoke about how they were a family and they protected and looked out for each other. The men spoke of their time as Marauders and how the discipline and teamwork they learned on the football field helped them to be successful businessmen, fathers, and leaders. Mr. Wheeler looked small and frail behind the current and former football players. He pushed his glasses up the bridge of his nose as he stepped to the podium with a typewritten letter in hand. He stared at the paper and cleared his throat.

"My son was Ben Wheeler. Six weeks ago, he killed himself in our home. Fifteen weeks ago, he was humiliated at a team initiation—"

"I'm sorry, Mr. Wheeler," Dr. Perry said. Mr. Wheeler looked up from his paper. "We sympathize with your loss, and our school mourns the loss of a fantastic kid. The initiation that allegedly took place on August thirtieth has not been corroborated by *any* of Coach Cowan's interviews."

Mr. Wheeler clenched the edge of the podium, his knuckles white. He continued, "He was so ashamed that he refused to go to school or practice the next week. He was promptly thrown off the team—"

"I'm sorry, Mr. Wheeler, I'm going to have to stop you again," Dr. Perry said. "All the kids sign a behavior contract that says if you miss three practices without an excuse, you are automatically—"

Mr. Wheeler pounded the podium, his glasses bouncing on his nose. "Shut up and let me speak!"

"Mr. Wheeler," Dr. Perry said, "we do not allow aggressive behavior here. For your own good, I'm going to have to ask you to leave."

Two police officers converged on the podium. Mr. Wheeler looked at the cops marching toward him. He leaned into the mic. "My son is dead." The auditorium was silent.

Mr. Wheeler nodded to his wife as he was escorted outside by the police officers. Mrs. Wheeler stepped up to the mic.

"I'll meet you outside," Carter said to Sarah as he stood. He marched to the short line behind the podium.

"Mrs. Wheeler," Dr. Perry said, "please be advised that we sympathize with your family, but we cannot have outbursts in this forum."

"Outbursts?" Mrs. Wheeler said. "What would you qualify as an outburst?"

"I know it when I see it," Dr. Perry replied.

"What I don't understand is why my son's life is less important than the reputation of the football team?"

"This forum is not for speculation," Dr. Perry said. "I can assure you that your son's life and the lives of all of our students are of paramount importance."

"Everyone who's ever played football in this audience knows about the hazing and the initiation—"

"I'm going to have to stop you right there. We have not found any evidence to support your claim."

Mrs. Wheeler narrowed her eyes at Dr. Perry. "I just want the hazing to stop. How can it stop, if we can't even admit it's a problem?"

"I'm sorry, Mrs. Wheeler, but your time is up. Please step away from the podium."

"I will not," Mrs. Wheeler said, her voice shaky. "How many thousands of kids have been subjected to this—"

"Mrs. Wheeler, that's enough," Dr. Perry said, looking behind him for the AV guy. "Cut the podium mic."

"She has a right to speak," Mrs. Little said.

The men seated at the long table glared at Mrs. Little.

The remaining two police officers approached the podium.

Mrs. Wheeler shouted, the mic dead. "You know what goes on. It wasn't just Ben. There've been kids with alcohol poisoning and post-traumatic stress—" The cops grabbed Mrs. Wheeler by her upper arms. She squirmed as they forced her up the stairs. "Let me go."

Carter pushed to the front of the line, his jaw set tight and his eyes wild.

"Because of the unruly outbursts," Dr. Perry said, "we'll adjourn this meeting."

"No," Carter said, loud enough for the entire audience to hear without the mic. "The Wheelers are telling the truth. I was there. Ben was tricked into allowing another player to smack him in the face with his penis."

The audience gasped.

Justin stood up. "He's a liar."

"Step down from the podium and leave the premises," Dr. Perry said.

"The cops are busy," Carter said, "why don't you come down and move me." Dr. Perry stayed in his seat. Carter looked at Justin. "I didn't say you did it." He turned to the audience. "He used a cucumber, but Ben didn't know it at the time. The point was to humiliate him, and that's what they did. Ben wanted to be a part of this team more than anyone, and they just looked at him like he was nothing." Carter turned back to the stage. "I think Ben would still be alive if it never happened. We're all to blame, myself included. The rest of us were forced into a party naked with two hundred girls watching us."

A handful of men and teenage boys laughed.

Coach Cowan stood and approached the end of the stage, glaring at Carter. "That's enough," Cowan said.

A few adults from the crowd piped up. "Let him finish."

Carter continued, "For those of you with daughters: listen up. We couldn't get our clothes back without having sex with a girl at the party." There was hushed whispering and several wide-eyed fathers. "Don't worry. A lot of girls lied to Justin and Zach over there"—Carter pointed—"so guys could get their clothes back. Only a handful of guys actually had sex with the girls. A lot of them just got blowjobs."

Some of the crowd began to shout at Carter, calling him a liar. Some began to shout at the school board and the superintendent, threatening changes with the upcoming election.

Two police officers marched down the steps toward Carter. He put his hands up.

"I'm leaving," he said.

* * *

Carter trudged down the linoleum hallway, his duffel bag slung over his shoulder. Kids hurried around him, fast-walking to beat the lunch rush. He elicited stares and scowls from the student body. He passed a cluster of football players. They were unconcerned about the long lunch lines forming. There would be friends saving them spaces or they'd simply cut in line.

"Bitch," one of them said as Carter passed.

He continued down the hall, unfazed.

After waiting in line, he sat down across from Sarah. They sat alone, at the end of a table large enough to seat sixteen. The buzz of voices blended together to form a constant stream of background noise.

Sarah frowned at his food as he sat down. "I'm making you lunch tomorrow. I can't watch you eat this shit. Do you know what they put in hot dogs?"

Carter shrugged and took a bite. "Tastes good."

She scrunched up her nose. "It's made from fatty tissues, head meat, animal feet, animal skin, blood, liver and other nasty stuff unfit for human consumption."

Carter put his hot dog on his tray. "Can we change the subject?"

She grinned. "How's the new job?"

"It's all right. Smelling like pine needles is better than smelling like French fries."

"It's so stupid that we kill perfectly healthy trees for decoration."

Carter gazed over her shoulder. Justin sauntered toward them looking like a mismatched music star. His jeans and cowboy boots were country, his Mohawk punk rock, his flannel grunge, and his pale skin and blond hair pure boy band.

Sarah turned around in her seat and scowled at Justin. Carter narrowed his eyes, his body tense.

"What up, Carter?" Justin said. "I just wanted to see how you were doin'. We haven't seen you lately. That's right." Justin snapped his fingers. "You quit like a little bitch."

"Walk away," Carter said, his hands gripping the edge of the bench seat.

Justin grinned at Sarah, his eyes locked on her. "Seein' that Christmas is comin' up, I had somethin' for your girl."

Carter moved around the table.

Justin pulled his zipper down, reached into his pants, and pulled a bun less hot dog from his boxer shorts. He held it at the opening of his jeans, like it was attached. He gazed down at Sarah and mouthed a kiss.

"Why don't you give it a little lick," he said. "You know you want—"

Carter coldcocked Justin with a right cross to the jaw. Justin's head snapped to the side, his brain bouncing against his skull. His body fell awkwardly as if his legs no longer functioned. He lay on the ground, seemingly asleep. Pandemonium erupted around him as kids laughed and jeered.

"Damn, he got knocked the fuck out!" someone from the crowd said.

Two school police officers pushed through the crowd.

Carter grabbed Justin's hot dog from the floor and shoved it into the boy's mouth. Justin lay sprawled on his back, his eyes closed, with a hot dog sticking from his mouth. Carter was grabbed from behind and shoved onto the table, his hands forced behind his back. He was handcuffed and hauled away.

* * *

The bar bent across Carter's shoulders as he squatted down. He pressed up with his arms and legs, exhaling as he stood. He took two choppy steps and set the bar down on the rack. A single light bulb cast dim shadows in the corners of the garage. He wore sweats in the unheated space.

The door from the basement opened and Amber waltzed through. She wore heavy makeup and heavy perfume. Her jeans were tight, her sweater low cut. Large gold hoops dangled from her earlobes. Carter scowled. She smiled, her lips glossed, her teeth white.

"Before you say anything," she said, showing her palms in surrender. "Your mom let me in. I'm just here because I want us to be friends. I really need to talk to you."

"I've got enough friends," Carter replied.

She frowned. "I'm sorry about what happened."

"Between us, or at school?"

"All of it. How long is your suspension?"

"A week. I'll be back after Christmas break."

"Justin deserved it, if you ask me."

Carter picked up a twenty-five-pound plate and hefted it onto the bar, sliding it into place. "Why do you care?"

She exhaled. "You may not believe this, but I loved you." She pursed her lips. "I still love you. I've never been in love before."

"I can't."

She looked down. "I know. I've been a complete mess since that day. You're all I ever think about. I just need closure."

Carter slid another twenty-five-pound plate onto the opposite side of the bar. "I don't know what you want from me."

"Can we just go somewhere and talk?"

"Isn't that what we're doing?"

She moved closer to Carter, whispering, her perfume flooding his nostrils. "Your dad's out there on the computer. He can probably hear everything we say. I don't feel comfortable talking here."

Carter stepped away from her, his eyes narrowed.

"Please, it won't be long. I promise."

"I'm grounded, except for work."

"Tell him you're goin' to work."

He exhaled. "Let me get my jacket."

Carter returned to the garage wearing his old army jacket over his black sweats. They exited under the garage door. Carter climbed into the passenger seat of Amber's Chevy Suburban.

She cranked the ignition and flashed a sideways grin toward Carter. "This truck bring back any memories?"

His face was expressionless. "Where are we going?"

"The park at South Run."

They drove into the gravel parking area. It was dark except for a single lamppost near the entrance and another near the portable toilets. The lot was empty. South Run Park consisted of acres of grass soccer fields, three baseball diamonds, and a large playground.

Amber cut the engine and killed the headlights. "Why don't we go sit on the swings?"

"Let's talk here."

"What's the point of coming to the park then? The stars are out. It's not even that cold. Come on."

Amber stepped from the SUV. Carter followed. The gravel crunched under their feet as they walked along the pathway toward the playground. To their right was the row of portable toilets, dim light reflecting off the blue plastic. The hair stood up on the back of his neck when he heard muffled voices from the toilets. In the distance, beyond the playground, he caught a glimpse of something large, something shiny, something metal. *Shit.* It was Zach's jeep, the chrome accents betraying the black exterior. Carter turned and sprinted back to the parking area, but three guys ran behind him, emerging from the far end of the portable toilets. Three more guys ran in front of him from the opposite end.

Carter stopped and shook his head. "You fucking bitch."

Amber laughed. "You got that right."

She strutted toward the parking lot. The six guys closed in, tightening the metaphorical noose. Everyone was dressed in black. Justin and Zach looked like enormous grim reapers. Luke and Noah stepped toward Carter with less confidence, the parking lot visible behind them. The other two guys, Mike and James, were reserve receivers that Carter had abused all season in practice.

"You ready for payback, bitch?" Justin said, his lips curled into a snarl.

Carter sprinted for the parking lot, his legs rubbery from the squats. Luke, Noah, and James blocked his path. Carter blasted into James, his forearm shivering off the kid's nose. James fell to the ground. Luke grabbed him from behind, and Carter slammed his head back into Luke's face. Stunned by the reverse head butt, Luke let go. Carter restarted toward the parking lot. Noah made a perfect angle tackle, his head in front as he drilled Carter into the grass. Carter struggled, but Justin and Zach piled on, pinning his arms behind his back. They yanked him to his feet, his arms secured. Noah took the first shots, one to the face and one to the stomach. They all took their shots, except for Luke. Carter was in a daze, blood dripping from his lip. His head hung, his body held up by Zach.

"That's enough," Luke said. "Let him go."

Justin shook his head. "Nah, fuck that. This motherfucker cheap shot me. Let's take him to the porta-john."

Zach and Justin hoisted Carter under the arms and carried him to the portable toilets, his feet dragging on the ground.

"The third one," Justin said. "That one's got the floater."

"Open the door," Zach said.

Noah opened the door and Zach and Justin threw Carter onto the floor of the plastic enclosure. It smelled like chemicals mixed with shit and piss. A few errant sheets of toilet paper were on the floor. Justin flipped the lid up and tried to force Carter's head inside the hole, but Carter didn't budge. His arms were rigid as he stared at a large brown turd floating in a sea of bright blue. Zach tried to help, but was unable to squeeze around Carter inside the plastic toilet. The flimsy structure rocked with his weight.

"You're too fucking fat," Justin said. Zach stepped out of the structure. Justin looked back at Noah. "Get your ass in here."

Carter grabbed some toilet paper from the ground. He reached down into the abyss and grasped the turd with the paper, his fingertips wet with piss and chemicals. Justin turned around, his mouth open, and Carter smashed the turd into his face. Justin staggered from the plastic structure, spitting and clawing at his face.

"I need water. I need water," Justin said. He turned and threw up, falling onto his knees.

Carter exited the structure, still holding the remnants of the shit encased in toilet paper.

"What the fuck?" Zach said, his jaw dropped, looking at the brown smeared on Justin's face.

Carter smashed the last bits of feces into Zach's mouth, helping to answer his question. Carter dropped the toilet paper to the ground and sprinted for the parking lot. Noah, Mike, and James gave chase, but they were left in the dust.

Carter ran from the park, occasionally glancing over his shoulder. He crossed the street into a middle-class neighborhood of seventies-style split levels. He knocked on three doors with cars in the driveways and lights on. The first two yielded no answer. An elderly man answered at the third house. There were thick square columns and a long open porch in front.

"Can I help you?" he said, eyeing Carter's battered face and dirty army jacket.

"Could I please use your phone?"

He narrowed his eyes. "You'll have to stay out here. I'll bring you the cordless."

"Would it be okay if I washed my hands?"

The old man frowned.

"My hands are dirty. I don't wanna touch your phone."

"I'll bring you some soap, and you can wash them in the hose."

"Thank you."

The old man nodded and shut the door behind him, the deadbolt latching. After a few minutes, the man returned with a bottle of dish soap and a cordless phone. The man told Carter to hold out his hands, and he sprayed some dish soap on them. Carter turned on the spigot, trying to hold the soap in his palm. He held his hands under the hose and washed the filth as best he could. He wiped his hands on his sweatpants and took the phone from the man. Sarah answered on the fourth ring.

"Hello."

"Sarah, it's Carter. Is your mom home?"

"She's not your type."

"I need a ride. It's kind of an emergency."

"Are you okay?" she asked.

"I'm fine. I'll tell you when you get here."

– 16 –

Blue Bunny Jammies

The Jeep spit gravel from the knobby tires as Zach and his crew exited the park across the street. Carter sat on the old man's front stoop, shielded by a holly hedge. He shivered as the sweat dried on his body. Julie's Honda crept past the house. Sarah peered through the driver's window. Carter ran out into the street, waving his arms. The red car stopped and reversed. He jogged around the Coupe, opened the passenger door and slid inside.

"Thank you," Carter said. "Where's your mom?"

Sarah gazed at Carter's face, her mouth open. "What happened? Are you okay?"

"I'm fine."

She clenched her fists. "It was Zach and Justin, wasn't it?" She reached out and squeezed his hand. A tear slid down her face. "Your eyes are already swollen."

Carter looked down. "I'm fine, really. I've had much worse. They hit like girls ... sorry, you know what I mean."

Sarah shook her head, her red hair moving against her cheeks. "I don't like that you've had worse." She reached over the center console and hugged him. "No more." She let go and sat up, her eyes puffy.

"I'm sorry," he said. "I should've prepared you on the phone. I didn't think you'd be so ..."

She sniffed. "Upset?"

"Yeah."

She frowned. "Of course I'm going to be upset. I really like you, Carter Lynch."

Carter smiled. "So do I—I mean I don't like myself—I mean I do like myself—I mean I really like you too."

Sarah giggled. "Let's go."

"Maybe I should drive," Carter said.

"I'm a good driver," she replied.

"Without a license."

"I have my learners."

Carter drove the Honda, telling Sarah the story of how he was lured to the park by Amber.

"I'm going to kill her," she said.

Carter continued, telling her how Zach and Justin and the other guys jumped him, holding his arms back as they took their swings. Her blue eyes were wide as he described how he was dragged into the portable toilet. She put her hand over her mouth as he described reaching into the hole to grab the fresh turd. She had a laughing fit when he described shoving the brown mushiness into Justin and Zach's faces.

"You didn't!" she said, still giggling.

He nodded.

"That is *so* gross."

"Don't worry, I washed my hands."

Carter pulled the Honda into their neighborhood of vinyl-sided townhouses.

"Do you wanna drop off the car at your house?" Carter asked. "Your mom might need it."

"Not likely," Sarah said. "She doesn't even know it's gone. She'll be in bed wallowing in her own misery at least through the weekend. Lincoln broke up with her."

"That's too bad," Carter said as he pulled into the visitor space across from his parents' house.

Sarah shrugged. "It was bound to happen."

Carter took a deep breath and glanced at Sarah. She was bundled in her red pea coat and gray scarf. His eyes panned down below her long coat. She wore white thermal pajama pants with blue bunnies. He looked up at her.

"Nice pajamas," he said.

She smirked. "You said it was an emergency."

He smiled. "I really like you, Sarah Cunningham."

She bit the corner of her lower lip. "Do you want to go in?"

He nodded. "We just have to be quiet. I'm still grounded."

Carter and Sarah strolled arm in arm toward the dark house. They slipped under the garage door and tiptoed into the basement. Carter glanced toward the computer, half-expecting his dad to be sitting there in the dark. Thankfully, he wasn't.

He motioned toward the open bathroom door. He pressed his lips to her ear and said, "I'm gonna clean up."

"Can I come in?" she whispered.

They entered the bathroom. He flipped on the light and shut the door, pressing the lock button on the handle. He peered into the mirror. His eyes were swelling. *I'll have two black eyes, but nothing major.* He touched his nose. One side of his long thin nose was sore. *Maybe a glancing blow.* He sucked in his lower lip, tasted blood, and pressed it back out.

He turned to Sarah. "Does my lip look fat?"

She pouted. "Yeah … it does."

She kissed him softly on his lower lip, then on each eyelid.

Carter opened his eyes with a grin. "All better now." He winced as he removed his army jacket and dropped it on the floor.

"Let me help," she said. "Raise your arms."

Carter held his arms up. She pulled his sweatshirt and T-shirt over his head and piled them in a heap next to his jacket. She ran her fingertips across his defined chest and stomach. She pressed against his stomach muscles and he lurched backwards.

She put her hand over her mouth. "I'm so sorry."

"It's okay. I'm just sore."

He slipped off his running shoes and stepped on the ends of his feet, pulling his socks off without bending over. Sarah removed her scarf and her jacket, hanging them on the door handle. Her breasts moved, braless beneath her thermal pajama top. Her nipples pressed against the fabric, a hint of pink visible between the blue bunnies. He put his hands inside the waistband of his sweatpants.

"Do you wanna turn around or something?" he asked.

She shook her head, her eyes locked on his. "Not unless you want me to."

He slid his sweatpants down his legs and stepped out. He stood in boxer briefs. She stared at the outline of his semi-erect penis. He turned on the shower and faced her again.

"It takes a minute to warm up," he said.

She nodded, pursing her lips.

Carter looked at her. "I think you're really… umm … beautiful." His face was hot. He looked down. "That was stupid, wasn't it?"

She put her hand under his chin, raising his gaze. "No, it wasn't."

He reached into the shower, warm drops pelting the back of his hand. "I'm gonna take these off and get in now."

She turned her back to him. He slid his boxer briefs down his legs. He glanced in the mirror, catching her eye watching him. In the shower, the hot water massaged his chest down to his groin. He thought about her body, soft and feminine, wrapped in pajamas. He glanced down at his penis pointing skyward. *Relax. This is Sarah. Do not blow this. Think about something else—anything else. How about the fact that you almost had your head shoved in a porta-john. Yeah, that would've sucked.* She sat on the toilet cover, watching the outline of his body through the rain glass.

After washing himself, he turned off the shower and grabbed the towel that was draped over the door. He dried himself and stepped out with the towel wrapped around his waist.

She smiled. "All clean?"

They carried their clothes into Carter's room. He turned on the overhead light and shut the door. He dumped his clothes into the hamper. She set her pea coat and scarf on his futon couch.

"You wanna watch a movie?" Carter asked, fumbling with his dresser drawer, one hand on the towel around his waist.

"Not really," she said.

"We could talk if you want."

"I don't want to talk."

"Are you hungry or thirsty? I could go upstairs and—"

She flipped off the overhead light and pressed the lock on the door handle. Dim light from the street lamp cut through the blinds in tiny slivers. She moved toward him like an apparition, her white pajamas glowing in the darkness. She placed her glasses on his dresser. Sarah stood, looking up at him with doe eyes, nibbling on her lower lip. She stepped closer, running her hands along his cheeks and down his upper body, as if she were trying to visualize him with her touch. She stopped at the towel, her hands resting on his obliques. Her breathing was shallow, her chest heaving. He pressed his lips to hers. Her mouth parted and their tongues touched. He pulled her closer with one arm, the other still holding his towel at his waist. She moved her arms up his back, her fingertips exploring. He let go of his towel; it stayed in place.

Carter tugged on her pajama top. Sarah raised her arms. He slipped it over her head and dropped it on the floor. Her breasts were full and teardrop shaped, her pink nipples erect. He pulled her close, her chest pressing against his. She toyed with his towel, the fold loosening until his makeshift skirt fell to the ground. She exhaled and ran her soft hands over his skyward erection. His hands ventured under the waistband of her pajama pants. She slid her pants and underwear past her thighs, letting them fall around her feet. Her legs were pale and toned—flawless. She had a small patch of red pubic hair. Sarah stepped out of her clothes and pressed her naked body against him. She smelled clean, like lavender and soap.

"Do you wanna move to the bed?" he asked.

She nodded, her lips swollen.

He grabbed a condom from his dresser and set it on the floor next to his mattress. Sarah slid under his covers and lay on her back. Carter slipped under the covers next to her on his side. They kissed. He moved his hand between her legs. She moaned and lifted her hips as he moved his middle finger against her clitoris.

"Have you ever …"

She shook her head.

"We don't have to."

She searched his face, her mouth open, her breath elevated, "I want to."

He reached over, grabbed the condom from the floor, and kneeled between her legs. She spread her legs wider to accommodate. She reached for his penis, her soft hands making him harder. He rolled the condom down his erection and lowered himself onto her, pushing the head of his penis inside of her. She gasped, her fingers gripping his upper back. He moved slowly, gradually increasing the depth. She directed him by alternately moaning when he was on the right track, and wincing when he went too far. Her wetness had created a round spot on his sheets the size of a softball.

Sarah moved her hips in rhythm with his, rubbing her clitoris against his pubic bone. His lips were locked on hers, their tongues weaved together. She moved in stronger motions, her hands on his hips, regulating his advances. He moved his lips to her neck. She moaned and exhaled, her eyes shut tight, her mouth open, her vagina convulsing. The moisture increased, allowing Carter deeper inside. He groaned as his penis spasmed. He pulled out and lay on his back, his ribcage moving up and down with each breath. She rolled onto him, her chin on his chest. She had a thin veneer of sweat between her breasts. He turned his head toward her with a brief smile.

"I'll be right back," he said as he squeezed out from under her.

"No," she said, pouting.

He wrapped up and disposed of the condom in the bathroom trash can and returned to Sarah's side. He lay on his back. She pecked him on his mouth, his cheek, and his neck, before settling her head on his shoulder, her leg and arm draped over him.

Carter's eyes were shut but he was wide awake. The warmth of her body radiated through him. He listened to the slow rhythm of her breaths, felt her warm exhalations breeze against his neck. He felt the softness of her thighs across his legs and the warmth of her vagina against him. Sarah's breast spilled onto his chest, forgiving and comforting. They stayed like that, Sarah sleeping, Carter trying to, until the low morning sun cut through the shades.

He blinked, drowsy, semi-conscious. *Douchebag is gonna be on the computer soon. I gotta get her out of here.* He started to pull the covers off, the cold air nipping that idea in the bud. *Just a few more minutes.* He replaced the cover and slipped back into the warm comfort of her embrace.

Loud knocking jerked Sarah's head from his shoulder. Carter rubbed the sleep from his eyes. There was knocking again, this time louder.

"Open this goddamn door," Jim said.

Carter's eyes opened wide. *Shit.* He put his finger to his lips. Sarah covered her mouth. Carter sprang to his feet and grabbed the towel from the floor, wrapping it around him. Sarah moved to the corner of the bed, behind the futon couch, throwing the covers over her head. Jim banged on the door again, almost breaking the hinges.

"I'm coming," Carter said before opening the door, holding his towel around him.

Jim stood, his bald head shiny, his arms crossed. "Why is your door locked?"

Carter's hair was disheveled, his eyes black. "For privacy. Unless you wanna watch me change."

"Watch it, smart ass." Jim narrowed his eyes at Carter's face. "What the hell happened to you?"

Carter's mouth was a straight line. "I fell."

Jim chuckled. "Yeah, fell into someone's fists. Serves you right. Maybe you ought a rethink that smart mouth of yours."

"I'm working on it."

"Are you workin' today?"

"From two to ten."

"You need to wash the car before you leave. Inside and out."

"The hose might be frozen."

His wide nostrils flared. "Then you better figure out a way to unfreeze it."

"Can I get dressed now?"

Jim glanced at the heap of clothes on the floor by Carter's dresser. He smirked. "Nice bunny pajamas. First you quit football, then you get your ass kicked, now you're wearin' wittle bunny PJ's." He laughed at his own joke, repeating "wittle bunny PJ's," in a high and mocking voice. "Alyssa's got some old Barbies in the garage if you want 'em."

Jim chuckled and stomped to his seat at the computer. Carter shut the door, locking it at the same time, so Jim couldn't hear the click. Sarah popped her head up above the futon couch. *What an asshole*, she mouthed. He put his knees on the couch and leaned over, kissing her on the mouth. She smiled through the kiss.

They dressed and exited through the bedroom window. Carter drove the red Honda two blocks down to Sarah's townhouse. He parked in front. Carter handed her the keys across the center console.

"I should go," he said, pecking her on the mouth.

She brushed her red hair back with her hand. "Do you want to do something later?"

He frowned. "I'm grounded and my dad knows what my hours are."

"I could sneak over to your house … late."

He smiled. "I'll call you as soon as everyone's asleep."

"Hang up after one ring," she said. "My mother keeps the phone right next to her in case Lincoln calls."

"I'll see you tonight then?"

"There's something I need to talk to you about," Sarah said. "It's really important."

He raised his eyebrows. "Are you okay?"

"This feud you have going on with Zach and Justin and the rest of the football team—it has to stop."

His mouth turned down. "It's not me. I'm just defending myself."

She put her hand on top of his. "You're misunderstanding me. I know it's not your fault, but it keeps escalating. They jumped you with six guys and tried to shove your head in a portable toilet. Setting aside the feces, those chemicals could really damage your eyes, and who knows what would happen to your insides if you swallowed any of it. And now that you smashed shit in their faces, I can't imagine they're going to let it go."

"It's fine, Sarah. I can handle it."

She squeezed his hand. "No, you can't. Not by yourself."

He rubbed the back of his neck, looking out the window.

"Look at me," she said.

He turned his head.

Her blue eyes searched his face, unblinking. "I'm going to talk to Mrs. Wheeler."

He scowled. "Sarah, don't. It'll just make it worse."

She yanked her hand away, her face red. "Worse than getting beat up and having your head shoved in chemical-laden sewage?"

He pursed his lips.

She crossed her arms over her chest. "You can be mad, but I'm telling her whether you like it or not."

He exhaled. "I'm not mad. I just don't want my girlfriend handling my problems for me."

She smiled and dropped her arms. "You think I'm your girlfriend, huh?"

His face was hot. "I hope so."

"Me too." She leaned over and kissed him on the cheek, her lips lingering. "Just let me help you, okay?"

"Okay."

– 17 –

Power Corrupts

Sarah jingled her keys with a wide smile as she approached Carter. He grinned. "I guess you passed."

"I'm legal now," she said, opening her pink satchel and dropping the keys inside. She fished out her wallet, opened it, and showed Carter her driver's license.

"You look pretty," Carter said, hoisting a Virginia pine onto his shoulder.

She frowned. "I wasn't ready. I have such a dumb look on my face."

Sarah shadowed Carter as he moved trees from the back of the lot to the front in an effort to consolidate the dwindling inventory of Douglas firs and Virginia pines. Wooden posts were set up along each row, connected by two-by-fours. The trees stood upright, resting against them. White lights were strung from the top of each post, illuminating the gravel lot.

He wore a knit cap and leather gloves. Sarah was bundled in her pea coat, scarf, and wool hat.

"You don't have to work tomorrow do you?" Sarah asked.

"Just a half-day," Carter replied, "then I'm off Christmas Day. Don't worry, I'll be off in time for dinner."

"I got the turkey today," she said. "I was thinking of making stuffing and getting some real cranberries and butternut squash and salad.

Do you think it's too much like Thanksgiving?"

"It sounds really good."

She stood shivering as Carter spaced the trees evenly. "I don't know how you can stand it out here. I'm freezing."

"I just keep moving. There's warm cider at the register. It's free."

Sarah's eyes widened at the mention and she bolted toward the one-story structure. She returned with her hands wrapped around a steaming paper cup. She took a sip.

"How is it?"

She smiled. "It's good. It's nice that they have warm cider for everyone."

"It's only for the customers."

She sauntered over, handing him the cup. "Here, try some. Nobody's here anyway."

"I don't think too many people wait until the twenty-third to buy a Christmas tree." He sipped the cider. "That *is* good." He handed it back.

"What happens after Christmas? Do you still have a job?"

"Sort of. The nursery's closed until March, but when it snows I'll be working on a sidewalk-shoveling crew. They pay double-time for snow. When they open back up in March, I can spread mulch and work here at the nursery. The owner said I can have as many weekend and after-school hours as I want."

"That's good."

"Yeah, at five-fifty an hour, I need a lot of hours." Carter set up a Douglas fir. "I did do pretty well with tips from people during the rush. Today's a bust, but last week I was making over a hundred dollars a day."

A Mercedes SUV rumbled into the lot, gravel crunching under the tires. A massive man with a blockhead and a dark suit stepped from the driver's side. The passenger door opened and Zach exited. His fresh crew cut was tilted toward the gravel, his wide shoulders slumped. Sarah and Carter gaped.

"This is the last thing I need," Carter said.

"He had to get that suit at Big and Tall," Sarah said.

The humongous man made a beeline for Carter and Sarah, with Zach loping behind like a tired dog on a leash.

"Carter Lynch," the man said with certainty.

"Yes," Carter said.

"I'm Mr. Goodman. My son has something to say to you."

Zach shuffled forward his head down. If he weren't six-foot-five, it would be hard to be intimidated by his chubby cheeks.

Zach stared at the dirt. "I'm sorry about what I did—"

"Look at him," his dad said.

Zach raised his head. "I'm sorry about what I did to you. It'll never happen again." Zach extended his massive meat hook.

Carter shook his hand. Zach's grip was light.

"Carter's jacket was ripped," Sarah said.

The three men looked at Sarah.

"Excuse me?" Mr. Goodman said.

"When Carter was attacked by your son and his *many* friends, his jacket was ripped. Now the only jacket he has is this old army jacket. Not very warm for someone who has to work outside in the cold."

"Sarah," Carter said.

"He was wearing that old jacket," Zach said. "We didn't rip—"

"Shut up," his dad said, pulling out his wallet. He opened the bill-fold and pulled out a hundred-dollar bill. "Will this cover your jacket?"

"It was six on one," Sarah added. "You're lucky there's not a civil suit … yet."

Mr. Goodman's face was red, the large vein in his neck throbbing. He flipped out a few more hundred dollar bills and handed the cash to Carter.

Carter stifled a grin and shoved the bills into the front pocket of his jeans. The hefty men turned and marched back to the Mercedes. Sarah giggled.

Carter shook his head. "You're unbelievable."

She smiled, purposely showing all her white teeth. "I told you Mrs. Wheeler would set them straight."

"But they get scholarships. They'll move on as if nothing happened."

"Zach got a scholarship?"

"He committed yesterday. I saw it in the gazette. Justin too. They're going to Virginia Tech."

"I'm sorry," Sarah said.

He straightened a Douglas fir. "It doesn't matter." He hiked to the back of the lot, Sarah following close behind, her cup in hand.

"Maybe after Christmas we can go get you a good work jacket. We could probably find a good after-Christmas sale. I doubt you want to shovel snow in that old thing."

"Okay," he said, hoisting a tree onto his shoulder.

He lumbered to the front, setting the tree in an open spot.

"I'm working on an article," she said after a moment. "I'm going to try to get it published."

"Oh yeah?" he said, adjusting the tree. "What's it about?"

"The North Potomac football team, the hazing, Ben ... you."

He turned to Sarah, looking her in the eyes. "Well if anyone could write it, you'd be the one."

"Could I interview you and use your name?"

"Sure, it's not like they can throw me off the football team."

She reached into her pink satchel, pulled out two folded pieces of paper and unfolded them. "Could you sign this release form?"

He laughed. "Seriously?"

"If I submit the article to *The Post* without release forms, they'll never run it." She handed him the papers with a pen.

"The Washington Post?"

"I know it's crazy. But even if they don't run it, I want to do the story, just so there's a record of what happened.

He nodded and signed the release, using his palm as a makeshift table.

"The other one is for your mom. Can you get her to sign that one?"

* * *

Carter pulled his cap over his head and buttoned his wool coat. He opened the front door of the townhouse, his duffel bag slung over his shoulder. The early morning sun and a blast of cold air invigorated him. He stepped out onto the stoop and descended the stairs. A handsome man in a suit and an overcoat hurried toward him. He had a newspaper wedged in the crook of his arm.

"Carter Lynch," he said.

Carter stopped. "Yeah?"

The man held out a white business card. "I'm Scott Gilbert from ESPN."

He took the card, scanning the information.

"I was hoping I could interview you about the article in *The Washington Post*."

Carter raised his eyebrows, his eyes wide. "They ran it?"

"You haven't seen it?"

Carter shook his head.

"Have mine," Scott said, handing him the newspaper.

"Thanks," Carter replied, taking it.

"I was hoping to get an interview with you. At ESPN, we're really fair. We don't do hit pieces."

"Sorry, I'm not doing any interviews. I just did the one for a friend."

Scott rubbed his freshly shaved chin. "If you change your mind, you have my card. For the record, I think that what you did took a lot of guts."

"Thanks."

Carter sat on his front step and opened *The Washington Post*.

SUICIDE, LIES, AND STATE CHAMPIONS
By Sarah Cunningham – Tuesday, January 21, 1992

On Friday, November 1st, 1991, the North Potomac High School football team won the Gunston District

Championship. On that same night, former reserve cornerback, Ben Wheeler, 16, committed suicide by carbon monoxide poisoning. The North Potomac Marauders of Alexandria, Virginia went on to win the state championship, and Head Coach Randy Cowan is riding the longest winning streak in high school football history.

Meanwhile allegations were made by Ben's parents, Jill and David Wheeler, that a humiliating initiation is forced on newly minted varsity football players. They believe their son Ben endured this initiation, nine weeks before his death.

On December seventeenth, 1991, a school board meeting took place to address the allegations. The North Potomac School District Superintendent, Dr. Richard Perry said, "Here at North Potomac High School we have a no-tolerance policy for bullying."

Dr. Perry conducted an investigation that involved one-on-one interviews between Coach Cowan and the football players. They did not find any evidence of bullying. Cowan said, "The kids told some funny stories, but nothing that was bullying or hazing."

Members of the public were allowed to comment at the meeting. Current football players spoke of the family-like bond between teammates. Several former football players remarked how playing football for the Marauders helped them to be better leaders and fathers.

Ben's father, David Wheeler, also spoke. He stood at the podium with a typewritten plea in hand. He never did finish reading the words on that piece of paper. Mr. Wheeler was interrupted twice by Dr. Perry. At the third interruption, Mr. Wheeler told Dr. Perry to shut up and to let him speak. He was promptly escorted from the auditorium by police officers. Mr. Wheeler gave me that piece of paper. Since he was not allowed to speak that day, I have sought to provide him with a new platform. Here are his words in their entirety.

> My son was Ben Wheeler. Six weeks ago, he killed himself in our home. Fifteen weeks ago, he was humiliated at a team initiation. He was so ashamed that he refused to go to school or practice. He was promptly thrown off the team. In a matter of days, my son lost the majority of his friends, the sport he loved, and his dignity. My wife and I are not looking for revenge. We're not looking to place blame. We're not planning a lawsuit. We simply want the hazing to stop. We do not want another child to suffer the way Ben did and so many others before him. I hope this issue isn't swept under the rug like it has been in the past. Thank you.

After the school board meeting, I interviewed dozens of current and former football players that corroborated initiations, spanning decades.

Sean Nicholson, class of 1974, had to sing in the school lunch room. He said, "Everyone laughed at me, but it was all in good fun. I think it brought us closer together as a team."

Dalton Barrett, class of 1983 was forced to run the length of the football field naked, with a cookie between his butt cheeks. "I didn't have to eat it—thank God. If we dropped it or if we finished last, we had to eat the cookie."

Stacy Jefferson, class of 1991 detailed a drinking game that continued until each and every player vomited. "We had one guy—he was only a sophomore—that wouldn't puke. He was so messed up that they had to take him to the hospital. I heard they just dropped him on the concrete in front of the emergency room and left. It's not like he died, but it was messed up how they left him."

Carter Lynch, class of 1993, and Ben Wheeler, along with a dozen teammates, were forced into the basement of a farmhouse. "The seniors gave us three choices for our initiation," Lynch said. "We couldn't leave the basement without completing one."

Lynch and his fellow recruits were forced to choose between allowing a senior to slap them in the face with his penis, inserting a cucumber in their rectum, and returning to the upstairs party naked, where nearly two hundred girls waited. "The catch was that if we wanted to get our clothes and our keys back, we had to sleep with a girl there," Lynch said.

The seniors expected all of the recruits to return to the party, where it was arranged for a female classmate to wrap them up in a jacket. "It was like some sort of stupid rigged test to get someone to come forward who they could then condemn for being gay," Lynch said.

Ben Wheeler chose first, choosing to let a senior slap him in the face with his penis. Everyone else chose to be let out into the party naked to have sex with a girl. Ben tried to change his choice, but he was not allowed. He was on his knees with his eyes closed as they mimed the sex act with a cucumber. He was sent back to the party fully clothed and alone.

"Everyone looked at him like he was nothing," Lynch said. "He was humiliated. He was never the same after that."

Carter Lynch is correct. Ben was never the same after that. He missed the first three days of school after the incident as well as football practice. Head Coach Randy Cowan requires each player to sign a behavior contract at the start of football camp. One of the rules states that if you miss three practices without an excuse, you will be kicked off the team. Ben lost his dignity at that party and then lost the sport he loved. Two months after the hazing incident, he took his own life.

These initiations have escalated over the years. What started as harmless fun meant to bring a team closer together, has become a dangerous ritual meant to humiliate.

As students, we are punished if we cheat or lie. We are expected to tell the truth to our teachers and coaches and principals. In return our leaders are supposed to lead. They are supposed to show us the right way to behave in a fair and just society. In this case, I think the adults in power failed Ben Wheeler and thousands of other children like him. The leaders of our young people should be held to the highest standards.

Because power corrupts, society's demands for moral authority and character increase as the importance of the position increases. – John Adams

– 18 –

School's Out for Summer

The halls were raucous. Kids ran around as if they were pardoned criminals. Some girls wore short shorts bordering on the obscene, while boys in baggy Bermudas provided contrast. Carter rummaged through his locker, separating the trash into a pile and the non-trash into his duffel bag. His jeans were starting to fray at the bottom. A soft finger traced the vein in his bicep.

"You ready to blow this joint?" Sarah asked.

She wore a cotton dress to her knees with a red belt.

He shrugged. "Yeah, I guess."

She frowned at him. "What's wrong? I thought you'd be ecstatic for the last day of school."

"It's not like I'm gonna be off on vacation. I'm already on the schedule for fifty hours." He tossed a paperback into his duffel bag. "The nursery's always shorthanded."

She grabbed his hand. "You could take some time off. We could go to the Shenandoah's and do those waterfall hikes."

"Sorry, I guess I'm just feeling burnt out." He took a deep breath. "It's like I just limped through the finish line, only to realize I have to run another race."

Devin sauntered toward Carter, his baggy jean shorts hanging to mid-calf, his flat-top three inches above his head. "What's up you two?"

"Hey, Devin," Sarah said.

"Congratulations," Carter said. "All state in the 200 is pretty crazy."

Devin shrugged. "I was actually second, but thanks. You should've run. We could've used another sprinter for the four by one."

"With work and everything ..."

"You got the rest of your life to work, only one more year to play sports."

Carter looked away.

Devin shook his head. "Come on, man, I know you wanna play. I heard you've been running up at the track at night. And I know you got those weights in your garage. You look like you've been using 'em."

"I said the same thing," Sarah said. "He does all these insane workouts. I don't see the point if he's not going to play a sport."

"I have to look good for you," Carter said to Sarah with a wink.

She rolled her eyes.

"You know, Coach Goodman's not that bad," Devin said. "I bet he'd let you back on the team. We have nobody at safety right now."

"I still can't believe they fired Cowan," Sarah said.

"Someone wrote a really good article," Carter said, flashing Sarah a grin.

Devin didn't let up. "Coach Goodman's been on our asses about the hazing too. He said if anyone's caught hazing they'd be thrown off the team."

Carter nodded.

"He's here today."

Carter nodded again.

"You should go talk to him," Devin said.

Carter looked at Sarah.

She held her hands up. "Don't look at me. It's your decision. I just want you to do what makes you happy."

* * *

Carter stared at the placard on the wooden door. *Head Football Coach Lyle Goodman.* He took a deep breath and tapped on the door. The massive man answered. Coach Goodman had a barrel chest, a block-head, and salt and pepper stubble. He narrowed his eyes.

"Carter Lynch," he said. "What can I do for you?"

"Can I talk to you?" Carter asked.

He frowned. "I can give you a couple minutes. I have a coaches' meeting at three." Coach Goodman lumbered behind the dark oak desk and eased into the leather chair with a groan. "Old knees," he said, placing his meaty forearms on the desk. "Have a seat."

Carter sat opposite.

Behind the coach were shelves loaded with pictures and memorabilia from his playing days at Virginia Tech and the Kansas City Chiefs.

Carter bit the inside of his cheek. "I'd like to get back on the football team."

Coach Goodman winced and sat back in his chair. "That won't be possible."

Carter's mouth was a flat line. "Why not?"

"Well for one, you admitted to being a part of that hazing mess. This program needs to heal. We need to distance ourselves from that nonsense."

Carter stood up. "I was forced to!"

Coach Goodman was expressionless. "For two, you and your little girlfriend extorted four hundred dollars from me. You're lucky I never called the cops."

"This is bullshit and you know it."

"You're not cut out to be part of a team. You're a cancer, pure and simple."

Carter marched to the office door and opened it.

Coach Goodman said, "Leave it open."

Carter slammed the door as he left.

* * *

The hamburgers sizzled as Sarah pressed down on the metal spatula. Carter sat at the kitchen table, staring out the bay window. She opened the oven door.

"I think the fries are ready," she said.

Carter stood and trudged to the stove, grabbing an oven mitt from the counter. Sarah moved aside as Carter pulled a metal tray filled with golden brown crinkle-cut fries. He shut the oven and Sarah moved back over the stove top. She placed squares of cheese on the burgers. Carter grabbed two plates and two glasses from the cupboard. Buns popped from the toaster. Sarah readied the burgers while Carter shoveled fries onto their plates. They sat down at the kitchen table.

Carter's eyes were glazed. He stared out the window, chewing slowly, as if eating were another burden to bear.

"I'm sorry," Sarah said. "I'm sorry for being such an idiot."

Carter looked at Sarah. "No, it's not your fault. The four hundred dollars was just an excuse. It wouldn't have mattered either way."

"Well it's not fair. We can appeal to the school board. I could write a follow-up article."

"Sarah, no." Carter shook his head. "I don't wanna play anymore. It was a stupid idea."

"I just—"

The phone rang. Sarah walked over to the phone and picked it up.

"Hello?" There was a pause. "Oh hey, Devin, did you want to talk—. Okay, hold on."

Sarah stretched the long cord to Carter.

"It's Devin," she said, her brow furrowed. "He says it's important."

Carter used his napkin to wipe the salt from his fingertips before grabbing the phone. "Devin, what's up?"

Carter heard cars and trucks in the background.

"You gotta get down to Zach's farmhouse," Devin said.

"Why?"

"Your sister's there and shit is getting out of control."

"Where are you?"

"At a gas station pay phone in the middle of nowhere. I had to get out of there. Tasha was really upset. We should've never gone. She said Zach grabbed her. Made some joke about how he had jungle fever. I confronted him, but what was I gonna do. He's huge and he had his boys with him. He kicked us out. When we were leaving, I saw Justin coming in with Alyssa."

"Shit."

Carter scribbled the directions Devin gave him on a scrap of paper.

He drove Julie's Honda Coupe through the darkness. Sarah was in the passenger seat, gripping the armrest on the door. A horn honked and high beams flashed as they flew past a slow moving pickup.

"Turn right! That's Cavanaugh Road," Sarah said.

The tires chirped as he turned from the asphalt road. Gravel spewed from the wheels as they flew down the country lane. Carter pulled over in the field among the other cars.

"Stay here," he said to Sarah. "I'll be right back."

"No way," she said. "I'm coming with you."

They jogged up to the front door. Sarah struggled to keep up in her flip-flops. Her camera was strapped across her chest. The buzz of voices intermingled with rap music was audible through the door. They entered without knocking. The living room lights were low. Football players and girls made out on the couch and the floor. Most were clothed, but some far less so. Bodies were intertwined and groping. They searched the twisted pack for Alyssa or Justin. No sign of them. They entered the dining room to the left. The crowd around the table cheered as Noah sank a quarter into a shot glass.

"Holy shit," Noah said, recognizing Carter.

The crowd turned to Carter and Sarah. Amber stood in her short jean shorts and cowboy boots. She had her arm around Luke, her hand in his back pocket.

"Where's my sister?" Carter said to no one in particular. The crowd was silent.

Amber laughed, cutting through the quiet.

"She's thirteen," Carter said.

"Someone might want to tell Justin that's felony statutory rape," Sarah added.

"She's upstairs," Luke said.

Amber scowled at Luke. Carter and Sarah ran upstairs. They opened and shut doors, disturbing consenting couples. The last door at the end of the hall was to the master bedroom. It was locked. Carter banged on the door.

"Go away, motherfucker, I'm busy," Justin said.

Carter backed up. Sarah stepped aside. He sprinted toward the door, lowering his shoulder. He blasted through the door, the jamb splintering. Alyssa was on her knees, topless, her upper body waiflike. Mascara ran down her face. Justin stood in front of her, his pants down, his hand around his erection. Zach stood in the background, fully clothed. He yanked his hand from his pants as the door crashed open. Sarah took a picture of the scene, keeping Alyssa's chest out of the shot.

"What the fuck?" Justin said his hand still on his penis.

Alyssa scrambled for her tube top. She put it on, standing and staggering toward Carter and Sarah. Justin grabbed her arm.

"Let her go," Carter said.

Sarah snapped another photograph. "Unless you want to be in *The Washington Post* for felony statutory rape," Sarah said.

Justin let go. "I didn't touch her." He pulled his pants up.

Alyssa stumbled away.

"Are you all right?" Carter asked. "Did he touch you?"

She shook her head. "Wanna go home," she slurred.

Sarah and Carter escorted Alyssa from the farmhouse unmolested. They supported her weight as she was unable or unwilling to walk on her own. Carter reclined the front passenger seat, and they set her down. Her micro skirt rode up her legs exposing black lace under-wear. Sarah pulled her skirt down and squeezed into what was left of the miniature back seat. Carter drove with the flow of traffic.

"What the hell were you thinking?" Carter said.

"Gonna throw … up," Alyssa said, barely audible.

"Pull over," Sarah said.

Carter pulled over on the shoulder of the two-lane highway. Sarah helped Alyssa out of the car and into the grass. Carter stood, lean-ing against the Honda, his arms crossed. Sarah held back her hair as Alyssa puked. After, they put her back in the reclined seat and contin-ued on their way.

"How long have you been drinking like this?" Carter asked.

She was breathing heavily.

"I think she passed out," Sarah said.

* * *

The townhouse was dark as Carter pulled into the visitor's space. He exited the Coupe and pulled the seat forward. Sarah stepped out. They walked around the car and opened the passenger door. Alyssa was snoring.

"Thank you for helping," Carter said.

Sarah kissed him on the cheek. "You're welcome. You need help getting her inside?"

"No. She's gonna walk herself inside."

Carter reached into the car, unbuckled the seatbelt and shook Alyssa. She groaned, her eyes sealed shut. He shook harder.

"Wake up," he said. "I'm not carrying you. Wake up."

Alyssa curled up tighter in the fetal position.

Carter frowned at Sarah. He reached inside and hauled his sister from the car, one arm under her knees and one behind her back.

"Can you open the garage for me?" Carter asked.

She giggled. "I thought you were going to make her walk."

Sarah pulled the garage door up. Carter pecked her on the mouth and slipped inside with Alyssa in his arms. Sarah shut the door behind them. Carter stopped at the basement door, turning the knob with some difficulty. He pushed inside, his forearm still supporting his sister. The lamp at the computer table flicked on. Jim stood from the swivel chair, his face red, his jaw clenched. Carter stood, holding onto Alyssa, whose skirt was hiked up. Her tube top left her midriff and shoulders exposed. She smelled like alcohol, smoke, and vomit.

Jim stalked closer like a lion about to pounce. "Put her down."

Carter set her feet down, but her arms clung around his neck. He dipped his head under her arms and set her down. She assumed the fetal position on the floor. Jim bent down, his face inches from hers.

"Wake up!" Jim said.

Alyssa's eyes shot wide open. She pushed herself against the wall, away from Jim.

"Stand up," Jim said.

"I'm sorry, Daddy," Alyssa said, blubbering.

"I said, stand up. Don't make me ask again."

Carter helped Alyssa to her feet. She stood, holding Carter's arm for support. She looked at the floor, tears dripping on the carpet.

"Why does she smell like a fuckin' brewery?"

Carter was silent. Alyssa sniffled.

Jim stiffened his jaw and put his hand under his daughter's chin. He forced her eyes up to meet his. "Where did you get the alcohol?"

"I don't know," she said.

She glanced at Carter.

"Did Carter have something to do with this?" Jim asked.

"No."

"Why did you look at him?"

"No reason."

He narrowed his eyes at Carter then back to his daughter. "Where were you?"

She looked down, but Jim jerked her head back. "It was a party, okay."

Carter bit the inside of his cheek.

"A middle school party?" Jim asked. "A bunch of eighth graders gettin' wasted?"

Alyssa was silent. Her eyes flicked to Carter.

"Why do you keep lookin' at him?" Jim said.

"I don't know," she said.

"How *old* were the *fuckin'* kids at this party?"

Carter and Alyssa were silent.

"Answer me!" Jim said.

"High school," she said, new tears spilling down her face.

"Lemme guess, graduation party?" Jim shook his daughter.

She nodded, sobbing.

"Did anybody touch you?" Jim said.

She shook her head.

"If I find out some eighteen-year-old piece of shit touched you, he'll be goin' to jail if I don't fuckin' kill him first." He glared at Alyssa. "And look at this shit you're wearin'. You look like a fuckin' hooker. What the hell's wrong with you?"

She glanced at Carter again.

Jim glowered at Carter, then at Alyssa. "Did he have something to do with this?"

"No," she said.

Jim clenched his fists at his side, turning his attention to Carter. "If you didn't have anything to do with this, why are you sneaking her in at midnight?"

Carter was unresponsive.

"And how in the hell is a little girl gettin' into a high school party?"

Carter shrugged.

"You better come up with an answer before I bash your *fuckin'* head in."

"It doesn't matter what I say," Carter said in monotone.

"Alyssa, get your ass upstairs. Now," Jim said.

She staggered past Jim, her head down. He waited, silently stewing while Alyssa trudged up the steps. Jim stared at Carter, his eyes wide open like Mike Singletary on a blitz. He rolled his neck.

"I know you're involved somehow," Jim said, rocking from one foot to the other. "This shit stinks like you."

"Let's get on with it," Carter said his hands by his side. "Take your shots so I can go to bed. You and I both know what's—"

Jim punched Carter in the jaw with a right cross, knocking him off his feet. Carter made no attempt to rise. He tightened his abdominals as Jim kicked him in the stomach, the force knocking him against his bedroom door. Jim bent over and put his hands around Carter's throat, squeezing like a vice. Carter didn't struggle. He didn't show pain or fear.

"If you ever take my daughter to a party like that again, I will fuckin' kill you." Jim let go of Carter's throat. Carter gasped for air. "You got me?"

– 19 –

Good News

Carter brushed his damp fingers through his hair. He tucked his button-down shirt into his black pants. He stared into the bathroom mirror. His summer tan was long gone, replaced by the light olive underneath. He patted his back pocket, feeling the bulge of his wallet, and his front pocket—nothing. He marched into his bedroom, scanning his dresser top and the foot locker. His bed was stripped bare down to the mattress. He grabbed his wool coat from the futon couch. He exited his room and glanced at Jim, hunched over the computer screen. Carter bounded up the basement steps to the kitchen. *There they are.* He snatched his keys from the counter. As he did so, the front door opened and slammed shut. Grace dropped a cluster of shopping bags with a sigh of relief. He moved toward his mother. She unbuttoned her pea coat.

"It's freezing out there," she said to Carter. She hung her coat on the banister. Underneath she wore a pencil skirt and long leather boots. She smiled, her caked-on makeup holding firm. "Don't you look cute."

"Thanks, Mom," Carter replied.

"Are those the pants I bought you for Christmas?"

Carter nodded. "Yeah, they're comfortable."

"They look good on you."

Carter eyed the shopping bags. "What did you get?"

"Oh, just some stuff for work. So, you and Sarah have any big plans tonight?"

"We're going out for dinner."

"That sounds fun."

He said goodbye to his mother before he left. He half-jogged to his Ford F-150 pickup truck. It was white, with several what-looked-like bullet holes on the right-hand side. They were the result of the previous owner's dent repair job. A snow blower was bungeed to the bed liner of the four-by-four. He yanked the magnetic signs from the door that said *Lynch Lawn Mowing* and tossed them behind the seat. He pressed the clutch in and cranked the engine. Thirty seconds later, he parked in front of Sarah's house.

Carter pressed down on the parking brake with his foot and hopped out of the truck, leaving it running. He climbed the steps and rang the doorbell. Sarah appeared in perfect synchronicity with the chime. Her hair was curled at the ends, burned into place. She wore eyeliner and lip gloss, but her face was naked, perfect as usual. Her black dress flowed just beneath her knees.

"You look beautiful."

She frowned. "Really? My mom let me borrow it. It was one of her more tasteful ensembles." She eyed Carter. "You look handsome."

He smiled and held out his arm. She entwined her arm in his and they strolled to the truck. He opened her door and she hopped in. He walked around the truck and slid into the driver's seat.

Carter turned to Sarah and said, "I have some really big news."

"I saw it already," Sarah replied. "I feel really bad for the girls. I guess we shouldn't be surprised."

Carter gave her a quizzical look. "What are you talking about?"

"You didn't see it on the news? I tried calling, but I got a busy signal."

"Alyssa was probably on the phone." Carter frowned. "She never clicks over on call waiting."

"So, you didn't see it?"

"You know I don't watch that stuff."

"I'm glad you're sitting down for this. Zach and Justin were arrested in Blacksburg on charges of rape."

"Jesus."

She shook her head. "Messed up, huh?"

He sat silent.

"You okay?" she asked.

"Yeah, it's shocking, I guess."

"It is." She nodded. "I hope they're put away for a long time."

"Me too."

She forced a smile. "So, what was your big news? Is it a bigger bombshell than that?"

"Thankfully no, but it's really good news. I can't wait to tell you."

She grinned. "Spill it."

"I wanna wait until dinner, if that's okay. It's a surprise." He leaned over and kissed her on the cheek. "Happy Valentine's Day."

* * *

They were in a booth on the top floor of *Mike's American Grill*, a three-story restaurant in the north of town. They looked out the window at the traffic below. The voices of patrons and waiting staff mingled with the cacophony of background noise. Eventually, despite the noise, it seemed quiet, as if it were just the two of them.

"Madam, sir. Your steaks," the waiter said. He placed the steaming entrees in front of them. "The plates are hot, so be careful."

Sarah smiled.

"Thank you," Carter said.

They stared at the filet mignon, asparagus, and garlic mashed potatoes.

Carter picked up his fork and steak knife, cutting into the beef. He took a bite. "Wow," he said. "I've had steak before, but never like this."

Sarah tried her own and agreed.

Halfway through the meal Carter said, "Do you wanna hear my good news now?" Sarah's face was still. "Or we can wait until after we've finished eating?"

"No, go ahead."

"Okay. As you know, my eighteenth birthday was last week. And being eighteen affords me some power that I didn't have a few weeks ago."

She put her fork down, her full attention on him.

He continued. "I did a ton of work last summer."

She nodded. "I remember. You were working sunup until sundown."

"Plus, I did a lot during the school year on the weekends and after school. And then, with all the snow we've had so far ... I have enough." Carter smiled wide, showing his upper teeth.

"Enough what?"

"Enough money to move out of my parents' house and to pay for my first year of community college."

She smiled. "I'm happy for you."

"You should be happy for *us*, because that's not all."

She raised her eyebrows.

He pulled his keys from his pocket and held up a single silver key. "This is the key to my very own basement apartment. I rented it from this older couple that lives in Landsdowne. It has a kitchenette, a bathroom with a shower, a bedroom, and a living room. They're so nice too."

Her smile faded.

"They said I can use their washer and dryer on Sundays. And guess who can come over and stay whenever they want? We can actually sleep all night *together*." He studied her face. "You don't look too enthused."

She forced a smile. "No, it sounds great. I'm really happy for you."

"Us."

"Of course, ... us." She smiled, her eyes still.

"Do you wanna know how I found the place?" He feigned enthusiasm, trying to inflate the deflating balloon.

"Sure."

"The older couple, the Woodruffs, you know, I told you about them before, my favorite clients. I saw that they had a 'For Rent' sign on their—" Sarah stared at her food. "What's wrong?" he asked.

She shrugged.

"This is really good for us. I've been dying to tell you all week. I wanted it to be a surprise. I thought we could go there after dinner."

She took a deep breath. "I have some good news too."

"That's great," he said, his stomach churning.

"I got a full scholarship to Northwestern."

He nodded his head, biting the inside of his cheek. "Wow, that's great ... for you." His shoulders slumped. "That is really great. You deserve it. If anyone deserves it, you do."

She smiled briefly. "Thank you. I'm really happy about it. I found out a few weeks ago. I just didn't know how to tell you. They have one of the best journalism schools in the country. I mean, I thought I could get in, but I knew I couldn't afford it. I never thought I'd get a scholarship. I think the article ..."

Carter pushed the remnants of his food around his plate.

"I'm sorry," she said.

Carter looked up, forcing a smile that failed to blossom.

"I know I was planning on George Mason so I could be here with you."

He set his fork on his plate. "I don't know why I can't just accept reality."

"The reality of what?"

"That I'm destined for failure. That I'm gonna be someone's punching bag, or someone's lawn boy, or someone's fall guy."

"Carter, stop. That's not true."

"It's like the moment I feel good about something, like really feel good, it blows up in my face."

"You're not making any sense." She reached across the table. He snatched his hand back.

"I'm not? I think I'm making perfect sense."

"Carter, stop. It's going to be fine. I'll come home in the summer and at Christmas. You work all the time anyway."

"And how long before you stop coming home, or you come home with a Northwestern boyfriend?"

"That's not gonna happen."

He crossed his arms. "How do you know?"

"Well, I don't *know*, but that's what I think." She shook her head. "Why can't you just be happy for me and see what happens?"

"So I'm supposed to just pretend like everything's fine until you decide to get rid of me."

She scowled. "If you want to keep me so bad, this isn't a good way to go about it."

He shook his head. "This is so fucked up. You kept this from me because you knew our relationship would be over the second you left."

"Well, I didn't think you'd completely blow it out of proportion."

The waiter sidled up to the table. "Can I get you anything else?" he asked.

"Could we have the check please?" Carter said, still glaring at Sarah.

"Of course," the waiter said. He retreated quickly.

"I'm not blowing it out of proportion," Carter said. "I don't think I'm making a *big enough* deal about this."

Sarah rolled her eyes.

"You don't even care, do you?"

"I'm starting not to."

"So, when you go to school surrounded by rich kids and they ask you about your boyfriend, what are you gonna say?"

Her mouth was flat. "I don't know."

"Let me help you then. You can tell 'em that your boyfriend goes to community college and he's really good at picking up dog shit and mowing grass. I'm sure they'll be impressed."

The ride home was silent. Carter kept his eyes focused on the road, his mind floating elsewhere. Sarah sat against the passenger door as far from Carter as possible. She stared out the window, her arms crossed. Carter parked the truck in front of Sarah's townhouse. She opened the door to get out before the truck had even fully stopped.

"Sarah—"

She turned, her eyes puffy. She slammed the door and ran up the sidewalk to her house. Carter blinked, tears welling up in his eyes. He drove a couple of miles down the road to Landsdowne. He parked in the visitor's space across from a brick-faced end unit and opened the wooden gate that housed the stamp-sized backyard. An outdoor light on the house illuminated the yard. A patch of grass was split down the middle by flagstones that led to a small concrete patio that matched the size of the wooden deck overhead. He followed the path to the back door of the walkout basement. Windows flanked the door. He pressed his key into the deadbolt, turned the latch and opened the door. He slipped off his dress shoes just inside the threshold. The living room was devoid of furniture. It was dark, but enough light from the outside lamp filtered in for navigation. He shuffled through the living room with his head down. He opened the bedroom door. A single bed sat against the far wall. The bed was made, with his bedspread pulled taut. Rose petals were arranged atop the comforter in a heart shape. He pulled off his jacket and dropped it on the floor. He brushed the petals to the carpet with a single swipe of his arm. Carter climbed under the covers and wrapped them tight around him. He lay on his side, his eyes open, long into the night.

* * *

His eyelids fluttered. He heard slow shuffling steps above him. The low morning sun shone through the basement windows, rousing him from an uneasy sleep. Carter stretched his legs and pulled the comforter from his body. His button down shirt was rumpled. He stood and staggered to the bathroom, wiping the sleep from his eyes. He urinated, washed his hands, and brushed his teeth. He grabbed his jacket from the floor and trekked across the empty living room. At the basement door, he slipped his shoes back on and exited.

Carter pulled his truck into the visitor's spot near his parents' townhouse. He trudged to the garage door and yanked on the metal handle. It was locked. He climbed the steps, opened the front door, and walked inside. Jim sat on the recliner, his nose in the newspaper. Grace was at the stove top, cooking scrambled eggs. Jim closed his paper and slapped it on the arm of his chair. He stood, glaring at Carter. He had a hole in his pajama bottoms near the crotch. He didn't wear underwear. A bit of his scrotum was clearly visible. Carter kept his eyes up after the initial grotesque exposure.

"Where have you been all night?" Jim said, moving to block Carter's path.

Carter stopped. "I stayed at *my* house."

Grace pulled the eggs from the burner.

Jim crossed his arms, his biceps bulging. "You're not gonna come and go like this is a fuckin' hotel. If you wanna live with your little girlfriend, you can't live here."

"Your father's right, Carter," Grace said, pointing the spatula for emphasis. "You are not permitted to live with your girlfriend. You may be eighteen, but you are *not* an adult until you can support yourself."

Carter shook his head and rubbed his temples. "I never said anything about living with my girlfriend." He clenched his jaw, scowling at his parents. "And another thing. He's not my father, and he never will be."

"Carter!" Grace said.

Jim's lips curled up for a split second. He grabbed a handful of Carter's shirt, pulling him close. "And when was the last time you heard from your father?"

"Get your hands off me," Carter said.

"Jim, let go," Grace said.

Jim chuckled and released his grip. Carter stepped back.

"Been a long time, hasn't it?" Jim said. "Your father wanted me to adopt you because he was such a cheap ass that he didn't even wanna pay your child support."

Carter shrugged. "I really don't care about either of you."

"Carter Matthew, what has gotten into you?" Grace said.

"I'm leaving," Carter said with a professional poker face.

Jim laughed.

"Stop this craziness," Grace said. "You're not going anywhere."

"Where the hell are *you* goin'?" Jim said.

"It's none of your business. I just came to get my stuff."

Jim clenched his fists, his face red. He moved into Carter's personal space. "Your stuff was purchased with *my* money, so it's *my* stuff."

"Not all of it," Carter said. "I've been paying for my own stuff."

Jim half-snorted, half-laughed. "You were a minor until what, last week? It's all mine. I shoulda been chargin' you rent."

Carter nodded, a smirk on his face. "Too bad you didn't have a contract. Now get outta my way. And if you touch me, I'll file assault charges. Don't think I won't."

"You can take your clothes, but everything else stays."

"Fine," Carter replied. "Move outta my way."

Jim stepped back, his eyes narrowed. Carter slipped past.

"This is silly, honey," Grace said to Carter as he started down the basement steps.

Carter shut his bedroom door, pressed the lock on the handle, and took a deep breath. He opened his closet. A box the size of a microwave sat on the top shelf. His heartbeat pounded as he pushed it aside. A wave of relief washed over him as he saw the shoebox, his makeshift piggy bank, taped up and safe. His relief turned to panic as soon as he picked up the box. It felt different. As he brought it down to eye level, he saw it. He felt nauseated. The tape was cut. He opened the top, confirming what he already knew. The box was empty. His money was gone.

His heart pounded in his chest. His mouth felt dry and frothy, like a rabid dog's. He ripped his door open and sprinted up the steps. Grace stood like a statue as her son blew by. Jim shot out of his recliner, standing flat-footed. One side of Jim's mouth curled up, almost in a smile. Jim must've expected the oncoming train to stop. The quickness and ferocity surprised him. Carter was at full speed when he launched himself at Jim's head. He was all forearms and elbows to his stepfather's face. Jim fell to the floor against the recliner. He was on his side, his bell ringing, his hands covering his head. Carter was a rabid animal, pummeling Jim's face. Some of the blows smashed Jim's fingers. Some smashed his nose, his jaw, his ears, his eyes. Jim's face bled; his nose was off-kilter. Eventually Jim's hands fell away, his body slack against the punches. Carter kept pounding until Jim's face was unrecognizable.

Two loud bangs woke Carter from his rage. He stood and looked up from the bloody mess he had created. Grace stood at the bottom of the steps pointing Jim's handgun at Carter's chest. The rectangular Glock shook in her hands. Carter gazed down at his stepfather. His face looked like pulverized meat, blood covering every speck of white except for his expansive forehead. His knuckles had blood and bits of flesh attached to them. His wrists hurt; he couldn't make a fist without searing pain. Blood droplets covered his shirt. He gazed at his mother. Her eyes were wide. Shame made him drop his gaze to her feet. They were obscured by the shopping bags piled near the steps, waiting to be carried upstairs. Tears slid down his face. Sirens pierced the air. Shortly thereafter, police officers in helmets and body armor burst through the front door. He didn't resist when he was taken down or when his hands were yanked behind his back. He grunted, the metal against his wrists cutting deep.

It wasn't until Carter was sitting in the back of the police car that he realized the full gravity of his actions.

– 20 –

Felonies and Misdemeanors

NORTH POTOMAC HIGH SCHOOL SENIOR, SENTENCED TO PRISON
By: Evan Schultz
June 16, 1993

North Potomac High School senior, Carter Lynch, won't be donning a blue cap and gown with the rest of his classmates at tomorrow's graduation. He will be off to a new start in an orange jumpsuit.

On the morning of February 15, 1993, Carter Lynch, 18, attacked his stepfather, retired First Sergeant Jim Arnold. The 41 year-old retired army NCO sustained multiple injuries. These included a lower jaw fracture, nasal fracture, vision loss in his left eye, and (TBI) traumatic brain injury. He is not expected to fully recover from his injuries. It is likely that he will continue to struggle with memory loss and fine motor skills.

Lynch pleaded guilty to Malicious Wounding, a class 3 felony, to avoid the more serious charge of Aggravated Malicious Wounding, which could carry a life sentence. Judge Henry Thompson imposed the minimum mandatory sentence: five years in prison.

After the sentencing, Assistant District Attorney for the prosecution, Jennifer Hockley said, "Eighteen-year-olds are tried as adults, period, whether they were eighteen for a day or ten months. We have to have standards. Mr. Lynch's violent actions will have detrimental lifelong effects on Jim Arnold's quality of life."

When asked about the alleged abuse Carter Lynch suffered at the hands of his stepfather Hockley said, "The bottom line is Carter Lynch is in perfect physical condition. Jim Arnold is not. My office successfully fought to make sure that Mr. Lynch would not be eligible for parole. He will serve every last second of his term."

Defense Attorney Steve Dean made the following statement. "With all due respect to the victim and his family, this case was not as simple as Mr. Lynch committing an act of violence. There were mitigating circumstances that I am not at liberty to discuss given the terms of the plea bargain. My office believes that justice was served in reducing the possible life sentence to five years."

* * *

The stainless steel stool that Carter sat on matched the table that it was affixed to. His hands were folded on the cold steel. He wore orange pants and an orange shirt, with a white T-shirt underneath. Men with blue shirts, ID badges, and dark trousers patrolled the room. Other men in orange, tattooed men, men with shaved heads, men in all sizes and colors sat across from their families and friends. Some spoke in whispers, some were jovial, some were formal. Some ate vending machine food. Some played with their children.

Carter stood as Sarah made her way across the linoleum, an ID badge attached to her thick T-shirt. She tiptoed through the scene as if she were afraid to touch anything. She approached with a forced smile, dark circles under her glassy eyes. Carter hugged her. She held on tight. A guard glared at them. Carter let go and sat down on the steel disc. Sarah sat opposite.

"Three seconds," Carter said. "I think we can have a three second hug before they get upset."

One side of her mouth turned up for a second. "How are you?" She searched Carter's face. His black eye was fading.

He smirked. "Maybe you could write an article about the hazing here."

"You look better than ..."

"Last time."

"Yes." She nodded, her hands folded in her lap. "Are the Wheelers still visiting?"

He smiled. "Every week. I keep thinking they're gonna get tired of coming, but every Saturday, they're here."

"Anyone else?"

"Devin came once with his dad. It was really nice of him. He's at football camp now, University of Richmond."

"I thought he was going to run track."

"He's doing both."

"Good for him."

"So, any news from the outside world?"

She scowled. "Did you hear about what happened with Justin and Zach?"

Carter mimicked her scowl. "Please tell me they didn't get off."

"They pleaded the charges down to sexual battery—an F-ing misdemeanor." Her face went red. "They'll be out in six months." She leaned forward. "Your lawyer *fucking sucked*." She whispered *fucking sucked*, so the guards wouldn't hear. "I'm sorry. I shouldn't have told you. It just makes me *so mad*."

Carter shrugged. "It doesn't matter. I'm pretty immune to disappointment these days. Besides, they still have to live with what they did, just like I do."

"True." Sarah's face softened and she sat upright. "What you did wasn't your—"

"So, the big day's coming up. Are you all packed?"

She shrugged and stared at her hands.

"What?" he asked.

She looked up. "I just ... Can I be really honest with you?"

He half-smiled. "I should hope so."

She wiped her eyes on the sleeve of her T-shirt. "A big part of me wants to leave. To just forget about all this."

He nodded.

"It's killing me seeing you here. I can't sleep. I just ..." she wiped her eyes again.

Carter stood, asking the middle-aged inmate to his left if he could have the box of tissues on his table. The woman sitting with him glanced at Sarah and handed the box to Carter. He thanked them and sat back down in front of Sarah. He pushed the box across the table. Sarah whipped out a couple of tissues and dabbed the corners of her eyes.

After a moment Carter said, "You just what?"

She shook her head. "Every day I wonder if you're hurt or dead or worse. I just can't."

Carter bit his lower lip. "I know." He smiled, but his eyes were still. "Next week you'll be in Illinois. Are you excited?"

"I am. Is that terrible?"

"No."

"I feel like a terrible person, like I'm abandoning you."

"What are you supposed to do, wait around for five years?"

Her eyes were wet. "If you tell me not to go, I won't go. If you need me to stay, I'll stay."

He frowned. "If you stay, I'll feel like I've ruined your life too. I can't live with that."

She nodded and wiped her eyes once more with her tissue. She sat up straight, forcing a smile. "You do look better. You look better than me. I mean look at me. I'm a mess. You'd think I was the one in prison."

"I'm sorry."

She shook her head. "Please tell me that you're going to survive this."

"It's getting better, but I'm not gonna lie to you. That first month was like living with a thousand Jims. They were testing me, to see if I'd stand up or not. It was really stressful. The predators were trying to decide if I was a mark. You don't know who to trust. Everyone's working an angle."

"But it's better now?"

"It's still prison, but yeah, it's better."

Sarah glanced around to make sure nobody was listening. "Did anyone hurt you … like, more than physically?"

He smirked. "You mean did someone hurt my feelings?"

She looked around again, leaning forward. "Sexually." She winced as if the word caused her pain.

He leaned forward, reached out, and put his hand on top of hers. "No."

She exhaled as if she were holding her breath. Her shoulders slumped, the tension in her body eradicated with a simple two-letter word.

He squeezed her hand. "Don't worry, I passed the initiation. I made friends with some of the guys that lift weights. They were shocked at how much I can bench press. I have a bunch of 'em on my program now. I even made some friends in my anger management class. A lot of guys with dads like mine."

"So what happens now?"

He swallowed the lump in his throat. "You're gonna go to North-western. I'm gonna be happy for you. And we'll see what happens."

– 21 –

Fresh Fish and Second Chances

The sound was on mute, Carter's focus dialed into the tip of the rotating football falling from the sky. He stepped in front of the receiver and leaped, his arms reaching for the clouds. His fingers were outstretched, his hands forming an open triangle. The receiver jumped behind him, grasping at his arm. The football dropped into Carter's grasp, his hands and fingers cradling it safely. He landed on his feet, a few yards inside the end zone. The receiver fell to the ground. He knew he should take a knee. It was over. There was nothing left to gain. But he saw nothing but green in front of him. He was off like a rocket, the precious cargo stashed tightly in the crook of his arm. He dashed down his team's sideline. Players and coaches jumped up and down in blue uniforms. He knew he was being chased, but he didn't look back. He knew this time it would be different.

Carter raced through the end zone. The man in the striped shirt threw his hands up. The sound returned. He flipped the football to the man and turned, scanning the metal bleachers of the old city stadium. It was half-full, but they were cheering—they were definitely cheering. The afternoon sun peeked through the scattered clouds. The clock on the scoreboard was 0:00. His teammates had already spilled onto the field. His fellow defenders that he'd left in the dust on his jaunt to the end zone caught up to him, burying him in the middle of a huddle of hugs and head slaps. It was a meaningless touchdown in a meaningless game, but it didn't feel that way.

After post-game handshakes, Carter and his teammates meandered toward the home bleachers. On his way, he was stopped by an older dark-skinned coach with a wiry build.

"Helluva season, Wheeler."

Carter smirked, his blue helmet in hand. "It would've been nice to win a few more."

"We're a young team." The coach laughed. "Well, everyone except you and me."

Carter chuckled. "Come on, Coach, I'm not *that* old. I have been meaning to ask you what it was like playing in a leather helmet."

"I see," Coach Clay said grinning. "Old man's got jokes now. You're lucky I can't make you run anymore. You will be gettin' my coffee though."

Carter shook his head with a smile. "And here I thought I was done with initiations."

"New coach gets coffee."

Carter held out his hand. "Thanks, Coach … for everything."

The old coach shook his hand. "It's been my pleasure, son."

Carter continued toward the home bleachers. David and Jill Wheeler stood behind the short chain-link fence that separated the game from the fans. They wore matching *Richmond Spiders Football* sweatshirts. David's forehead had grown past the middle of his head, and what was left of his hair was salt and pepper. Jill took good care of herself, but time marched on, adding wrinkles to her face and gray to her hair.

Carter walked off the grass, across the swathe of asphalt that circled the football field. He stopped at the fence. David and Jill were on the other side, beaming ear to ear. Carter shook David's hand and hugged Jill.

"You played such a great game," David said. "You should've seen your mother on the touchdown. She was jumping up and down screaming."

Carter laughed. "I can picture it. I didn't hear anything though."

"I think everyone else did," David said with a grin.

Jill mock-frowned and tapped the top of his hand like he was an unruly child. "I wasn't that loud." She turned to Carter. "We're just so proud of you, honey."

"Thanks, Mom, it means a lot."

David pushed his glasses up the bridge of his nose. "So when do you start recruiting?"

"They want me on the road as soon as finals are over," Carter replied.

"Have you thought about the graduation ceremony? I know the fall term isn't a big deal, but we'd like to see you walk."

"I haven't even thought about it."

"Your mom and I have been talking." David glanced at Jill, then back to Carter. "We'd like to have a graduation party for you."

"That's really nice, but ..." Carter thought of Ben. "That sounds great, Dad. I can't wait."

"It's settled then," Jill said, smiling. "Is there anyone special you'd like to invite?"

"Maybe just Devin and Rochelle," Carter replied. "We can keep it small."

"And their boys," Jill said. "They are *so* adorable."

"Speaking of Devin," David said, "did you get a chance to see him? He was here."

"No, he didn't tell me he was coming."

"He's right over there, talking to Coach Clay," Jill said, pointing across the field.

Carter glanced over his shoulder at Devin and Clay. "I should go say hello," Carter said.

Before leaving his fan club, Carter confirmed the place and time for their postgame dinner. He hugged Jill once more and shook David's hand before heading across the tarmac back toward the field. Devin strutted toward Carter with a wide grin on his face. He wore an old blue windbreaker with a miniature Richmond football helmet stitched into the upper left corner. Carter held out his hand, but Devin hugged him, smacking him on the back.

When Carter pulled away, Devin said, "You know you broke my record."

"What record?"

He smiled. "Longest interception return for a touchdown. Mine was ninety-nine yards. Yours had to be at least a hundred and two." He chuckled. "You should've knocked the damn thing down. You're such a showboat."

Carter laughed.

"I mean who in the hell picks off a Hail Mary pass in the end zone when the opponent's down by four. But no, not only do you pick it off, but you gotta run it back a hundred yards. That was some Deion shit, you know that."

Carter shook his head, grinning. "I thought about downing it."

"Yeah, but you saw all that green." Devin laughed. "You looked pretty fast for an old man."

Carter smiled. "Just to give you a heads up, Jill and David are gonna throw me a graduation party. I'd like for you and Rochelle and the kids to come."

Devon nodded. "We'll definitely be there."

"I wanted to thank you. None of this would've happened without you."

Devin shook his head. "I just opened the door. You had to do the work."

"It must've been a heavy-ass door."

After saying goodbye to his friend, Carter strolled to the end zone. He scanned the stadium; it was mostly empty and quiet. His eyes settled on the field. The grass was thinner in the middle. Rays of sun cut through the scattered cloud cover. He stood for a moment. He smiled to himself and walked off the field for the last time. He continued through the open chain-link gate to the bleachers. The locker room was under the stands. He entered through an open roll-up door and strolled inside, his helmet in hand. He borrowed some scissors from the training room on the way to his locker.

In the locker room, many players were already showered and dressed. They had parties to attend. The air was humid from the showers. It smelled like sweat and soap and mold, with a spritz of cologne. Carter opened his metal locker and hung his helmet. He unlatched his shoulder pads and pulled his jersey—number twenty—and his pads off at the same time. He grabbed the scissors and sat down on the wooden bench. Carter cut the white tape that covered his shoes and ankles. He removed his cleats and set them in the bottom of his locker.

A dark-skinned young man wearing a towel tapped Carter on the shoulder as he walked by. "Nice game O.G.," he said.

"You too," Carter replied.

Carter continued undressing, before slipping on his flip-flops and trudging to the shower bank. He stopped at the line of sinks and mirrors. He grabbed a paper towel from the metal dispenser and dampened the paper under the faucet. He looked in the mirror. Black charcoal and wax were smudged in a thick line under each of his blue eyes. His jaw was a little stronger and stubble grew on his face and neck, but in many ways he still felt young, like his time away had simply been a press of the pause button. He spent several minutes wiping the black grease from his face.

After showering and changing into his street clothes, Carter tossed his laundry bag in the bin and strolled into the asphalt parking lot. His duffel bag was slung over his Richmond football windbreaker. He wore a blue knit cap with a red spider stitched into the front. A woman sat on the tailgate of his old pickup truck. Her glasses were small, black rimmed, stylish. Her red hair was shoulder length, wavy. Her lips were full, her face pale and young. She wore a skirt suit with heels and thick tights. She gripped a handheld recorder. At the sight of him, she stepped off the tailgate and brushed off the back of her skirt.

She bit the corner of her lower lip as he approached. Carter's stomach turned on the inside, but he maintained a calm exterior.

"Hi," she said.

He ignored her greeting, dropped his bag and pulled her into a hug. She reciprocated. After a moment they disengaged.

His eyes were wide as he looked her over. "Sarah … wow, I'm surprised."

She smiled, her eyes glassy. "Is that a good surprised or a bad surprised?"

"It's good." Carter shook his head. "It's just I haven't seen you since …"

"I went to Northwestern."

He paused as he processed the information. "Nine years ago."

"I know. I'm sorry." She sucked in her lower lip and pushed it out. "I also know that sorry doesn't even begin to cover it."

He chuckled.

"What's so funny?"

"I guess I was right. You remember the fight we had on Valentine's Day?"

"Wow, Carter Lynch, do you forget anything?"

He laughed. "I said Northwestern would be the end of us, and I guess I was right." His smile faded.

"You weren't right about everything that night."

"I wasn't?"

"You said you were destined for failure. You were definitely wrong about that."

"Wow, Sarah Cunningham, do you forget anything?"

"Technically it's Sarah Burns."

"Technically it's Carter Wheeler."

She smiled wide. "Which I love by the way. I can't tell you how happy I am for you."

"What are you doing in Richmond, Sarah Burns? I can't imagine you came all the way down here to catch up."

"I'm not sure if you're aware, but I write human interest stories for *The Post*."

He smiled. "I am aware. I read all your stuff."

"I thought you didn't like the news."

"I don't. I just read your stuff." He narrowed his eyes. "I can't imagine you came all the way down here from *The Washington Post* to watch a 1-AA team go four and seven."

"Actually, I did. And for an interview with you?" She winced.

"About what?"

"About you, about what you went through at North Potomac and prison and how good you've done here."

He exhaled, his excitement deflating with his breath. "Not sure I wanna dredge all that up. You should've called first."

She half-smiled.

"That's why you didn't call. You figured I'd be more likely to say yes in person."

"Does that make me a terrible person?"

"Pushy maybe, and a good reporter, but not a terrible person."

She chewed on her lower lip. "So you'll do it?"

"I'm not *that* easy." He narrowed his eyes, searching her face. "I'll tell you what. If you answer my questions, I'll answer yours."

"Fair enough," she said.

* * *

Carter and Sarah sat in a window booth in a quiet diner. Sarah's hand-held recorder sat on the table in front of her. Carter finished the last of his cheeseburger.

"Aren't you supposed to go to dinner?" Sarah asked.

He swallowed. "It's not for a few hours. I'll eat again."

She shook her head with a smile. "I'm going to start recording if that's okay with you. Do you mind if I ask the first question?"

"Go ahead," he said.

She pressed a button on her device. "What was the toughest thing that you went through in prison?"

He thought for a moment. "You remember how I told you that the predators in prison try to test all the new guys?"

She nodded. "I remember."

"I had a cellie."

"Cellie?"

"A cellmate."

"Got it."

"This was toward the end of my sentence," he said. "My original cellmate was a good guy. He was in for voluntary manslaughter. His name was Jarrod. Some dude groped his girl at a club. They had words. Later when they were leaving, this dude wanted to fight him. Anyway, Jarrod ended up killing him in the fight. It was a freak accident. He knocked him out and the guy hit his head on the sidewalk. Anyway, he got out about a year before I was supposed to get out. I was hoping that they would leave me in my cell alone, because I didn't wanna get used to another cellie. I mean, I heard some horror stories from some of the guys I was friends with. Nasty stuff like guys not keeping up with their hygiene. Some sexual assaults. Anyway, they did send me a fresh fish."

She raised her eyebrows. "A fish?"

"Someone fresh to the prison system."

She nodded.

"He was a young guy too—Josh. He was drinking and driving and killed someone. The judge threw the book at him—*ten years*. He was eighteen, and I think that's why they put him with me. I think they thought I'd understand. Anyway, Josh was miserable. He was crying at night. I tried to tell him not to do that, because the other guys could hear him. So I had this eighteen-year-old kid that was falling to pieces, and the predators were licking their chops. This kid really had the prison deck stacked against him. He already had one strike against him because he was white. He had another strike because he was small and weak, and another because he was crying and acting like a punk." Carter took a deep breath. "I did my best to protect him. I introduced him to my friends and asked them to look out for him. I took him to the weight pile with me to lift. And it worked ... for a while. Nobody touched him for like, eight months. Everyone started to like him too. He was actually really funny." Carter bit the inside of his cheek.

"And after the eight months?" Sarah asked.

"He got cocky. He thought we had his back. He started gambling, betting on football games. He got in over his head and he tried to get out of it by doing what gamblers do."

Sarah raised her eyebrows.

"He double-downed on the Super Bowl, betting on the Packers to win and cover twelve points. Green Bay was supposed to be a lock. They were the defending Super Bowl champs. Denver had never won a Super Bowl. In fact, they had lost four of them. A lot of people said Elway would never win one. An AFC team hadn't won in thirteen years. And to top it off, Denver was a wildcard team, and a wildcard team had only won a Super Bowl once. Everyone thought Green Bay was gonna blow 'em out. Of course Denver upset Green Bay and Josh had a debt he couldn't repay." Carter frowned and gazed at his hands.

"What happened?" Sarah asked.

Carter looked up, his face expressionless. "He was gang-raped and murdered."

Sarah's eyes went wide. She placed her hand over her open mouth. "That's awful."

"It felt like Ben all over again."

She placed her hand back on the table, and nodded in commiseration.

"That's prison. You don't accept favors and you don't get into debt."

"What happened after you got out? Did the Wheelers take you in? I'm assuming you finished high school in prison?"

Carter shook his head with a smirk. "Unh uh ... I answered your question, now you have to answer mine."

She matched his smirk. "You're right. Let me have it."

Carter swallowed. "Why didn't you ever come back?"

She stared at the table. "I knew you'd ask that."

"Of course I'm gonna ask that."

She looked up. "It was too painful. I just wanted to forget. It was also because ..." She winced. "I met someone."

He nodded. "I figured."

"I was stupid and young. I didn't know how to deal with any of it." Her eyes were glassy. "I'm really sorry. I was a coward." She gazed out the window as she spoke, her voice barely above a whisper. "I still think about it to this day. I should've just pretended that the Northwestern scholarship didn't exist. I should've stayed." A few tears spilled down her face. She made no attempt to remove them. "It was like all these bad pieces had to fall into place for that to happen, and if I had just taken out one small piece, things could've been different." She grabbed a napkin from the metal dispenser on the table and wiped her face. She looked at Carter. "I was wrong. What I did was selfish and wrong. And I'm sorry. I wanted to tell you that a long time ago, but the more time that went by the harder it was to admit what I'd done. It was easier to do nothing, to move on with my life. I mean, I was eighteen and in a new state for the first time, with tons of new people, people like me." She dabbed her eyes, sighed, and forced a smile. "I was surprised you didn't tell me to fuck off in the parking lot."

He chuckled. "I was angry when you didn't visit that first Christmas, but my mother told me something that day that I'll never forget."

She furrowed her brow. "Your mother came to visit?"

"Sorry, I mean Mrs. Wheeler. I haven't seen Grace since she stole my money and pointed that gun at me."

A waitress in black pants and a white shirt ambled toward them. "Can I take that?" she asked Carter. He handed her his empty plate.

With the waitress out of earshot, Carter continued, "Mrs. Wheeler told me that we never know how long someone's gonna be in our life. We just have to love and appreciate them in the time we have. Our situation may have seemed like this terrible thing that never happens to anyone. But the truth of the matter is we weren't unique. This stuff happened to about every guy I was in with. When they first got in, people would visit … friends, family, girlfriends. The visits would be less frequent over time. Eventually, people would stop coming. Guys would get Dear John letters."

"I'm so sorry."

He shook his head. "You shouldn't be sorry for living your life. I'm glad you did. I mean look at you. You're the best journalist in D.C., you look beautiful, you're married." He smiled. "When I said that I was gonna be happy for you, I meant it. I'm just glad we had the time together that we did."

One side of her mouth turned up in a crooked smile. "My life isn't quite as bright as the picture you paint."

He frowned. "You're the only journalist that can keep my attention, so as a loyal reader I can say that you're the best. Any fool can see how beautiful you are. And—"

"I've been divorced for a year and a half."

He grinned.

She shook her head. "I thought you were supposed to be happy for me?"

"I am. I'm happy for you that you're divorced."

"Uh huh."

His face went still. "I'm sorry. Are you okay?"

"I'm fine. I should've never married him to begin with."

"Is he the same guy from Northwestern?"

"Yes." She frowned. "I went straight from you to Daniel with barely a breather. You know in some ways I'm my mother's daughter. She could never be alone, and I think I was that way too."

"And now?"

"I think it's been good for me to be on my own. I know myself better now."

"This may sound like a stupid question, but why are you still using Burns as your last name?"

She sighed. "Because I'm known professionally under that name. And then, if I change back, everyone knows you're divorced. I think

I'm gonna bite the bullet though. I've got some time off coming up." She crossed her arms and mock-scowled. "You've asked about ten questions in a row. It's my turn."

He put his palms up in surrender. "All right."

She folded her hands together on the table. "What happened after prison? Did the Wheelers take you in? How did you end up in Richmond?"

"The Wheelers did take me in. They had moved to Richmond while I was in prison. Jill was teaching at this terrible city school, but she loved the kids. She still loves 'em. With the internet, David could work from home. They liked the slower pace down here and the cheaper real estate. I'm not even sure if they asked me to live with them. I think we both sort of assumed. They picked me up from prison and took me to their house. They already had a fully furnished room for me. I asked them if I could take their name."

"You told me once that you were going to change your name. Do you remember that?"

He nodded. "I do."

"And then you started going to the University?"

"Not exactly. I finished my diploma in prison and I took some college classes. I think it amounted to like a year of college credit. But I wasn't sure what I wanted to do, so I just took any job that I could get. I wanted to help out my parents. I didn't wanna be this twenty-three-year-old sitting on their couch. As you can imagine, the job market wasn't great for a felon with a high school education. I worked for a temp agency for about a year. Mostly entry-level warehouse and construction stuff. Then Jill told me about a groundskeeper job at Richmond. She heard about it from our neighbor who's a professor there. The professor put in a good word for me. I was shocked when I got the job. The pay wasn't great, but it had decent benefits, and I got to use the athletic center. So after work, I'd work out. One day I was running sprints on the track. Don't ask me why. At the time I had no intention of playing football. So I see Devin watching me with his hands on his hips and this huge smile on his face. I hadn't seen him since that one visit before he left for football camp my first year in prison. I would've looked him up, but I figured he already graduated. Anyway, he was just working out. He had a job working in admissions. He's the Dean of Admissions now."

"Wow," Sarah said. "He's what, twenty-seven?"

"Yeah, same as us." Carter rubbed the stubble on his chin. "Anyway, he had me over for dinner at his apartment that night. And we became really good friends again. Besides my parents, he was the only friend I had. We started working out together, and he started telling me that I should walk onto the football team." Carter chuckled. "I thought he was joking, but he kept pushing me. He wouldn't let it die. One day he challenged me in the forty-yard-dash. He told me that he really wanted me to be at my best, so we took a few days off from working out so that our legs would be fresh. The day came and he had the forty marked out exactly on the track. He even brought some kid from the track team with a starting gun. I mean he was really serious. I just thought it was funny, you know, Devin just being competitive. We ran three forties. Devin beat me on every one, but barely. Devin was really fast—he still is. He might've been faster than he was in college. So there was this old dude in the stands watching us. Afterward, he came up to Devin. They knew each other. Of course Devin had set the whole thing up."

She smiled. "I gathered."

"The old guy was Coach Clay, the defensive backs' coach. Clay asked me if I'd be interested in walking on in the summer. So I enrolled at Richmond and walked on. My parents were thrilled. They insisted on paying for school."

"You didn't get a scholarship?"

"Not the first two years. I played on special teams, but there's only so many scholarships to go around. They did give me a scholarship for my junior and senior season."

"And you've been the leading tackler for the past two years. Have you thought about the NFL?"

He laughed. "There's not much interest in a twenty-seven-year-old 1-AA safety with concussion problems."

She grabbed his hand on reflex, an old but familiar wave of concern washing over her.

"I'm fine," he said before she could speak. "I had a cat scan, and I'm okay. I did have a half-dozen or so concussions. I think I had a couple in high school, but I didn't know what it was back then. It's probably for the best that I stop playing. A lot of former NFL players are dying left and right. Not that the NFL is knocking on my door anyway, but I'm definitely done. It was a lot of fun, and I'm grateful for the friends I've made, but it's time for something else."

"Coaching?"

He smiled. "You heard?"

"I interviewed Coach Clay in the press box. He said your defensive coordinator got the head job at William and Mary, so Clay's moving up to D-coordinator, and you're going to be the new defensive backs coach."

"That's the plan."

She smiled. "Congratulations. You'll make a great coach. I'm really happy for you."

"My recruiting territory's in Northern Virginia."

"Are you going to make a trip to North Potomac?"

"I'll have to. They have a lot of good players. I doubt I'll have much luck there. Coach Ware never did like me."

"You might be surprised. I interviewed him yesterday. He was actually in your corner, but Cowan and then Goodman were calling the shots."

Carter chuckled. "Remember when you got Goodman to give me four hundred dollars?"

She giggled for a moment. "You needed a jacket."

They were quiet, the silence comfortable. He held her hand, massaging her palm with his thumb.

She gazed at Carter. "When you come to town, do you want to have lunch or dinner or something? I could cook for you."

"And then what?" he said, stone-faced.

She leaned across the table and pressed her lips to his. Her lips were soft. She smelled like … Sarah. His stomach tumbled as if he were on the downslope of a roller coaster. She sat back. "Maybe we can see what happens?"

He smiled. "I really like you, Sarah Cunningham."

For the Reader

Dear Reader,

I'm thrilled that you took precious time out of your life to read my novel. Thank you! I hope you found it entertaining, engaging, and thought-provoking. If so, please consider writing a positive review on Amazon and Goodreads. Five-star reviews have a huge impact on future sales. The review doesn't need to be long and detailed, if you're more of a reader than a writer. As an author and a small businessman, competing against the big publishers, every reader, every review, and every referral is greatly appreciated.

If you're interested in receiving my novel *Against the Grain* for free and/or reading my other titles for free or discounted, go to the following link: http://www.PhilWBooks.com. You're probably thinking, *What's the catch?* There is no catch.

If you want to contact me, don't be bashful. I can be found at Phil@PhilWBooks.com. I do my best to respond to all emails.

Sincerely,
Phil M. Williams

Author's Note

This book is a work of fiction, but my goal was to create something real. I wanted to give the reader a realistic glimpse into the world of high school football. Yes, this was an extreme example, but the majority of the content in this book was adapted from news stories or my own personal experiences. As a college freshman, I remember being forced to sing in the dining hall for the seniors. It was rather benign good fun for most, but nerve-racking for me as an introvert. The second part of the initiation involved drinking until vomiting. I refused to attend the "party". I hope I strayed from the clichés that plague this genre and created something true.

I'd like to thank my wife Denise, first and foremost. She's my first reader. And she always will be. I love you.

Thank you to everyone that I've played football with or against. The best of the bunch: Adeel, Cornell, Scott, and Mark. Thanks to my coaches, Clay, Coach Sturgeon, and Coach Renner in particular.

I never really understood football until I became a coach. I've learned a ton from the entire staff at NL, Kris and Roy especially. Those early years were tough. I suppose that made back-to-back all the sweeter.

Made in the USA
Las Vegas, NV
08 May 2021